TRUST *my* HEART

OTHER BOOKS BY CAROL J. POST

Harmony Grove Series

Midnight Shadows
Motive for Murder
Out for Justice

Cedar Key Series

Shattered Haven
Hidden Identity
Mistletoe Justice

TRUST *my* HEART

CAROL J. POST

Waterfall
PRESS

This is a work of fiction. Names, characters, organizations, places, events, and incidents are either products of the author's imagination or are used fictitiously.

Text copyright © 2016 Carol J. Post
All rights reserved.

No part of this book may be reproduced, or stored in a retrieval system, or transmitted in any form or by any means, electronic, mechanical, photocopying, recording, or otherwise, without express written permission of the publisher.

Published by Waterfall Press, Grand Haven, Michigan

www.brilliancepublishing.com

Amazon, the Amazon logo, and Waterfall Press are trademarks of Amazon.com, Inc., or its affiliates.

ISBN-13: 9781503937697
ISBN-10: 1503937690

Cover design by Michael Rehder

Printed in the United States of America

TRUST
my
HEART

ONE

Decision making's a bear.

Well, not all decisions, just ones that had the potential to ruin her life.

Jami Carlisle tilted her face upward and expelled a frustrated sigh. "Okay, Lord, I need some advice. Robert's getting tired of waiting, and frankly, I can't blame him."

She stepped onto an outcropping of rock that jutted over a small creek. Early morning sunlight filtered through the canopy overhead, painting the flora varying shades of green. Somewhere nearby, a cardinal whistled its cheery song. The McAllister woods were her refuge, her place to gather her thoughts and regroup. It didn't matter that they weren't hers. They adjoined her property, and she'd been coming there as long as she could remember.

She released a sigh. "Robert's expecting me to say yes." Actually, everyone was expecting her to say yes. The whole town had the two of them engaged and all but married the moment he'd taken her hand at the harvest party hayride in eighth grade. They'd each dated others through the years, but last summer it had turned more serious, and in the eyes of the people of Murphy, North Carolina, that was enough to cement it—she was marrying Robert.

With another sigh, Jami dropped to the cool surface of the rock and let her sneakered feet dangle over the edge. Just below, water trickled over a downed limb and around protruding rocks on its lazy path to lower ground. A breeze rustled the trees above, harmonizing with the soothing sound of the creek. But the peace she usually found there eluded her.

"This shouldn't be so difficult." She lifted her eyes skyward. "Robert's a good man. He's kind and responsible, and he's a Christian." There weren't many people she felt as close to as Robert.

So what was she waiting for? A sign? She snickered at the image that popped into her head, one of those black billboards with bold white letters:

JAMI. MARRY THE MAN.

-GOD

If only it were that easy. "Lord, help me know what to do."

She drew in a long, slow breath, heavy with the musty, organic scent of the woods. For the past eight years, Robert had been there for her, ready to lend support and a shoulder to cry on when another boyfriend bit the dust. There'd been several. Most of those relationships never made it to the serious stage. A couple had. And when their demise came, Robert was there.

She couldn't ask for a better friend. Based on everything she'd read, friendship was important for a happy marriage. But shouldn't she feel *something* when Robert kissed her? Was it too much to ask for a man who could make her stomach flip-flop and her pulse race by simply walking into the room? Someone whose kisses left her breathless?

She released a snort. She'd read one too many fairy tales as a child. Or too many romance novels as an adult. Prince Charming wasn't going to come in and sweep her off her feet, no matter how long she waited. She needed to quit stalling and take the plunge.

"Okay, Lord, this is it." She slapped both hands against the rock, palms down. "I'm going to do it. Tonight I'm going to tell Robert I'm ready and the answer is yes."

There. Mind made up. Life-altering course straight ahead. She would talk to Robert, then call her two best friends. She could hear Holly's response already—"Holy cow! Jami's finally decided to tie the knot. Someone take her temperature. She must be sick!" Holly always was a bit of a drama queen.

But she couldn't guess Sam's reaction. Sam liked Robert. All her friends did. But Sam insisted she wouldn't be having such a hard time committing if Robert were the one. But Robert *was* the one. He *had* to be. It was commitment in general that was so hard. And getting married was the most serious one she would ever make.

She dropped her gaze to the water, where a small branch had become trapped in the current. It clung to a rock for a brief moment, only to be recaptured and swept away. She picked up a stone and tossed it into the water. She'd finally done it. After almost a year of putting it off, she'd made her decision. And it left her feeling much like that small branch being carried helplessly downstream.

"Lord, please let me know I'm making the right choice."

After a final glance at the creek, she pushed herself to her feet and headed in the direction of home. Today was her last day of freedom before starting her job with the newspaper, and she had a lot to do. The first order of business would be breakfast. Then she had boxes to unload—four years of dorm life crammed into the interior space of a Pontiac Sunbird.

If she worked fast enough, maybe she would have time for a trip into town to catch up with friends before meeting Robert for dinner.

She hadn't seen anyone yet since her return. It had been early enough when she'd gotten home. But she hadn't been able to muster up the gumption to go out.

She'd left Michigan State at four that morning, and six hours later, her AC gave up the ghost. After driving the next seven with both windows down, she'd made it to Murphy at six that evening, exhausted and looking like a redheaded stunt double for the Wicked Witch of the West. A sturdy hairbrush, a long shower and a good night's sleep had done wonders. Now she felt like a new person. Except for the two-ton elephant sitting on her chest.

She shook her head. There was no reason to feel that way. She'd made her decision, back there at the creek. She stepped from the trees into her own backyard.

Yeah, the decision was made. But somehow, she didn't feel any more settled coming out of the woods than she had going in.

—⚉—

Grant McAllister pulled into the only available parking space in a two-block stretch and backtracked down the sidewalk toward the Daily Grind. The hotel clerk had promised he'd find a good cup of coffee there. Actually, he'd seen the place yesterday, tucked into the row of shops lining that side of Valley River Avenue. He'd been in the area for an appointment with a lawyer, a meeting that had left him reeling.

Although he'd never met Elizabeth McAllister, he knew a lot about her. At least the things that mattered. His mother had seen to that, filled him in on all the sordid details. His whole life, his grandmother had wanted nothing to do with him. Learning he was sole heir to her estate was the last thing he'd expected.

It wasn't a pleasant surprise, either. Twenty years ago, when his mother was working two jobs to keep food on the table, his grandmother's money would have been welcome. Now he didn't need it, and this trip south was more of an inconvenience than anything.

He swung open one of the glass doors and stepped inside. The Curiosity Shop Bookstore stood in front of him, with the Daily Grind ahead and to his left, a wide hallway separating them. Apparently, the Daily Grind was the place to be at eight thirty on a Thursday morning.

He ambled toward an empty stool, the latest issue of the *Cherokee Scout* rolled up in his hand. A cheese-and-egg biscuit and cup of coffee should hit the spot. And his usual quick skimming of the paper would keep him up to date on happenings in the world. Then again, maybe not. A fraction of the thickness of the *New York Times*, what lay on the bar in front of him probably wouldn't offer a whole lot in the way of international news.

A perky female voice cut across his thoughts. "Haven't seen you around. Are you vacationing?"

His eyes followed the voice, heavy with a mountain twang. An older woman sat perched atop the stool next to him, crowned with a halo of fiery orange hair that could only have come from a bottle.

"No vacation." That was coming soon enough. "I'm here on business."

She wiped her fingers on the paper napkin in her lap and extended her hand. "Bernie Hopkins."

"Grant McAllister."

"Well, I'll be. You're the McAllister boy. How long have you been here?"

"I flew in from New York yesterday."

"The city or the state?"

"Both."

Her gaze swept him from the collar of his Gucci polo to the toes of his Ferragamo loafers. When she again met his eyes, she nodded. What she'd been looking for, he wasn't sure. Apparently she'd found it.

"I hope you can squeeze in some R and R while you're visiting. We've got some of the prettiest country on God's green earth."

A young woman approached from behind the counter and took his order. But Bernie wasn't finished yet. As soon as the attendant stepped away to make his café mocha, she picked up where she'd left off.

"Y'all staying out at the McAllister place?"

"No *y'all*. It's just me. And no, I'm staying at the Holiday Inn." There were no five-star hotels in Murphy, but the Holiday Inn was clean and comfortable, and he didn't have any complaints.

"I don't blame you. That house has sat empty since Elizabeth McAllister was moved to the nursing home five years ago. I bet there's all kinds of critters taking up residence in there."

Grant smiled. "No critters, unless you count some hyperactive spiders and an overabundance of dust bunnies."

She threw back her head and laughed, a loud, boisterous sound that wasn't nearly as annoying as it should have been. Anything less wouldn't have seemed natural. Everything about her was bold and loud—from her bright red hair to the brilliant pink-and-purple fabric of her pantsuit to her way of engaging perfect strangers in conversation. She picked up her coffee cup and washed the Danish down with a loud slurp. "So you're single? No wife? No girlfriend?"

He cocked a brow at the intrusion into his privacy. But something told him this fiery-haired Bernie wasn't much for convention.

"I'm not married." He'd made that mistake once. Two years and a quarter of a million dollars later, he was once again single.

"Don't worry, you're still young." She gave his hand a couple of pats. "You've got plenty of time."

He stifled a snort. Thirty wasn't exactly young. And if single was an ailment, he wasn't looking for a cure.

She downed the rest of her coffee and set the cup on the wooden bar. "I'd better get to the paper. It won't run without me. Actually, it would, but that's beside the point." She slid off the stool. "While you're here, though, you have to check out our sights."

The young woman returned with his egg-and-cheese biscuit and steaming cup of coffee, then removed the napkin and mug left by the flamboyant Bernie.

Bernie raised a hand in farewell. "I'm sure I'll see you around."

"For a few days, anyway." That estimate was overly optimistic. It would probably take weeks to figure out what to do with his surprise inheritance.

As soon as he'd arrived yesterday, he'd checked out the house—a huge stone monstrosity that looked as if it hadn't hosted occupants since the Civil War. Cockeyed shutters framed several cracked windows, and the wooden deck that spanned the back leaned precariously. Inside were two floors of rooms crammed full of furniture, art, books and other belongings. He smiled wryly. He could plan and prepare a seven-course meal and memorize an entire horn concerto, but sorting through his grandmother's stuff felt like cutting the White House lawn one blade at a time.

Once finished with his biscuit, he brushed the crumbs from his fingers and sipped his coffee. This afternoon, he had an appointment with a Realtor. And he needed to call the investor whose name the attorney had given him.

But first he had to go face the mess of a house that waited for him several miles southwest of town. If it were just his grandparents' belongings, it would be a no-brainer. Because frankly, he didn't care what happened to their things.

But he would give anything to hold a piece of the past if it included his father.

Jami stepped under the green awning in front of Downtown Pizza Company. The mouthwatering smells almost woke up her appetite, which had been on strike for the past hour. Robert would have finished work and should be pulling up at any moment. She probably had all of two minutes to calm her nerves and convince her protesting stomach that it was time to eat.

She drew in a deep breath. She hadn't finished her chores, but she'd gotten far enough along to squeeze in some visiting before dinner. Since they were both in town, she'd called Robert to tell him to meet her at the restaurant. It saved him the seventeen-mile round-trip to her house and back. And gave her an out if their reunion didn't go so well.

No, that was ridiculous. Everything was going to be fine, despite the butterflies taking flight in her stomach. Actually, these weren't butterflies. They were something much less dainty. Maybe moths. Big, hairy ones.

She cast a glance over her shoulder in time to see a familiar silver Scion ease into a parking space three down from hers. The door swung open, and Robert stepped out in black dress pants, a pale blue long-sleeved shirt and a coordinating striped tie. Granted, he was coming from his accounting office, but no matter where he went, he dressed well. His clothing choices reflected his personality—rigid, particular, precise.

He moved down the sidewalk toward her, then swept her into his arms and spun her around. "Welcome back." When he again put her on her feet, a wide smile split his face. There wouldn't be any welcome-home kiss until later. Robert wasn't much for public displays of affection.

After he paid for their meals, she started through the buffet line. Boasting a salad bar and several choices of pizza, both main course and dessert, Downtown Pizza Company was the CiCi's of Murphy. She'd been coming most of her life and had yet to be disappointed.

She filled one plate with a moderate serving of salad and plopped two slices of pizza on the other one. At shortly after five, the place was pretty empty. They'd beaten the dinner crowd. Over the next hour, it would fill up.

She took a chair against the wall, and Robert sat opposite her. Once she got started, her appetite would kick in. At least she hoped so.

"Are you all unpacked and settled in?"

"I got a good jump on it. Got the cleaning finished, anyway." She'd paid the neighbor kid to mow a few times over the past nine months, but inside, everything had been pretty dust covered. Other than her two brief trips home for Christmas and spring break, the house had sat vacant, and it showed. Pain stabbed through her.

That first step inside had been the hardest, the moment she'd felt her mother's absence the most. There had been no breeze blowing through open windows, fluttering the sheers and spreading around the tantalizing aromas of freshly baked bread and that night's casserole. Instead, everything had been musty and still. Even aired out, the house had a deserted, forlorn feel, as if it had sat empty so long all its energy had seeped out.

"I know you miss her." Robert's voice was low.

She gave him a weak smile. His sympathetic nature was one of the things that made him such a great friend.

"Yeah, I do." The summer after her junior year of college was when the cancer had come back, so she'd put her education on hold and stayed in Murphy. Near the end, her mother had made her promise she'd finish her final year. The last part of July, the cancer won. The middle of August, Jami headed to Michigan.

She shook off the melancholy thoughts and smiled at Robert. "Fill me in. What's the latest gossip?" Their recent contact had consisted of a few hurried phone calls between research papers and finals. Not conducive to acquiring all the juicy details of life in Murphy.

"No interesting gossip, I'm afraid."

"Did Missy have her baby?"

"Babies. Twins." He picked up his pizza to take a bite, then wiped his hands on his napkin. "Elizabeth McAllister died last week. A stroke, I think."

She frowned. Depending on what the heirs did with the property, she might have to curtail her walks. "Any other news?"

"Samantha ran away with a traveling salesman."

"Holly, maybe, but not Samantha." Sam was the grounded one, the voice of practicality that kept her and Holly out of trouble.

He reached across the table to take her hand. "I've missed you. I can't believe I've got to fly out tomorrow for my cousin's wedding. I'm tempted to skip it and stay here."

"You can't. You're a groomsman."

"A minor detail." He squeezed her hand, and a little of the lightheartedness fell away. "And if that isn't bad enough, I have that trip with my two other cousins. So I'll be gone three weeks. What was I thinking?"

"You planned this almost a year ago. Two weeks touring Europe is the trip of a lifetime. Relax and enjoy it."

He heaved a sigh. "When I get back, we'll work on our wedding plans."

The moths that had settled down while they chatted went into a frenzy, and her insides drew into a knot. What was wrong with her? She'd made her decision. So why did she feel like a prisoner listening to the cell door clang shut?

She forced a casual smile. "Why rush things?"

"Rushing? We've dated off and on now for, what, eight years?"

Nine, if she counted the hayride. But most of that had felt more like friendship.

He continued. "I'm twenty-five, and you're twenty-three. I've got my accounting practice, and you're finished with school. We've been talking about marriage for months. There's no reason to wait."

No, *he* had been talking about it. She'd been pulled along for the ride. Now her foot was itching for the brake pedal. "You're talking wedding plans, and I haven't said *yes* yet." She released a wry laugh, born more of uneasiness and frustration than humor. "Actually, you haven't asked."

"Yes, I have."

"Not exactly." Every time he broached the subject, it was to tell her that once she finished school, they'd move ahead.

"Maybe not, because I thought it was a given. But I'm asking now. Jami, will you marry me?"

She twisted her napkin in her lap as she listened to the dings and rings and buzzes coming from the arcade area. Her gaze traveled to the vines trailing along the ceiling, the wall painted a faux concrete-block design. It was a fun, casual atmosphere, a great place to get together with friends.

But a wedding proposal? Where was the candlelight, the romantic music and the white linen tablecloth? The getting down on one knee and taking her hand, the hinged satin box? Robert was too practical for all that. Those sappy, romantic gestures were nonsense. Part of those wedding plans he mentioned would be taking her ring shopping to pick out something she liked.

Robert snapped his fingers near her face. "Earth to Jami."

She swallowed an annoyed sigh. He'd said it like he was joking, the same as he always did. But she recognized the quip for what it was—one more admonition to get her head out of the clouds.

Another moment passed in silence. For the first time, doubt flickered in his eyes. "You're going to marry me, aren't you? Come on, we're perfect together."

She opened her mouth, but nothing would come out. He was right. They *were* perfect. They'd grown up together and knew each other's secrets. Spending time with Robert was like wrapping up in a down comforter in front of a roaring fire at Christmas, a hot cup of cocoa in her hands. She was comfortable with him, just like she was comfortable with Holly and Sam.

And that was the problem. There was no spark because Robert was just another close friend.

She shook her head. "I can't."

"You can't right now . . . or ever?"

She picked up the paper napkin in her lap and started tearing small pieces from its edge. The moths were gone. The few bites of salad and single slice of pizza she'd managed to eat had congealed into a doughy lump. "I'm sorry." She forced the words through her constricted throat. "All I feel for you is friendship."

His brows drew together, and his gaze dipped to the table. For several moments, he sat in silence, straightening the napkin holder, making each side perfectly parallel to the edges of the table, then doing the same with the salt and pepper shakers. His jaw was tight, and a vein throbbed in his right temple. Robert didn't do outbursts of emotion. But the pain swimming in his dark eyes was unmistakable. Her heart twisted, knowing she was the one who'd put it there.

He again met her gaze. "Have you met someone else?"

"No." Her tone was emphatic. "There's no one else."

He gave a small nod, then stood. "You know, Jami, you can't live your whole life afraid you'll repeat your mother's mistakes."

Her jaw dropped, but he'd already turned and was walking toward the door, his pace brisk. Missy and her husband, John, walked in just then, each holding a baby carrier. Several others had entered over the past thirty minutes. The dinner crowd was arriving.

Jami crumpled in her chair, doubt chasing regret through the corridors of her mind. Was that what was wrong with her, why none of her relationships worked out? Was she really letting fear keep her from a happy, satisfying future?

No, Robert was wrong. Fear had nothing to do with it. She just had high standards and wasn't willing to settle. Besides, she wasn't always the first one to bail. She'd been the dump*ee* as many times as she'd been the dump*er*. Neither was much fun.

She wadded up her napkin and retrieved her purse from the chair beside her. What if she'd just made a huge mistake with Robert? What if she realized, years down the road, that her standards were out of reach, that what she was holding out for didn't exist? By then, Robert would be married to someone else.

Whatever happened, one thing was sure.

Tonight she'd lost one of her closest friends.

TWO

Jami settled in at one of the desks lining the left wall of the *Cherokee Scout* office. Not sure how her stomach would react to a full breakfast, she'd opted instead for a protein shake. And even that seemed revolting.

She'd had a rough night. After her shortened dinner with Robert, she'd gone home to her empty house and tried to find something to distract her. She'd given up reading almost immediately and decided on a movie. That wasn't any more successful of a diversion than the book had been. While the characters worked through their issues, she played the events of the evening over and over in her mind and kicked herself for letting things with Robert go on as long as they had.

But this morning, her problem was 100 percent nervousness. It was her first day on the job, and she felt every bit as green as she probably looked. Thinking about the experience of those around her didn't do anything to quell her jitters. Most of the *Scout*'s employees had been there for years and were top-notch.

She drew in a deep breath and squared her shoulders. Maybe she didn't have the experience they did, but she had enthusiasm and persistence and education. That shiny new diploma at home was solid proof of the latter.

Besides, Bernie would be sitting right next to her, helping guide her over the bumps. She was as long-term as some of the others and wore two hats—staff writer and part-time ad person. And she'd been instrumental in getting Jami the job.

Jami's eyes drifted to the desk to her left, which was currently unoccupied and had been since she'd arrived. Bernie had waltzed in ten minutes ago and made a beeline for David Brown's office in the back corner.

As the publisher, and her new boss, David had already met with Jami, taking her through the facility and explaining what was expected of her. During the half hour since then, she'd skimmed through last week's paper and jotted down several story ideas.

She shifted her gaze to the back office as Bernie emerged and crossed the large room. Most of the bottom floor of the *Scout* was open, with rows of desks and a long counter separating the work area from the lobby.

Bernie stopped at the desk beside Jami's and plopped into the chair. "It's good to see you. Are you glad to be home?"

"Yeah, I am." Especially now that the situation with Robert was settled. She was embarking on a new life—completely unattached, a reporter instead of a student, an independent adult.

"The next three months are going to be a whirlwind."

Jami raised her brows. "They are?"

Now Bernie's expression mirrored her own. "A September wedding?"

No. He didn't. "Robert told you we're getting married, didn't he?"

"No, he told Beulah, and Beulah told me."

Jami groaned and put her head down on her desk. "That's even worse." Beulah Fines wasn't just Robert's aunt. She was Murphy's most notorious gossip.

"So you're not marrying Robert. What made you change your mind?"

She lifted her head to frown at Bernie. "I didn't change my mind. He's been talking about it, but I never said yes. Last night I gave a distinct *no*."

"Interesting." Bernie nodded slowly. "Beulah said you guys were having a September wedding and going to Key West for your honeymoon. After that, you were going to be moving into his house in town and putting yours on the market."

She shook her head. "While I was finishing school, he was planning out the rest of my life." He'd always been a take-charge kind of guy, but that was extreme even for Robert.

"I can't say I'm disappointed to hear there won't be wedding bells. I like Robert, but when you were around him, you always seemed like a bird with its wings clipped."

"I never thought of it that way." But Bernie had a point. It had happened so gradually she hadn't even noticed. There were the little things, like his penchant for being early, which required she set her watch ahead, his gentle lectures when she made choices that didn't turn out so well and his playful jabs about her lack of structure and having her head in the clouds. But lately, the lectures and playful jabs had felt more like criticism.

"I think you need to get out and celebrate your freedom. What have you wanted to do but couldn't with Robert around?"

She thought for a moment, then broke into a smile. "Get a puppy. Robert always insisted they're not practical for people who work full time."

Bernie dismissed the argument with a wave of her hand. "Ah, pooh. Who says you need to be practical? If you want a puppy, you should go by the Humane Society tonight and take one home."

Jami nodded, a sudden sense of freedom sweeping over her. "I just might do that."

Bernie crossed an ankle over her knee and settled back in the chair. "Guess who I ran into at the Daily Grind this morning. Elizabeth McAllister's grandson. And whoo-wee, is he a fine one!"

"Isn't he a little young for you?"

"I'm not thinking of me, silly girl."

"Well, don't think of me, either. I'm not looking." Her name was going to be mud once Beulah got ahold of the news the wedding of the century was off. The last thing Jami needed was to check out the newcomer. At least she would have a short reprieve. Since Robert left for Wisconsin early this morning, he probably hadn't had the time or the desire to fill his aunt in on the latest development.

"Methinks thou protesteth too much. But that's okay. He's staying at the Holiday Inn, and you're going to go see him."

"What?" She blurted the word. Several people looked their way, and she lowered her voice. "What are you talking about?"

"Your first assignment. I already ran it by David, and he agreed wholeheartedly."

Jami narrowed her eyes. "This isn't another one of your harebrained matchmaking schemes, is it?"

"You're unjustly accusing me, my dear. When I walked into David's office, that was the furthest thing from my mind. Remember, I thought you were engaged to Robert."

"And now?"

Bernie tilted her head and shrugged. She was an incorrigible matchmaker. She just wasn't very good at it. Over the years she'd orchestrated dozens of disasters. Her few successes were people who'd gotten together *in spite of* her matchmaking attempts rather than *because of* them.

"I'll never tell. But you'll be doing a feature article on the McAllisters—the estate, the McAllisters themselves, all the secrecy surrounding them. And," she added with a wink, "this red-hot grandson."

With that, she turned to face her monitor and began to click away on the keyboard. Jami shook her head. In spite of all the matchmaking Bernie had tried for others, she'd never found that special someone for herself. He would have to be one jewel of a man to put up with all her eccentricities.

Jami flipped the page back on her legal pad, exposing a clean one. At the top, she wrote *McAllister Feature*, emphasizing it with a double underline. This assignment was going to be fun. She would get to do some in-depth reporting, digging into the past, uncovering the mystery that had always shrouded the McAllisters. Thirty-something years ago, they were the crème de la crème of Charlotte society and awed the residents of Murphy with grand entertainment and lavish parties. Then, with no explanation, they sold everything, holed up at the Murphy estate and became hermits. Her job was to find out why.

She would start with an online search and see what she could pull up on the McAllister family. She would also pore over old issues of the *Cherokee Scout*, maybe even talk to Hilda Parker, who'd been head librarian for a couple of decades before retiring a few years ago.

But her most valuable source would be Flora Jenson—if she could find her and if Flora would talk. She'd been the McAllisters' housekeeper for upwards of forty years and the only one to step foot inside the sprawling house since the day the doors of hospitality had closed for good. After Franklin McAllister died and Elizabeth McAllister was moved to Shady Meadows, Flora went back to Charlotte, and no one had seen or heard from her since.

Jami picked up her pen and wrote *google McAllisters*, then *Hilda Parker* and *Flora Jenson*, scrawling a star beside the latter name. That was enough to get her started. But she wasn't finished.

Regardless of what nefarious plans were circling through Bernie's head, she had to add one more name:

Red-hot grandson.

―⁕―

Grant stepped from his room and pulled the door closed. The same as at home, he'd started out the day with exercise. The hotel's information on its amenities said limited fitness center, with *limited* being the operative word. It was nothing like what he was used to, but five miles on the treadmill had given him a pretty good workout. After a shower and a change of clothes, he was ready to face another day at his grandparents' place.

He headed down the hall toward the elevator. When he had finished his shower, he'd discovered he had a message. A Jami Carlisle was trying to reach him. He'd made the call, hoping for a prospect interested in the McAllister estate. Instead he'd gotten a newspaper reporter.

He shook his head. He didn't do interviews, under any circumstance. He'd learned that lesson two years ago. The tabloids had had a heyday with his high-profile divorce, taking every word his socialite ex-wife said as fact and plastering it on the front page. The whole thing had left him with a bad taste in his mouth when it came to reporters. As far as their integrity, or lack thereof, he ranked them right up there with certain politicians.

In another life, he'd have had a hard time turning this one down. She seemed so sweet. She spoke with a musical lilt, a soft drawl that's only hint of the North Carolina mountains was a slight lengthening of the shorter vowels. And she sounded young, maybe even brand-new at reporting. As she'd pleaded with him to let her interview him for the little weekly paper he'd carried to breakfast, he'd listened, patiently letting her have her say.

But this wasn't another life, and once she'd finished, he'd dashed her hopes without a twinge of remorse. Because no matter how sweet Jami Carlisle sounded, beneath that innocent exterior was the motto of every ambitious reporter—*anything for a story*.

He opened the door of the lobby and stepped under the hotel's porte cochere. When he pressed a button on the key fob, the lights on his rental car flashed once and the locks clicked up. He'd just reached the front quarter panel when an older-model Pontiac Sunbird pulled into the parking lot and shuddered to a stop in the next space. Hopefully it wasn't the newspaper reporter. In his experience, one word described a reporter going after a story—*relentless*.

He reached for the door handle of the Mercedes, still focused on the Sunbird. If this was Jami Carlisle, he had her pegged right. She was young, maybe even fresh out of school. What he was looking at was definitely a starter car, a please-keep-running-until-I-get-through-college-and-can-afford-something-better car. He remembered those days well. An '88 Honda Civic had gotten him all the way through law school.

As he slid into the driver's seat of the Mercedes, the door to the Sunbird flew open. A young woman sprang to her feet and hurried around the front of his car. Either someone was extremely eager to discuss the purchase of the estate or he was about to be accosted by a cute but determined newspaper reporter.

She skidded to a stop at his open door. "Grant McAllister?"

He hesitated. He could say no. Or he could pull the door shut without saying anything. Except he wasn't a liar. And although he was often accused of being firm and unyielding, he was never rude.

"Yes, I am."

She thrust out her hand. "Jami Carlisle, reporter for the *Cherokee Scout*."

He accepted the handshake, but before he could respond, she rushed ahead. "I know I already asked, and I know you said no, but I dropped by to ask you to reconsider. Just one little interview. I promise it'll be painless. I'll even treat you to lunch at the Murphy Chophouse." She talked fast, her words sounding winded, likely from nervousness rather than the short sprint around his car.

She tilted her head, her lips curved up in a pleading smile. That would have affected him in another life, too. So would the rest of what he was seeing. Auburn hair with golden highlights flowed in soft waves around her face and over her shoulders, and her green eyes sparked with enthusiasm. The gray tailored jacket hugged her curves. Black high-heeled sandals peeked out beneath the matching pants, a splash of burgundy adorning her toes.

But he was long past being swayed by a pretty face. He shook his head. "Thanks, but no thanks." The Chophouse was good. He'd had dinner there last night. But he would pay for his own meal and eat alone.

She heaved a sigh and shifted her weight to one foot. "Oh, come on, it's my first paid assignment. I can't go back and tell my new boss I couldn't even get the interview."

"Sorry, miss. I can't help you."

She lifted her brows in a pleading gesture. What she lacked in sophistication, she made up for in exuberance. "Please?"

He tempered the rejection with a soft tone. "Look, I wouldn't be any help for your story. I never knew my grandparents. The McAllisters disowned my father when he announced his marriage to my mother."

"Oh." Disappointment flashed across her features, but almost instantly, her face brightened. She smiled more broadly, and his gaze traveled to her mouth. Her lips glistened with gloss tinted the same shade as her toenail polish. "You can still help me out. I'll need photos of the house, something on what you're planning to do with the place, any prospects you might have, information about you and your mom and dad . . ."

He shook his head and reached for the door. "Sorry."

"Please? I'm not beyond begging."

A pang of something shot through him. It felt an awful lot like guilt. Why couldn't it be a pushy, obnoxious middle-aged guy trying to get the story? Why did it have to be someone so sweet and fresh and wholesome?

But he couldn't give in. Once he had, to give the press his side of the story. He'd learned some valuable lessons—words are easy to spin, even impartial people have a viewpoint, and there's no such thing as off the record."

"Sorry, sweetheart. You need to go chase another story." He shut the door, started the car and backed from the space. As he pulled onto Holiday Drive, he glanced to his left.

He shouldn't have. His young reporter stood in the same place he'd left her, lower lip pulled between her teeth, watching him go. His chest tightened. The poor girl, stuck with the world's most stubborn interview subject for her first assignment.

He eased to a stop at Highway 64, then made a right turn, pushing aside the image of sad green eyes. He had things to do, and he didn't need to get tied up with some small-town newspaper reporter. This whole Murphy detour was putting a major crimp in his plans. Before the phone call from his grandmother's attorney on Monday, he'd been just two weeks away from total freedom. A much-needed break.

For the past twelve years he'd driven himself. Actually, he'd *always* driven himself, for as long as he could remember. But during the twelve years since high school, he'd been obsessive about it, finishing college and then law school at the top of his class, then getting hired by a prestigious New York City law firm. Now, five years later, he was on the brink of making junior partner. He was ticking off every goal on his smooth climb to the top.

So why wasn't the sense of accomplishment there? Why wasn't he experiencing the satisfaction success always brought?

He reached for the radio dial and let it scan. After landing on one gospel and two country and western stations, he turned it back off. Finding a Mendelssohn symphony played by the Boston Philharmonic wasn't likely to happen.

He heaved a sigh. He was probably just suffering from burnout. Twelve years without a real vacation would make anybody crazy.

Whatever was wrong with him, he was getting ready to remedy it. He had it all planned out. While in Murphy, he'd sort and dispose of the first-floor contents. And he would list the property with a Realtor, possibly sell to the investor whose name the attorney had given him. Then he'd fly back to New York and wrap up everything there. A final trip to Murphy would have the last of his grandparents' possessions sorted and, if he was lucky, a contract signed.

Then for two months, the man who always had a plan for everything was going to hit the road with absolutely no plan at all.

Jami sat at her kitchen table, spoon suspended over a half-full bowl of cereal. "Don't look at me like that. You already ate."

Two sets of sad brown eyes met hers, and twin tails wagged.

The trip to the Valley River Humane Society hadn't gone at all like she'd planned. She'd intended to just look. After all, getting a puppy was a big decision, a fifteen- or twenty-year commitment, not something to be taken lightly. She'd planned to do her research, decide on a breed and purchase all the accoutrements of pet ownership before making her choice. But those good intentions had fallen by the wayside. Maybe Robert was right. Maybe she *was* too impulsive.

Well, at least one thing had gone according to plan—she hadn't brought home a puppy.

Penny had shown her several litters, but when she'd gotten to the cage on the end, her heart had melted. Inside were two long-haired dachshunds, looking up at her with such hope it broke her heart. Then one gave a pitiful wag of her tail and tried to nuzzle her hand through the front of the cage.

Her plans to eventually get a puppy flew out the window. Instead, she became a dog owner—times two. And seven-year-old sisters Bailey and Morgan became part of the Carlisle household.

She shoved her spoon into the bowl and brought the last bite to her mouth. Dark eyes followed her every movement. "If you give the breakfast you inhaled time to settle, you'll feel satisfied. I promise."

She hoped so, anyway, because she had no clue what she was doing. She pulled a neon pink Post-it from the dispenser on the table and made herself a note—*Library, book about dog care*—then plopped it next to the green one with her grocery list.

Life had changed in a hurry. Two days ago she was agonizing over whether to marry Robert, anticipating the start of her dream job and not even remotely considering adding a pet to her household. Thursday night, Robert walked out of her life, maybe permanently. Last night she slept nestled between two warm, furry bodies. And this morning, she would work on wearing down a stubborn, unbending interview subject who was more tight-lipped than a CIA operative guarding the nation's military secrets. The dream job wasn't quite as easy as she'd hoped.

Howard Blackburn didn't help things. Not that he was trying to make her look bad. At least not intentionally. He'd been a reporter for the *Cherokee Scout* the last thirty-something years and recently retired, leaving the opening she had filled. In the eyes of the people of Murphy, he'd reached almost iconic status. So far, eight people had pointed out what big shoes she had to fill, what a great reporter Howard was and how Howard *always* got the story. And that was just yesterday, her first day on the job. Nothing like a little pressure.

But she was up for the challenge. Maybe this Grant McAllister *was* stubborn. But he was about to find out she could be quite stubborn herself.

Jami rose from the table and retrieved her empty bowl, stepping over Morgan on her way to the sink. Both dogs watched her pick up a foil-covered plate. She had just that morning baked the chocolate chip cookies it held. Supposedly, the way to a man's heart was through his stomach. She wasn't interested in getting to Grant's heart. But if chocolate chip cookies would help wear down his resistance, this morning's activities would be well worth it.

When she walked from the room, both dogs raced past her to stand at the front door, fuzzy black bodies quivering with excitement.

"No, you can't go with me. You have to stay here."

Bailey responded with a bark and an enthusiastic wag of her tail, and Morgan pranced back and forth in front of the door. Hopefully they wouldn't destroy the place while she was gone. She didn't have crates to put them in, but she could at least minimize any possible damage.

She closed both bedroom doors, then moved to the small room she used as an office. Several stacks of papers littered the desk, one consisting of bills, one with research for story ideas and one composed of miscellaneous paperwork, along with a pile of yesterday's mail. Three Post-it notes topped the stacks, information she didn't want to forget but hadn't yet had time to deal with.

Robert had always complained about how she kept her writing and school projects, saying she worked in chaos. Granted, it didn't *look* organized. But she always knew where to find everything. If her work area was chaos, it was at least organized chaos.

After squatting to receive sloppy kisses on both cheeks, she slipped her purse over her shoulder and stepped out the front door. Cutting through the woods would get her to the McAllister mansion as quickly as driving. But she hadn't set foot on the property since the morning after she got home. Now that Grant was there, traipsing through the McAllister woods didn't feel right anymore.

So she got into her car and followed Ranger Road to where it ended at Panther Top. Her goal for today's visit would be to get Grant to drop his guard. She would show up as a friendly neighbor welcoming him with a plate of cookies. She wouldn't even mention the story. If he could get to know her in a nonthreatening way, maybe he would agree to an interview later.

By the time she turned onto Panther Top, she was already having second thoughts. She was a straightforward person. And a lousy actress. If she pretended to be something she wasn't, he'd see right through her. And she could kiss her story good-bye.

She pushed the thought from her mind and turned into the gravel drive. The wrought iron gates were open, a first for as long as she could remember. But there was nothing welcoming in the sight. Kudzu had taken over both sides of the drive, turning the shrubs and trees beneath into looming, nondescript shapes. The long gravel road snaking its way through the property had almost disappeared under years of unrestrained growth.

Then the trees thinned and cleared, and the mansion lay before her, as neglected as the grounds. The drive circled around a huge two-tiered stone fountain, a vague hint of long-forgotten grandeur. At some point over the years, the statue at its top had toppled over to rest facedown in the now-empty basin. If Grant decided to keep the place, he would have his work cut out for him.

She braked to a stop next to his Mercedes. When she'd talked to him at the Holiday Inn, she'd been too focused on trying to get the interview to pay much attention to what he drove. Now she took the time to eye the car with appreciation. *Nice.* Silver with a convertible top. Actually, the car wasn't his. With the Massachusetts tag, it had to be a rental. What kind of person rents a Mercedes? Someone wealthy and sophisticated, that's who. And she was showing up on his doorstep with chocolate chip cookies.

After a stabilizing breath, she retrieved her foil-covered gift, trying to calm the butterflies taking flight in her stomach. What if he told her to go? What if he took the plate, thanked her for her thoughtfulness and closed the door, leaving her standing on the porch? Or what if he saw it was her and didn't even open the door? Well, she would have to make sure that didn't happen.

"I can do this." Her voice was a squeak. A couple of those butterflies had made it into her throat. She swallowed hard and tried again. "I can do this." Better.

Yes, she *could* do this. Maybe she was new at reporting, but she wasn't born yesterday. She was confident—comfortable with people and comfortable with herself. She would melt his objections with her smile and wow him with her wit. And try hard to not think about how far out of her league he was.

She squared her shoulders and started up the front walk. If she could get those butterflies to cooperate, the rest would be a breeze.

THREE

Another photo album landed atop the growing pile slung carelessly across the wood floor while Jesus stared down from the opposite wall. Grant wasn't totally comfortable with his silent observer, but he wasn't surprised, either. That was another tidbit his mother had given him about his grandparents—how they were such good churchgoing people. Like so many others he'd known, it was all for show.

He picked up another album and flipped the pages, giving each no more than a cursory glance. Soon it joined the others. Album after album, all devoted to his grandparents. Wedding pictures, trips, social events. Hundreds of photos and not a single one of his father. His dad grew up in this house. At least spent summer vacations here. There should be something in all the mess definitively branded *Gary McAllister*. But it was as if he'd never existed.

Grant tossed the book he held onto the floor. He didn't need to look at the rest of the photos. It was his grandparents' wedding album. There would be no pictures of his father there. He dropped to his knees and packed the albums into a box. After closing it up and scribbling *trash* across its top, he carried it into the parlor to join the two others already there. Why hadn't he found a single picture of his father? Granted, he still had 90 percent of the place to go through, but he should have come across something by now.

The doorbell interrupted his private gripe session, and he glanced at his watch. The Realtor wasn't due for another hour. The investor wouldn't arrive until midafternoon. When he stepped into the foyer and approached the double doors, someone stood on the other side of one of the oval glass inserts. The image was broken and somewhat distorted. But it was clear enough to know he wasn't looking at the Realtor or the investor. The pesky newspaper reporter now stood on his front porch. Sheesh, what would it take to get rid of the woman?

He swung open the door. It didn't matter how cute she was. Never again was he going to have things he said twisted and spun to fit someone else's idea of a good story. If *firm* didn't work, he'd resort to *rude*.

"I already told you, no interview."

She held up a hand in denial. "Today's Saturday. I left my reporter hat at the office. This is a neighborly visit."

He frowned. "We're not neighbors."

"Yes, we are. The back corner of my property butts up to the back corner of yours. I've been hiking through your woods for years." She flashed him a friendly smile. When Jami Carlisle smiled, her eyes joined in, underscoring the gesture with a confirming sparkle.

She extended her hand, and his gaze dipped to her foil-covered offering. He wasn't going to be bamboozled by rosy lips and sparkling green eyes. Or whatever was on that plate.

Another dazzling smile lit her face. "Chocolate chip cookies. I baked them this morning. I know your stay is probably temporary, but I still wanted to show you some of the warm friendliness Murphy is known for and welcome you to the neighborhood."

"Thanks." He took the plate from her hands. If he invited her in, he'd probably live to regret it.

"If there are any services you need—someone to clean, a contractor, ministries to donate any unwanted items—I can probably help you. I've lived here all my life."

"Thanks. I might take you up on that."

Several seconds ticked by in silence, tense and uncomfortable. Actually, *he* was the only uncomfortable one. She maintained a casual pose, weight shifted to one foot, right arm hanging loosely at her side, left thumb hooked around the strap of the purse hanging from her shoulder. It was apparently easier being the pursuer than the pursued.

Okay, thirty minutes. He could use a break, anyway. "Would you like to come in?"

The smile climbed higher. "I'd love to."

As soon as she stepped over the threshold, her eyes circled the room and widened in awe. "This is pretty impressive."

"You wouldn't have thought so a couple days ago. When I first walked in, with the power off and the drapes drawn, it was like stepping into a cave." Or a tomb.

Even with everything lit up, he didn't view the old place with the same appreciation she did. To him, it was a monumental inconvenience, one more thing to deal with before embarking on his two months of freedom. But she was right. Under different circumstances, he would find it pretty impressive himself. The curved entry walls rose almost thirty feet, melting seamlessly into the domed ceiling. A massive stairway wrapped two-thirds of the room, and a huge crystal chandelier hung in the center. Paintings lined the walls, following the rise of the stairs.

"I've never even been inside, so this is pretty cool." She turned to face him. "Even though we've been neighbors most of my life, I never met the McAllisters. No one came to visit, and they never left."

"I guess my grandparents weren't very friendly." That was an understatement. Based on everything his mother had told him, the elder McAllisters were stuck-up snobs.

He strode toward the parlor, and Jami followed, chatting as she walked.

"For the last twenty-five or thirty years, they kept to themselves. But it wasn't always that way. They used to entertain on a regular basis. Then it all stopped. No one came or went from here again, except the housekeeper. Every Wednesday she would slip out and disappear for a few hours. Whatever she was doing, she didn't do it in Murphy. Probably wanted to avoid the questions."

"Strange." Pretty intriguing, actually. But he was here to dispose of their stuff and get on with his life, not investigate a mystery. He removed one dust-covered sheet from the couch and a second from the coffee table. "Have a seat. I'll even share my cookies."

She settled onto the couch and gasped. "The window's broken."

He followed her gaze to where a large rock lay beside one of the chairs, untouched since being hurled through the large window. Shards of glass had found their way between the drapes and littered the hardwood floor. "I know. That's how I got in the day I arrived."

"You broke the window?"

Grant laughed, his reaction sudden, spontaneous and totally unexpected. That was what pleasure felt like, something he hadn't experienced in . . . a while. And it had come from the least likely source. But Jami had an innocence about her he found refreshing. "No, I didn't break it. But I didn't get a key until I met with the attorney. So I reached through the empty frame, unlocked the window and climbed in."

He removed the foil from the plate and, after offering her a cookie, took one himself and sank his teeth into it. It was warm and moist and, if he had to guess, made from scratch.

"Two other windows are broken. But I'm surprised that's the only vandalism, considering the place has sat empty for five years."

She nodded. "I'm sure all the stories helped you out. No one got any braver than to run up and bust out a few windows."

"Stories?"

She took a bite of her cookie and continued. "All the kids think this place is haunted. Even when the McAllisters lived here, everyone was afraid to get anywhere near it. You know how kids make up scary stories. In Murphy, this is the setting. They say the ghost of the dead son roams the halls, and on a full moon—" She stopped suddenly, color creeping up her cheeks. "I'm sorry."

"It's all right. I never knew my dad. He was killed in an accident before I was born."

"I never knew mine, either. He wasn't sober long enough to get acquainted." She forced a smile, but there wasn't any humor behind it.

Okay, maybe this idealistic, young newspaper reporter wasn't as sheltered as he'd thought. She likely had some surprises hiding beneath that innocent exterior. But he wasn't sticking around long enough to find out. He polished off the cookie he held. "I'd offer you milk, but all I have is bottled water."

"Water's fine." When he returned, she took the bottle from him. "So how long are you here?"

"Five more days. I'm flying out next Thursday. Meanwhile, I'm trying to get as much of this stuff sorted as I can."

He frowned at the boxes stacked against the adjacent wall. A lot of personal effects had been packed up before he arrived. Judging from the layers of dust on the boxes, it wasn't recently. "It's nice someone tried to take care of some of the packing, but I think it's been more of a hindrance than a help."

"My guess is Flora boxed some things up before she left."

"Who's Flora?"

"Flora Jenson, the McAllisters' housekeeper, and for the past thirty years, the only one of the staff left. After your father's accident, your grandfather sold all his holdings in Charlotte, and overnight, he and your grandmother became recluses."

As Jami talked, his pulse picked up speed. Flora Jenson would have known his father. "I'd like to talk to her."

"You can't. I already tried. She said she won't disrespect Elizabeth McAllister's memory by allowing me to sensationalize her story."

"Whoa, I guess she told you."

Jami smiled. "She did. I tried to convince her I don't write like that. But she wouldn't budge."

Grant reached for a cookie. The poor girl was running into resistance everywhere she turned. He actually felt sorry for her. Just not sorry enough to give her the interview she'd asked for. "I'm guessing you found a listing for her."

"Yeah. You thinking of calling her?"

"I bet she'd talk to me."

"What makes you think that?"

"Number one, I'm not a newspaper reporter. Number two, I'm Elizabeth McAllister's grandson. I'm an orphaned boy, searching for my roots. How could she refuse that?" He grinned at her, a gesture as uncharacteristic as the spontaneous laughter. Apparently the laid-back mountain atmosphere was draining away some of his ever-present tension. Or maybe it was Jami's effect on him.

She returned his smile. "You've got a point. If she suddenly decides to get talkative, I'd appreciate it if you'd put in a good word for me. I really *am* harmless."

With those sincere eyes and the sweet smile, he could almost believe it. But she was a reporter. So no, she wasn't harmless.

She laid her water bottle on the table and reached for a second cookie. "I guess you'll be back and forth for a few weeks until you get all this cleared out."

"I'll make one more trip back to wrap up the last of it. Then I'm taking off for a couple of months." Nothing was going to cut into that two-month sabbatical if he could help it.

She nodded. "Vacation?"

"Something like that."

"Where are you going?"

He raised his brows. "A little nosy, aren't we?"

"I'm supposed to be nosy. I'm a reporter. So where are you going?"

"No idea. Away. Wherever my mood takes me."

She watched him, her expression intent. "Funny, you don't strike me as a fly-by-the-seat-of-your-pants kind of guy."

"What kind of guy *do* I strike you as?"

She pursed her lips. "A planner, someone who thinks things through in advance."

He opened his water bottle and took a swig. She had him pegged. *Structure* was his middle name. That was probably how he'd gotten himself into the rut he was in. Maybe throwing away some of that structure would help him get out of it.

"You're pretty good at analyzing people." Maybe too good. He put his bottle on the coffee table. "Anyway, I want to get as much wrapped up this trip as I can. After my second trip, I'll have the contents auctioned off and donate whatever's left over."

"When you get to that point, there are several thrift stores that could use this stuff. We've got REACH for battered women and both Logan's Run and the Humane Society for animals, to name a few."

"Abused women or helpless, little animals. That's going to be a tough decision."

"Maybe you can do more than one. It might be easier than choosing. Let's see, what else might you need while you're here? I can recommend some restaurants, a good church, if you practice a faith . . ."

"I did an online search for places to eat, and I've been content with what I've tried so far." He wasn't going to even acknowledge her other suggestion. His attending church was about as likely as his granting her interview request.

She cast a glance at the three boxes on the other side of the coffee table, each with the word *trash* written in black marker on top. "Would you like me to drop those by the landfill this afternoon?"

"I can take them. I don't want to inconvenience you."

"It's no trouble. I'm going anyway, my usual weekend run. We don't have trash pickup out here." She cast a glance at the boxes. "So what's in there, anyway?"

"Photo albums, letters from my grandmother."

Her brows pulled together, forming small vertical creases between them. "You're throwing them away?"

"I'm just interested in things that belonged to my dad, so if you'll drop this junk by the landfill, I'll say good riddance."

"Don't you want to hang on to them for a while? I mean, what if you change your mind?"

An itchiness crawled through his veins, the sense of annoyance that had become an increasingly frequent companion. He tamped it down. "Remember, my grandparents disowned my dad and never wanted anything to do with me or my mom. Now they're dead and gone. It's too late for them to make things right." He'd successfully curtailed the annoyance. But bitterness had lent a hard edge to his tone, and he couldn't seem to soften it.

Jami shrugged. "It's your decision. I'll get rid of them if that's what you want." She swallowed the last of her cookie, then took another swig of water. "Any bites on the house and property?"

"Not yet." He sat back on the couch, glad for the change in subject. "I'm meeting with a Realtor at eleven, and I've got a three o'clock appointment with an investor from Charlotte."

Her face fell, and creases of worry settled in. "Durham Vanguard."

"You know him?"

"Several of us do."

Judging from her tone, she didn't think much more of the man than he did. During their brief phone conversation, Vanguard had come on strong, slicker than a car salesman at month's end. As soon as he heard the McAllister name, phony camaraderie gushed through the line. More than once, Grant had been tempted to disconnect the call. But he'd gritted his teeth and held on. If their dealings would result in a quick sale, he could put up with a lot, even an overbearing, puffed-up blow bag. It was a brief business transaction, not Christmas dinner.

Jami set her water bottle on the coffee table and angled her body on the couch to face him more fully. "He's had his eye on this place as long as I can remember. There's a vein of gold running through some of the properties on Ranger. We've also got gemstones in the area."

"So he wants to do mining?"

She nodded. "When I was a kid, a couple of the residents tried, on a small scale. The gold is deep, embedded in a vein of quartz. Vanguard is apparently sure he can make it profitable." She shrugged. "He's hit most of us up at some point or another. I think he was hoping we'd be able to persuade the McAllisters to sell. But none of us want his operations out here. He'd completely destroy the beauty of the land."

She stared back at him with the same pleading gaze she'd used in the Holiday Inn parking lot. It wasn't going to be any more successful here than it had been there. What he did with the property was a business decision, something he made with his mind, not his emotions.

She set her empty water bottle on the table and stood. "Your Realtor will be here in another forty-five minutes. If you want to help me load this stuff, I'll let you get back to your sorting."

He picked up a box, then followed her to her car. Once he had all three loaded, he rested a hand on the faded metal roof. "Thanks for taking them. And thanks for the cookies and the visit. I enjoyed both." More than he'd expected. The irritability that had gripped him while sorting through his grandmother's stuff had all but disappeared.

"Me, too." She slid into the driver's seat. "See, I kept my word—no interview. Just a friendly, neighborly visit. But after today, all bets are off. Come Monday morning, I'll be back in reporter mode, determined to get my story." Her lips curved upward in a quirky grin.

"Thanks for the warning. So I guess I should make myself scarce."

"No, I'm not that scary. Determined maybe, but in a lovable way."

She was teasing, but he had to agree. Her hounding him was almost fun.

Fun. The word had become a foreign concept, at odds with his drive to finish his education and climb the corporate ladder. The melancholy that had settled over him when Bethany walked away with his heart had put the simplest pleasures even more out of reach.

He stuffed his hands into his pockets, then watched the old Sunbird circle the dilapidated fountain and head toward the road. She'd warned him. Come Monday, she would be back in reporter mode. Maybe he should just give her the interview. Then she'd leave him alone. One pesky reporter out of his hair.

Instead of relief, the thought left him with a vague sense of disappointment. Maybe he didn't want her to leave him alone.

He shook his head. What was wrong with him? Even at his worst, he was always decisive and in control. He mapped out his course and charged ahead, not one to second-guess himself.

Now he didn't know what he wanted. The problem was Jami stirred something in him, and it threatened to completely upset his ordered life.

The jury was still out on whether that would be good or bad.

—⚏—

Jami skidded to a stop a few parking spaces down from the Daily Grind. She was running late, which wasn't anything unusual. To Robert, it had been a constant source of annoyance. To her other friends, it was just something to tease her about.

This morning, though, was worse than normal. First, she'd overslept. Once showered and ready, she had hurried to the front door and hit a puddle, which sent her foot flying from under her and her body landing in an unladylike sprawl. Her hip and elbow were still screaming in protest. She didn't even know who to blame. Both dogs had looked down at her with eyes equally contrite, then rolled onto their backs in submission. With her unplanned change of clothes and second shower, her usual five to ten minutes late had grown into almost twenty.

She sprang from the car and sprinted down the sidewalk. As soon as she swung open the glass door, a figure just inside turned. Her pulse picked up, and her stomach made an unexpected flip. She tried to ignore both, chalking them up to nervousness, pressure to get the story.

Grant eyed her with suspicion, underscored by a hint of teasing. "Are you stalking me?"

"No. Actually, I am, but that's not why I'm here. I'm meeting friends for coffee." She stepped inside and let the door swing shut. "Follow me, and I'll introduce you."

After several greetings and hugs from the people who hadn't seen her since her return from school, she finally reached the table where Holly and Samantha waited. Holly's lips were quirked upward, her eyes lit with unspoken questions. She was as bad as Bernie. Jami would set her straight as soon as Grant was out of earshot.

"Holly, Sam, this is Grant McAllister. I'm doing an article on his family, and he's going to help me." She gave him a wink. "He just doesn't know it yet."

Without confirming or disputing her claim, he shook Holly's hand, then Sam's. For a brief moment, his gaze snagged on the side of Sam's face. Below the ever-present baseball cap, pale, mottled skin stretched tightly across her right cheek, over her jawbone and down the side of her neck, the result of a barn fire. Jami hardly noticed the scars anymore. Sam's exuberance and love for life were so infectious her physical imperfections seemed to slip quietly into the background.

Grant gave Sam a warm smile, but a coarse voice rose above all the others in the Grind, drowning out his "Pleased to meet you." Bernie moved toward the bar, clad in a neon-green pantsuit trimmed in hot pink. The clothing was typical Bernie. The hair wasn't. Last night must have been dyeing night. Besides the usual orangey-red hue, she'd somehow managed to get streaks of purple running throughout. Not many people could pull off a look like that—only twentysomething rock stars and one flamboyant, old newspaper reporter.

Bernie's gaze shifted toward them, and she made a beeline for their table. "Well, hello, ladies. And gentleman. You're all lookin' mighty fine this mornin'." She patted her poufy locks. "What do you think of the do?"

Holly nodded. "I like it. But tell me the truth. Was it planned?"

"Yes and no. Last time I accidentally ended up with some orange streaks, which got me thinking. So this time I went for dramatic instead of the same old, boring thing."

Jami laughed. "Bernie, you couldn't be boring if you tried. But you definitely succeeded with the drama."

Bernie hooked one arm through Jami's and the other through Grant's. "Let's go get some coffee."

After guiding them to the counter, she hiked herself onto the only unoccupied bar stool. Next to her, Hank Dorchester sat, sipping a cappuccino. When he didn't immediately turn, she heaved a sigh.

"What kind of a gentleman are you? A lady sits next to you and doesn't even get greeted. Didn't you hear me come in?"

Grant watched, obviously amused. But Hank didn't seem to notice Bernie's conspicuous entrance. He took another long sip, then set the cup on the counter in front of him. When he finally turned to face Bernie, his gaze swept the length of her before bouncing back up to settle on the halo of red hair. "Bernie, you're so loud I can hear you coming even when you don't open your mouth. Although *that* rarely happens."

For the next several moments, Bernie's guffaw drowned out whatever conversations were going on around them, and she slapped a hand on the wooden counter. "Hank Dorchester, you're an ever-lovin' mess."

After the server had waited on them, Jami gathered her Danish and coffee and turned to Grant. "You're welcome to sit with us if you'd like."

"Thanks, but I don't want to crash your breakfast with your friends." He raised his cup of coffee in farewell and turned in search of other seating.

As Jami made her way back to the table, Holly continued to watch her with the same knowing half smile. But it was Sam who spoke.

"Let me guess. Bernie somehow finagled an assignment that would force you to spend some time with this Grant McAllister."

Jami put her coffee on the table and slid into a seat. "You got it."

"I don't think I'd fight Bernie on this one." Holly's eyes were still on Grant. "What does he do?"

"I'm not sure. But he doesn't seem very thrilled with the inheritance. I get the impression he doesn't need the money."

It wasn't just his attitude toward the estate. It was everything about him. The designer clothes that gave him the appearance of having just stepped off the cover of *GQ*. The way he carried himself—confident, suave, sophisticated. The air of classiness that surrounded him.

"Good-looking *and* successful. You better nab him."

Jami shook her head. "I'm not looking, and I don't think Grant is, either. Right now, I've got other concerns. I need that interview, and he's not budging."

Samantha sank her teeth into her egg-and-cheese biscuit. No coffee and Danish for her. When she strayed from her usual morning concoction of freshly juiced vegetables mixed with some kind of green powder, it was never for anything remotely decadent. "So what are you going to do?"

"I'm going to convince him to let me interview him. I've got to. I can't fail at my first assignment." She puffed out a frustrated sigh. "I'm afraid the next person who tells me what a great reporter Howard was is going to find my fingers wrapped around their throat."

"That would be quite a headline for the *Cherokee Scout*." Samantha looked past Jami and tilted her head. "I think Grant's having trouble finding an empty table."

When Jami turned, Grant was moving past a family of tourists, with some kind of croissant sandwich in one hand and a cup of coffee in the other. She lifted an arm to motion him over.

Holly lowered her voice to a whisper. "When it comes to Bernie's matchmaking schemes, you've got to admit Grant is a better choice than Eddie."

Jami groaned. "He was so full of himself. He couldn't pass a storefront without flexing or rearranging his hair." She shook her head. "I didn't think I was ever going to get rid of him. When I found out Bernie had been egging him on the whole time, I could have strangled her."

Samantha laughed. "When you finally got rid of him, she tried to hook him up with me."

Grant laid his breakfast on the table and slid onto the only empty stool. When his shoulder brushed hers, Jami's heart picked up speed. The more time he spent with her, the more likely she was to get the story. That was the only reason for her reaction.

But she couldn't argue with Holly's assessment. Grant *was* good-looking. The angled lines of his face, straight, proud nose and chiseled jaw radiated strength and masculinity. His eyes weren't just blue. They were that brilliant green-blue color of the Caribbean Sea. Judging from his jet-black hair, he apparently took after his mother's side of the family. He looked nothing like the pictures she'd seen of his redheaded Irish grandparents.

He picked up his sandwich. "Sounds like you're talking about Bernie. I get the impression she's a character."

Jami rolled her eyes. "You don't know the half of it. She's made it her personal mission to make sure everyone within a ten-mile radius of downtown Murphy has found their special someone."

Grant nodded. "I figured that out within a few minutes of meeting her."

"The problem is she's not very good at it." Sam grinned. "I've been on the receiving end of those matchmaking schemes more times than I can count."

Holly gave her a sympathetic smile. "Jami has, too. I used to feel so sorry for you two. Wherever she dug up these guys, she was scraping the bottom of the barrel." She shook her head. "I was blessed. I somehow escaped Bernie's notice."

Sam frowned at her. "That's because Bernie didn't think you needed any help."

No one could argue with that. All her years at Murphy High, Holly had boys flock to her, unable to resist the silky blonde hair, blue eyes and million-dollar smile. She never left home without making sure her makeup was flawless and her hair was straightened and brushed to a fine sheen. But the primping hadn't been needed. She'd always been pretty without it. Now, at twenty-two, it was graduate school instead of high school and hot rollers instead of a straightening iron. Although she probably still spent as much time on her appearance as most students spend studying, she'd mastered the art of making it look effortless.

Holly waved away the compliment. "One thing we can all agree on is that, at almost fifty-eight years old, Bernie's not likely to change."

Grant's gaze shifted to the bar, where the object of their conversation was eagerly devouring a Danish. "She must be happily married."

"No." Samantha and Holly spoke at the same time, and Sam continued. "Never has been. I haven't even known her to date."

"Sam's right," Jami said. "She's too busy playing matchmaker for everyone else."

Grant raised his brows. "That's a little hypocritical. Have you ever considered turning the tables on her?"

Holly's eyes widened, and a slow grin spread across her face. "I love it. We can do some matchmaking of our own."

Sam rubbed her hands together. "Bernie and Hank."

"Hank?" Grant's brows went up a second time. "The guy in the overalls sitting next to her at the bar? They act like they can't stand each other."

Jami smiled. It was fun including Grant in their scheming. "We think it's an act, that they really have a secret crush on each other."

Holly took a bite of pastry, then talked around it. "So how are we going to get them together? We can't just set up a blind date."

Jami thought for a moment. "Bernie's birthday is a week from Friday. What do you say we start with flowers? We can have them delivered to the paper, make her think they're from a secret admirer."

"That's a great idea." Holly again lowered her voice. "So what do we put on the card?"

Sam didn't hesitate. "Roses are red, violets are blue. I can't go on if I don't have you."

Grant shook his head. "Based on the short exchange at the bar, that doesn't sound like Hank at all."

"How about this?" Holly said. "My love for you is immense. When you're near, the sun is always shining—"

"And when you're far away," Sam cut in, keeping the same dramatic tone Holly had used, "heavy, black clouds overshadow the sky."

Jami giggled. "You guys aren't any help at all. If it's too mushy, she'll know it's a prank."

Grant leaned forward. "How about this? From someone who thinks you're one special lady."

"Perfect." Sam held up her juice bottle in a toast. "To scheming."

Grant raised his mug, and Holly followed. "To love."

"To love," Jami repeated. And the clink of porcelain and glass sealed it.

FOUR

Grant stepped under the red awning of ShoeBooties Café and drew in a deep breath, savoring the mouthwatering smells. He'd discovered some decent restaurants during his four days in Murphy, and it looked like ShoeBooties was going to be another one to add to the list.

When he stepped inside, the hostess smiled at him. Sara, according to her name tag. "One?"

He nodded. He was used to eating alone, even at home. Usually he read or perused files he'd brought from the office. Tonight he had his iPad, along with a mental list of what he hoped to accomplish. What he didn't get finished there, he would do when he got back to his room.

The young woman led him to a two-person booth in the corner. In the center of the table, a tea candle burned inside a red glass vase. It was the perfect setting for a romantic evening out. There was even live music, a young man playing a keyboard a few feet away.

But there wouldn't be any romancing going on at his table. He would spend the next hour reading e-mails and reviewing documents. Janet, his paralegal, had been in touch every day since he left New York, helping to ensure the transition went smoothly. Today was no exception. She'd texted him earlier in the afternoon, so he already knew what he would find when he opened his e-mail—trial management conference notes, a settlement offer and a couple of briefs.

All his cases had been farmed out to other lawyers in his firm. Preparing someone to take over the newer ones had been easy. The ones approaching trial were the challenge—files bulging with motions and notices and mounds of discovery. But Janet had been with him since day one and was making the whole process as painless as possible. During his week back, he would tie up any loose ends.

Then he'd be ready to take off. Hopefully everyone at the firm would be ready to move forward without him. He'd still have his phone and iPad, which would make him easily reachable. But he'd rather they not use them.

After Sara walked away, he flipped the cover back on his iPad. He'd just pulled up his e-mail when an excited squeal cut into his thoughts. "Jami, girl! When did you get back?"

Jami? He looked up from his device. *Relax.* There were probably dozens of Jamis in Murphy. At least a handful or two.

As he waited, Sara stepped around the wall separating the dining area from the entrance. Jami was right behind her. The *Cherokee Scout* Jami. She'd probably followed him there. Or trolled the streets of downtown, looking for his car. Maybe he should have chosen something less conspicuous.

He ignored the sudden lightness in his chest and heaved a sigh. His trip to Murphy wasn't going at all as he'd planned. Not only was he being relentlessly pursued for an interview, he was a victim in some crazy lady's matchmaking scheme. One that had no hope of success. A quirky, free-spirited soul like Jami wasn't likely to be interested in a stick-in-the-mud New York City lawyer.

And she wasn't exactly his type, either. The few women he'd dated had been cultured, with elegant grace and a cool beauty. Women who roamed the upper echelons of society as if they were born to it. Like Bethany. Though look where that relationship had gotten him.

Jami was nothing like his ex-wife. She possessed a special blend of blunt honesty, wry humor, and obvious contentment with who she was. And a guy would have to be blind to not be drawn in by her warm smile and expressive eyes.

He shook off the thoughts. Tall, stately and sophisticated or short, quirky and down-to-earth—it made no difference. Hell would freeze over before he would once again be ready to risk his heart or his bank account.

Sara turned to Jami. "Table or booth?"

Jami looked around the restaurant, then pointed his direction. "Booth. That one." Without waiting to be seated, she made a beeline for his table.

Great, now he wouldn't get anything done. He stifled a snort. Who was he kidding? He'd worked most of the day at his grandmother's place, and when the entire afternoon had passed without Jami intruding, he'd been disappointed.

"Mind if I join you?"

He quirked a brow at her. "I was right. You *are* stalking me."

"I already told you I was. May I sit?"

He motioned toward the opposite bench. "Are you planning to follow me back to New York?"

"Nope." Her lips were turned up in one of those sassy smiles. "I'm planning to get the interview before you leave, so I won't have to."

"You're awfully confident."

"No, just determined."

Before she could sit, a waitress approached and gave her as enthusiastic of a welcome as Sara had, complete with a hug. Judging from what he'd seen at the Grind that morning, Jami was well liked by the people of Murphy. He wasn't surprised. That quick wit and enthusiasm were like magnets, drawing people to her. He'd been caught in the pull himself, which probably wasn't a good thing.

The waitress took their drink orders, and Grant watched her walk away. "You called her Aunt Lily. Is she really your aunt, or is that an affectionate title?"

"She's my aunt. While I was growing up, she and my mom had a bed-and-breakfast together. Through my teen years I helped out on weekends. I really enjoyed it—hanging out with my mom and aunt, interacting with the guests. Having spending money was pretty cool, too." She sighed, and a sense of nostalgia seemed to settle over her. "Several times since then, I've thought about how cool it would be to open one myself someday."

"What happened to your mom and aunt's place?"

"After my mom got sick the first time, they sold it."

"Does your mom live here in Murphy?"

"She did." Pain filled her eyes. "She died a year ago. Breast cancer."

"I'm sorry."

She lifted her chin. "Thanks, but we had a lot of good times. She knew where she was going, and I think she left this life without a single regret."

"That's more than a lot of people can say." He tried to keep the hardness from his tone, but it seeped in anyway. It happened every time he thought of his grandparents. "What about your father? Is he still alive?"

She looked over at him and shrugged. "I have no idea. He walked out on us when I was in the third grade. My mom was pushing him to get help, but he decided he'd rather give up his family than his booze."

He studied her while she spoke. The bitterness he expected to hear in her tone wasn't there. Instead she just sounded resigned. "You don't seem angry."

Lily approached with their drinks, then took their orders. After she left, Jami stared into the flickering flame and traced a small figure eight on the polished wooden surface of the table.

"When I realized he wasn't coming back, I was crushed. For the next two years, every birthday and the whole week before Christmas, I would eagerly check the mail and wait by the phone, sure he'd finally remember me."

"Did he?"

"Nope, not once." She continued her smooth, slow pattern, around and around. "Finally when my tenth birthday passed with no card or phone call, I dried my eyes and decided I wasn't going to shed another tear for him. I thought I was all grown up, you know, double digits. After that night I never cried for him again, and through my teen years, I hated him."

"What changed? You must have gotten past it at some point."

"I have my mom to thank for that." She finally met his eyes, her face alight with love and gratitude. "She was forgiveness personified, an awesome example. For years, she prayed for me. Finally, everything she'd been telling me sank in, and I realized I was only hurting myself. He has to answer for what he did, but I have to answer for my reaction to what he did. When I finally let go of the anger, it was as if a big weight had been lifted off me. Now when I think about him, I'm just sad."

He shook his head. How could a man walk away from a daughter like Jami? "I'm sorry. I never knew my father, but he didn't leave by choice."

"It's okay. My mom did a great job filling the role of both parents. Of course, she had a little help. Besides my aunt and uncle and cousins, the church people really took us under their wings when my dad left. I always felt like part of a big, loving family."

He nodded, an odd emptiness settling inside, the sense he'd missed out on something special. His mother had filled the dual role well, too, but she'd done it alone. At least from the time he was four years old and they moved to New York. There'd been no loving church family to offer encouragement and support. Just random Christians whose faith was nothing but talk, like the wealthy McAllisters who kept their hands fisted and refused contact with a hurting widow. The landlord who claimed to be a saint, then trumped up repairs so he could keep their security deposit. Even Bethany. She and her parents had gone every Sunday. It was a large church, with lots of wealthy members. He'd gone a couple of times. It had felt more like belonging to a club. Apparently that was all the effect attendance had on his former in-laws, too, because instead of acknowledging their daughter's wrongs, they'd taken her side on everything.

Maybe there *was* a level of compassion and generosity among some church people, but he certainly hadn't seen it.

"How is everything going, the house and all?" Jami's words pulled him back to the present.

"Slow. I'd hoped to be further along by now." At the rate he was going, he wouldn't even be finished with the first floor by the time he left on Thursday. And he'd found nothing belonging to his father. It was as if Gary McAllister had never existed. "How about your article?"

"Aside from the stubborn, bullheaded grandson?" She gave him a crooked grin. "It's going well. I got some great information from Hilda Parker. She was head librarian for about twenty years. She's ancient now, but she's got the mind of a thirty-year-old."

"Good." He didn't feel so guilty holding out on her if she'd be able to get the information for her article elsewhere.

"She's rounding up some pictures for me. Her son used to play with your dad when he would come during summers and holidays."

His pulse picked up. "She has pictures of my dad?"

"She's pretty sure she does. I was planning to give you copies of whatever she can find."

"Thank you. My mom has only one album of photos with him." Throughout his childhood he'd pored over and over them, wishing he could make the man in the images materialize before him, if not in real life, in his dreams. Occasionally he did. "In all the pictures we have, he's an adult."

As Lily placed a garden salad in front of each of them, excitement coursed through him. Four days of searching had gotten him nowhere, but Jami had already hit the jackpot. And she had planned to share with him whatever she obtained, not in exchange for him granting her an interview, but because she knew what it would mean to him.

He stabbed a forkful of salad. She was right. He *was* stubborn and bullheaded, even though she'd said it with a teasing smile. He couldn't head back to New York without giving her anything for her story.

"When did you want to come out and take your photos?" Four days, and he was already throwing up the white flag of surrender. No, not surrender. Just a little give-and-take.

"I wasn't trying to bribe you with Hilda's photos. I was planning to get those for you anyway. Now, the chocolate chip cookies . . ." She flashed him a teasing grin. "Those were a bribe."

He returned her smile. "You're welcome to take all the pictures you want. But I'm afraid I won't be much help as far as an interview. I don't know anything."

"You can tell me about yourself."

No way was he going anywhere near that. "I'm not a very interesting person."

"The people of Murphy would find you interesting. I don't even know what you do."

"CIA agent."

Her eyes widened. "Are you serious?"

"No. You're pretty gullible, aren't you?"

"I'm not. I just haven't figured you out yet. So seriously, what do you do?"

"I'm a defense attorney representing insurance companies. See, I told you I was boring."

"Do you play any musical instruments, or are you involved in any athletics?"

He smiled. Funny how easily she'd slipped into interview mode. "I used to play French horn but haven't picked it up in a while. And no athletics, unless you count my home gym."

"What about family? Based on what Bernie told me, there's no Mrs. McAllister back home."

"Nope. Been there, done that, bought the T-shirt. Then had to mortgage it to pay for my mistake."

She grimaced and shot him a sympathetic smile. "That bad."

"Every bit. And that's all I'm telling you." Of course, she could do an Internet search of his name and pull up the entire scoop.

"How about if I come over tomorrow? I can be there around nine."

"Sounds good."

She stabbed her last bite of salad but instead of bringing it to her mouth, gestured with it as she spoke. "So how did the meeting with your Realtor go?"

"Pretty well. But she doesn't expect a quick sale."

"And Vanguard?" Something told him the nonchalant tone she managed took some effort.

"It went well. He made me an offer I couldn't refuse, and we're closing on the place in thirty days."

Her jaw dropped, and her face fell with it. "You're selling to Durham Vanguard?"

"You *are* gullible. Adorably so, I might add."

"I am not gullible. I just keep forgetting there's a wry sense of humor hiding beneath all the sternness."

"So you think I'm stern."

"Stern and gruff. Cocky at first, but I'm amending my opinion on that one." The bite that had traveled around on her fork finally made it to her mouth, and she followed it with a swig of iced tea.

"Stern, gruff *and* cocky. I'm not sure what to think of that."

Lily came to remove their plates. When she left them alone again, he continued.

"The serious answer to your question is I haven't decided. I told him I'd let him know."

Her features relaxed in a sort of cautious relief, like someone who'd been given a reprieve but not a full pardon. "So there's a good chance you won't?"

The hope in her eyes went straight to his gut, and he had to remind himself again it was a business decision. But even with business decisions, sometimes intangible factors came into play. "Not in the foreseeable future. I think I would have to reach a certain level of desperation."

"And what level is that?"

"Flat broke, living in my car and struggling to fend off starvation."

She laughed, a pleasant, musical sound that wove through his mind and wrapped around his heart. The candlelight and music were getting to him.

"So you weren't exactly impressed with him."

"I don't think I've ever met anyone quite so full of himself."

"Frankly, I haven't, either."

Vanguard's offer was good. Fair market value and then some. And the man was ready to act now. Finding another buyer would likely take months. But he could wait it out. He wasn't hurting for money. Not by a long shot.

He would give the Realtor a chance. Several chances, if need be, because the thought of letting Vanguard get his hands on the property filled his gut with lead. His dislike for the man had started with that phone conversation. The face-to-face meeting had only intensified those feelings. If the Realtor could find a buyer, it would be better for everyone involved. Including Jami.

As much as he hated to admit it, he cared what she thought. She'd woven herself into the hearts of the people of Murphy.

If he wasn't careful, she was going to find her way to his own.

"Excuse the mess. I think my gardener flew the coop."

Jami sidestepped the brambles and other undergrowth that had taken over the McAllister gardens and smiled back at Grant. "No problem. I'm always up for an adventure."

She wasn't about to complain. When Grant offered to let her take pictures, she'd almost dropped her fork. She hadn't been nearly as confident as she'd let him believe.

She leaned forward to step over a small downed tree, bracing herself on its trunk before straightening to shoot a series of photos. The neglect framed in her lens had obviously started long before Elizabeth McAllister's departure. It wasn't just the yard. The house showed the same lack of care. The back deck sagged, its weathered boards graying, cracked and warped, and the top portion of the chimney lay scattered about its base, a haphazard jumble of stones and mortar.

She dropped the camera to let it dangle from the strap around her neck. "I think that about wraps it up outside." She made her way back around to the front of the house, Grant next to her. "So what do you know about the McAllisters?"

"Nothing. Remember, I never met them."

"Surely your mother told you something."

His jaw tightened, and he walked in silence so long she gave up hope of an answer. Finally, he drew in a slow, deep breath. "Elizabeth and Franklin McAllister were Charlotte socialites. They had lots of plans for my dad. Falling in love with the daughter of poor Hungarian immigrants wasn't one of them." His words were heavy with sarcasm.

"They tried hard to break them up, even offered to pay my mother if she would disappear. She told them to keep their money, and they eloped."

"And the McAllisters disowned him."

He nodded. "When my mom and dad got back from their honeymoon, my dad tried to reconcile with his parents."

"How did that go?"

"We'll never know. He didn't make it home. But since my grandparents refused to have anything to do with my mom and me, I can make an educated guess. We weren't good enough for the high-and-mighty McAllisters."

Jami cringed at the resentment lacing his tone. He wasn't letting his grandparents off the hook, even after their death. And judging from his attitude toward marriage, he hadn't let his ex-wife off the hook, either.

She flashed him a sympathetic smile. "You know, as long as you let it eat at you, you're giving them a certain amount of control over you."

"Now you're a psychologist?"

"No, just someone who's been there. Life's a lot better when you let it go." She ignored his frown and continued. "So why do you think she left everything to you? She could have donated her fortune to charity."

He shrugged and opened the front door, letting her go in ahead of him. "Who knows?"

"Maybe she regretted the way she treated you and your mother and was trying to make up for it."

"It's too late. We could have used it when my mom was struggling to keep us fed. I don't need it now."

His tone had softened only slightly. That stern facade didn't just hide a wry sense of humor; it also hid a lot of hurt and betrayal. If only he could experience the same freedom she had. She knew what it would take. Getting him to see it would be another thing altogether.

He closed the door and held out a hand, palm up. "Feel free to wander through."

"I will." She lifted the camera to her face and squinted through the viewfinder. The small green brackets framed only half of the stairway. She snapped the photo anyway, then captured the upper half before letting the camera once again dangle.

For the next several minutes, she took pictures, oohing and aahing as she went. Even with the lack of care over the years, the attention to detail was amazing. So were the furnishings and artwork. The paintings and sculptures alone would fetch a small fortune.

She pushed open a door, then let out a low, appreciative whistle. A fireplace was nestled into one wall, a padded leather chair flanking each side. Built-in bookshelves covered the other three walls, floor to ceiling. Every shelf was full. She stepped forward and ran her finger across the spines of several classics, likely original editions. "This is a book lover's dream."

She moved back to survey the room again. Grant stood in the open doorway, leaning against the jamb, watching her. His pose was relaxed, and he wore a half smile. "I had the same reaction the first time I walked in. I've always been an avid reader."

"Me, too. If I wasn't in school or hanging out with Holly and Sam, I had my nose in a book." Reading was still her favorite pastime. She could easily picture herself curled up in one of the big leather chairs, surrounded by the sight and scent of old books, a roaring fire next to her and one of the classics open in her lap.

Grant pushed himself away from the doorjamb and walked into the room. "When I was a kid, we moved around a lot. Mom would go wherever she could make the best money. And while the babysitter watched her soaps, I read. Always being the new kid, I found it easier to connect with the characters in my books than the people I went to school with."

Warmth infused her chest. In spite of his refusal to grant her an interview, he'd just given her a rather personal glimpse into his childhood. That cozy image she'd created moments earlier flashed through her mind again, except this time Grant was occupying the other chair. She pushed the thought aside and flashed him a sympathetic smile. "I can imagine it's not easy being the outsider. Kids can be cruel."

She snapped several pictures, then stepped back into the hall. Around the corner, an open double doorway led into another room. This one was huge, probably twenty by thirty, with marble floors and intricately carved molding beneath a ceiling of decorative wood panels. Three sets of French doors led onto the deck spanning the back.

"This is the ballroom." She spun slowly, taking in the detailed carvings, huge mirrors with heavy gold frames and crystal chandeliers that captured and disbursed whatever stray shafts of light found their way through the dirt-caked windows and doors. "Can't you picture it? Ladies in their colorful gowns, hair piled atop their heads, jewelry glittering in the lamplight. Men in their starched shirts and dark suits. Servants slipping in and out with their trays of delectable sweets and crystal champagne glasses."

He wasn't smiling, but his brows were raised, and there was a hint of amusement in his blue eyes. "I think your writer's imagination is working overtime."

"I'm not a writer. I'm a journalist." Well, she was both, but the former she didn't broadcast. She couldn't claim to be a writer when she had yet to finish something.

"Same difference."

She raised the camera and snapped a picture. "No, journalists don't make things up."

"They just embellish the truth."

Her gaze snapped to his face. The distrust she'd seen in his eyes when she first confronted him in the Holiday Inn parking lot was back. His refusal to let her interview him wasn't because of a desire for privacy. Sometime in the past, he'd had a bad experience.

"They're not supposed to. And I can assure you this one doesn't." She turned away from him to take shots from several angles.

"So what do you think this room *was* used for?"

"Entertainment, for real." She continued working as she talked. "The McAllisters regularly threw lavish parties. Some of the older people in town still talk about them."

"See, you *do* know more about the McAllisters than I do."

She leaned against the doorjamb and snapped one more picture. This one had Grant in it. She might end up keeping it. He stood in a relaxed pose, one hand in his pocket, the other resting at his side. His expression was serious, which, from what she knew of Grant, was typical. She hadn't witnessed very many spontaneous smiles. But that didn't detract from his good looks. It just made him look that much more distinguished—strong, masculine, brooding, a bit untouchable.

"I've learned a few things." The things that were public information, anyway. Not the kind of details that made for compelling, in-depth reporting. "Your grandfather made his money in Charlotte, in banking and real estate. Right after your dad was born, they bought this property and had the house built. Although this was a second home for them, they kept the place fully staffed—gardener, maids, cooks, butler—and the parties they held were something else."

Grant moved toward her. "That explains the kitchen. It's pretty state of the art for sixty years ago."

When she walked into the room, she had to agree. Cabinetry and countertops stretched to ridiculous lengths along three walls, the expanse broken by two double sinks and a pair of matching cooktops. Two islands in the center offered more workspace.

He motioned toward the far wall. "Someone could replace these two old Frigidaires with a couple of stainless steel side by sides, update the ovens and stoves, add a couple of commercial dishwashers and a convection oven, and they'd have a chef's dream."

She lifted her brows. "For a guy, you're awfully enthusiastic about a kitchen."

"I don't cook much anymore, but I used to do it a lot. I was actually pretty good at it."

She studied him, then wrinkled her nose. "I'm having trouble picturing you in an apron and chef's hat, slaving away over a hot stove."

"It's not that far-fetched. I learned to cook for self-preservation. My mom's idea of a gourmet meal has always been a frozen dinner and salad-in-a-bag."

"I've got you beat there. My mom was an awesome cook." She moved around the kitchen, taking shots at different angles, until she once again stood next to Grant. "Why don't you cook anymore?"

"Just busy." He turned away, but not in time to hide the hardness that had settled in his eyes. He made several slow swipes of his hand across the butcher-block surface of the island, clearing away the dust in a widening arc. It drifted downward, joining the thin layer already blanketing the hardwood floor. "I guess I'm going to need the name of a good cleaning person before the Realtor shows the place."

"I think we can arrange that." Whatever his reason for no longer cooking, it wasn't because he was busy. Nor was it something he wanted to discuss with her.

He turned to face her, brushing the dust from his hand. "Are you ready to tackle the second floor of this tour?"

She followed him back to the foyer and up the curved stairway. At each end of the second floor was a master suite, complete with a sitting area and huge bath. One was masculine, the other distinctly feminine. Two other bedrooms lined one side of the long hall. The door on the opposite side was closed . . . and locked.

She dropped her hand and turned to study Grant. "Something you don't want the local newspaper reporter to see?"

"Since it was locked when I arrived, I have no idea."

"So *you* don't even know what's in there."

"It's the only locked room in the place. There aren't even any locked closets."

She stared at the door, her lower lip trapped between her teeth. "How are you at picking locks?"

"Pretty rusty. My burglary days are long over."

Her gaze shot to his face, but there was no hint of teasing there. "You used to break into houses?"

A smirk quivered at the corners of his mouth, hidden amusement that almost broke the surface. "You *are* gullible."

She poked him in the ribs. "I'm not gullible."

He twisted and grabbed her hands, obviously ticklish. His touch sent an electric charge shooting through her, one she tried her hardest to ignore. But the sensation wouldn't go away. His hands were strong, even a little calloused. Probably the result of lifting weights, the home gym he mentioned earlier.

She pulled from his grasp and looked up at him. His smile was broader now, and it did funny things to her pulse. All the oxygen seemed to leach from the room. She drew in a quivery breath and turned back to the door, breaking the connection before she said or did something stupid. She had no business feeling that way about anyone at the moment, and certainly not Grant.

"I wonder what the McAllisters thought was so important it needed to be locked up."

"I'm sure I'll run across a key somewhere. If not, I'll call a locksmith."

She shook her head. His nonchalance was making her crazy. "Aren't you going nuts, wondering what's in there?"

"I *am* a little curious. I've just been too busy to do anything about it."

"A little curious! If this was my place, I'd be kicking in the door. I mean, it's like this big mystery, begging to be solved." Especially with the secrecy surrounding the McAllisters. There were likely answers in that room. A great angle for her story.

"So you think there might be skeletons in the McAllister closet."

"Think about it. They suddenly disappear from society." She held up an index finger, then followed it with two others. "No one goes in or out for thirty years. And now this mysterious locked room. What do *you* think?"

"I think they were serial killers, and this is where they hid the bones of their victims." His tone was flat, deadpan, a teasing glint in his eyes the only hint he wasn't serious. She was starting to figure him out.

She grinned up at him. "You never know. But if you're interested, I can put you in touch with a good locksmith. Like right now." She pulled her phone from the pouch on her belt and scrolled through her contacts.

"You keep the locksmith's number programmed into your phone? You must lock yourself out on a regular basis."

"I *have* locked my keys in the car a few times." Maybe she shouldn't admit it. Grant seemed too put together to have engaged in any of her absentminded foibles. "That's not why I have the locksmith's number, though." She punched a final button and put the phone to her ear. "Brian happens to be my cousin, Aunt Lily's next-oldest son."

Once she reached him, she provided a brief explanation and handed Grant the phone.

A minute later, he ended the call. "He'll be here in thirty minutes."

She finished taking pictures and had just made her way downstairs when the doorbell chimed. As soon as Grant swung open the door, Brian stepped inside and engulfed her in a bear hug. Of all of her cousins, if she had to choose a favorite, it would be Brian. They shared no family resemblance. He was a good ten years older than her, fair skinned, freckled and built like a linebacker for the New York Giants. But for as long as she could remember, they'd shared a special bond.

When she made introductions, Brian grasped Grant's hand and shook it enthusiastically. "So where is this locked door my cousin is dying to get into?"

"Up here." Grant waved a hand and led him up the steps.

Jami hesitated. There was likely a reason that room was locked. Would Grant want her there when the door was opened for the first time?

She shook off her doubts and headed up the stairs. Grant didn't invite her, but he didn't ask her to leave, either.

If she was going to compete with Howard's legacy, she would have to be bold enough to pursue the story. The worst thing Grant could do was throw her out.

FIVE

Grant watched Brian make quick work of the lock. "You made it look easy."

"Comes with experience. There's not much I can't get into." He grinned at Jami and gave her a playful wink. "I've become a pro at Pontiac Sunbirds."

She punched him in the shoulder. "Hey, that's not fair. I've only locked my keys in the car twice."

"Three times."

"Okay, three times. In how many years?"

Brian paused, apparently doing the math. "Seven."

"So that's less than once every other year."

Grant watched the exchange, the warmth filling his chest tinged with longing. Jami was lucky to have family nearby. With both of his parents being only children, he'd missed out on cousins. Aunts and uncles, too. His maternal grandparents had passed away by the time he reached his teen years, so most of his life, he'd had no family except his mother.

Brian stepped aside. "Come on in. I'll have the lock rekeyed in no time."

Grant entered and scanned the room. It was a typical teenager's bedroom. Black bedspreads with bold splashes of color covered two twin beds, and model cars and sailing ships were prominently displayed on high shelves wrapping three sides of the room. Two large paintings hung on one wall, and a wooden desk stood in the corner, beneath a poster of the Beach Boys.

He turned to study the paintings more closely. One was a picture of a boy of about four holding a big tabby cat, the other a young man in a band uniform. His jaw went slack, and the room seemed to tilt. What he was seeing was impossible.

Jami stepped up beside him. "This was your dad's room." Her tone was low, almost reverent.

He stood motionless, still staring at one of the paintings. "My dad played the trumpet."

"That's a French horn." She gasped and spun to look at him. "That's you, isn't it?"

He nodded. "The cat in the other painting is Rusty. That's my mom's parents' backyard."

"But how . . ." Her voice trailed off, confusion deepening the furrows in her brow.

"I don't know." He blinked several times, trying to clear his mind. But his brain seemed to be stuck in neutral. "I never met the McAllisters. My mom said they wanted nothing to do with me."

"Those two-by-four-foot paintings say otherwise."

She was right. What he was looking at cast doubt on things he'd believed all his life. But if his grandparents had wanted to see him, why hadn't they tried to contact him?

Brian stepped forward and held up a set of keys, reminding them of his presence. "Here you go. All finished."

Grant dragged his gaze from the paintings, then reached for his wallet. "Thanks for coming out so quickly."

"Glad I could help."

Once Brian was gone, Grant crossed the room and opened the door on the back wall. The odor of mothballs and cedar assaulted his senses, increasing the air of mystery. This closet had probably sat undisturbed for years. He swung the door wider.

The space was large, a walk-in closet with shelves and rods spanning three sides. Two rows of clothes hung neatly on hangers, arranged by type—jeans, then dress pants, then a couple of suits on one side, and short-sleeved shirts, long-sleeved shirts, sweaters, and jackets on the other. Either the McAllister housekeeper's duties extended to maintaining closets in tip-top shape, or his father had been extremely organized. Since his own closet looked much the same way, it was probably the latter.

Letting his hand fall from the doorknob, he stepped farther inside. The shelves above the closet rods were empty except for a pair of roller skates, a baseball mitt and a reclining stuffed Tigger. Two stacks of boxes stood against the back wall. He reached for one of the top boxes, then dropped his arms. Was he about to uncover some of those skeletons he'd joked about earlier?

He cast a glance over his shoulder. Jami stood a couple feet from the open doorway, her expression somber. He should tell her to leave. She had plenty of pictures for her story. He opened his mouth to tell her as much, then snapped it shut again. What would be worse, Jami discovering the truth along with him, or having her speculate about it? She couldn't make anything up or print her own ideas of what might be in those boxes. But she could pose the questions and let her readers draw their own conclusions.

He picked up a box and walked from the closet. He would let Jami stay. If his grandparents harbored secrets, so be it. They were no concern of his.

After setting the box on the floor in the middle of the room, he returned to the closet to carry out each of the others, until all six rested at haphazard angles around the room. He dropped to his knees. The first four held stuffed animals, toy cars and trucks, a train set and some children's books. He handled each item with care. These were things his father had played with. He fingered through the pages of *Tom Sawyer*. Had his father shared his own love of reading?

He set the book aside and picked up a stuffed seal. The other plush toys were varying levels of almost new to new, but the seal's gray fur was worn, its stuffing compacted. It had obviously been a favorite, squeezed and hugged and held. Well loved. He brought the toy to his chest and closed his eyes, the longing to know the man who had owned it almost overwhelming.

A soft rustle drew his attention, and he lowered the stuffed toy, self-consciousness seeping through him. Jami had crossed the room and now sat watching him from the edge of the bed. She was quiet and subdued, apparently unwilling to intrude. It was just as well. He wasn't up for conversation anyway. He repacked the four boxes but kept one plush toy out. Most of the items he would donate, to be enjoyed by other children. The beloved stuffed seal he would keep.

When he lifted the flaps on the fifth box, his breath caught in his throat. Delicate script danced across a padded silver-and-blue cover—*My First Year*. He lifted it from the box, exposing a photo album. Below that were more albums. His heart began to pound. Finally, what he'd been looking for, pictures of his father.

He dragged the box toward the bed, then eased down next to Jami and opened the book. Inside was a birth announcement. Photos followed, interspersed with lots of stats—length, weight, favorite things, dates and descriptions of each small accomplishment. He tilted the book toward Jami, finally breaking the silence. "Check out this boat."

A grinning young boy looked back over one shoulder, clutching a smooth metal wheel taller than he was. In the background, white fiberglass and sleek wood trim stretched on and on. Someone had penned the words *First Sailing Trip* over the top.

Jami whistled. "That's not a boat. It's a small cruise ship."

His chest tightened. His grandparents' financial success just made their refusal to help sting that much more.

He thumbed through the pages and studied the pictures, emotion swelling in his chest, love for the father he'd never known. The books beneath were more of the same, album after album devoted to nothing but his father's childhood. He hadn't just found a key to his past. He'd hit the mother lode.

He pulled another album from the box. His father was much older in that one, probably in high school. Jami pointed to a photo of a teenager dressed in a band uniform and holding a trumpet.

"Your dad played in the band."

"I know. My mom did, too, flute. So I come from musical parents."

"How come you don't play anymore?"

He lowered his eyes to the album in his lap. His father stared back at him, proudly holding his instrument. His own was tucked away in its case at the back of his closet.

"Just busy." It was the same excuse he'd given her for quitting cooking. And judging from her frown, she wasn't buying it any more this time than she had before.

The truth was he'd given them both up together. After his marriage blew up, it just wasn't the same. Gourmet meals prepared and served alone, performances without Bethany in the audience. They were like banners announcing his failure. And he'd never tolerated failure well.

So he'd quit entertaining, quit the orchestra and thrown himself into the one area he would always be a success—work.

He turned to find Jami studying him, a sympathetic smile curving her lips. "I'm sorry you stopped."

Yeah. Sometimes he missed it. Just not enough to push himself to pick it back up, to go face all those people he'd spent so much time with and see the pity in their eyes. Too many private details of his life had been made public, some true, some Bethany's form of revenge. There'd been plenty of anger on both ends—his for suffering the ultimate betrayal, hers for the perceived wrongs that had led to that betrayal.

He dropped his gaze to the book and turned the page, pushing the thoughts from his mind. Next was a group picture, the entire band.

Jami shifted beside him. "I studied both piano and clarinet in junior high."

"Oh? I didn't know you played."

"I don't know if *played* is the right word for it. But I had really encouraging teachers. My piano teacher encouraged me to pursue the clarinet, and my clarinet teacher encouraged me to stick with piano."

He laughed, the gloominess burning off like early morning fog. "That's bad."

"Wait till you hear me sing. I make babies cry."

Still smiling, he closed the book and reached for another one. "I bet you're not half as bad as you think you are."

"Stand next to me in church sometime and you'll be changing your tune." She grinned. "No pun intended."

He closed the last book, then returned everything to the box. This one would definitely go back to New York. He stood and dragged over the final one while Jami watched from her place on the side of the bed. This box was larger, its top mashed in from the weight of the others. He bent over and raised the flaps. A scrapbook lay on top, another take-back-to-New-York item, as treasured as the photo albums. He placed it in his lap and opened the front cover. Inside was a short article and picture of a kindergarten graduation clipped from a newspaper—*a New York newspaper.*

Blood pounded in his ears, gradually building to a roar as he flipped through the book. This wasn't his father's scrapbook. It was his own. His grandparents had watched him, or someone had. The pages were filled with newspaper clippings, graduation bulletins, concert programs, every accomplishment he'd ever had, at least the publicly recognized ones. Interspersed throughout the book were photos, probably taken at a distance with a zoom lens.

Jami shook her head, her jaw slack. "Did your grandparents hire a PI to follow and photograph you all these years?" Her voice was the softest whisper. "If they didn't want any contact with you, why would they do that?"

He sat in silence, his mind spinning. He didn't have an answer. The scrapbook in his lap was proof they'd done exactly that. What he couldn't guess was why.

He laid the book aside and looked into the box. Several smaller ones were stacked inside, all sealed, as if ready for shipping. He picked up the first and read the label. It was sent to him in Raleigh, North Carolina, from Elizabeth and Franklin McAllister. Stamped next to the address was *return to sender* in red capital letters. The date on the postmark was a week before his first birthday.

He stared at the package, conflicting thoughts tumbling through his mind. That gift was contrary to everything his mother had told him. His grandparents hadn't ignored him. They had reached out with a gift. But he'd never received it.

He pulled another package from the box, this one sent in December, and then another, mailed around the time of his second birthday. Three gifts, all from his grandmother, addressed to him and returned unopened.

Jami drew in a deep breath. "Were they sent to the wrong address?"

"I don't know." He laid the packages aside. "We lived with my mom's parents in Raleigh until I was four, but I don't know the address."

Apparently it was different from what was on those packages. His gut tightened as a wave of unease swept through him. It *had* to be the wrong address. The alternative was unthinkable—that the one person who'd been his constant all his life had deceived him from the start.

Jami rested a hand on his forearm. "I'm sure there's a logical explanation. The address is probably wrong, and since your mom didn't have her own place at the time, they had trouble locating you."

"Thanks." He put his hand over hers and met her eyes. They were filled with sincerity and a warmth that touched something deep inside him. His foundation was shifting, leaving him scrambling for a foothold. But Jami was there, offering stability and encouragement. His hand tightened over hers, and an odd longing filled him, the desire to connect, to draw strength from someone and to offer his in return.

To no longer be alone.

He mentally shook himself. What was he thinking? He'd been alone all his life. In childhood, while his classmates excluded the new kid and his mom worked two jobs, he found his company in books. And in adulthood, while he focused on success, he hadn't taken the time to intimately connect with anyone except his wife. And he hadn't even done that right. While he'd poured himself into his career, she'd filled her time with her charitable fundraising activities and sought comfort in the arms of his best friend.

No, *alone* was what he knew.

He wasn't cut out for anything different.

—⚬⚬⚬—

Credits rolled on the big-screen TV. Three paper plates and an empty Papa's Pizza box sat on the coffee table beside a half-finished two-liter of Coke. Jami released a sigh and scratched Bailey behind the ears.

Samantha grinned over at her. "That sounded like a sigh of longing."

"She's missing her man."

Jami frowned at Holly. "Robert's not my man anymore." In fact, the way they'd left things, he probably wasn't even her friend. He hadn't tried to contact her since the awkward proposal at Downtown Pizza. No phone call, no text, no e-mail. No pleas to give their relationship another chance. Either he was taking the breakup exceptionally well and had already moved on, or he was so hurt and angry he wanted nothing to do with her. More than likely, it was the latter.

Holly shook her head. "Robert's not the man I'm talking about."

"Well, Grant's not my man, either." Although she *was* missing him. She'd spent a good bit of the day yesterday taking pictures and talking to him. Then today she'd followed through with her promise of lunch at Murphy Chophouse.

She was no longer on edge around him. The sense he was in a whole different realm had disappeared somewhere between warm chocolate chip cookies at his place and scheming at the Grind. She liked being with him—that dry sense of humor, the unexpected teasing, even the brooding.

Yesterday she'd seen a side of him that surprised her. Actually, it had done a whole lot more than that. As he'd knelt among the open boxes, eyes closed, the worn-out stuffed seal held tenderly against his chest, she'd almost cried. There was so much more to Grant than the cool, hard exterior he presented to the world.

She looked over at Holly again, who was watching her, a knowing glint in her eyes.

"You have to admit you're attracted to him."

"I'm guessing so are ninety percent of the other women he meets. Even Bernie says he's hot."

Sam grinned. "With Bernie, that doesn't mean anything."

Jami pushed the pizza box out of the way to rest her feet on the coffee table. "I just broke things off with Robert. I don't need to add another failure to my already-poor track record."

"Your track record's not *that* bad." Holly paused. "Well, maybe it is."

"It's okay to make mistakes," Sam said. "You just have to try to learn from them. First off, stay away from the guys who seem to eat up attention from women."

"Like Steve?"

Holly rolled her eyes. "He played on the Michigan State football team. Everyone knows athletes are major players."

Yeah, Steve was a player, all right. She'd been surprised when he'd taken an interest in her in algebra class. Over the next few weeks, he'd had her walking on air as he took her places and introduced her all over campus as his girlfriend. When she found out he'd slipped one of the cheerleaders into his dorm room, she'd crashed back down to earth in a ball of fire.

Sam continued. "And don't date guys who are too into themselves."

Holly nodded. "That's good advice. When they constantly talk about themselves, bragging about their accomplishments, those are instant red flags. They tend to be selfish. You want a guy who's into *you*."

Yep, she'd had her share of guys who thought way more of themselves than they should. Those relationships hadn't lasted long. When a man was more interested in himself than her, she lost patience fast.

"What about Jerrod?" Not all of her exes were jerks. "He wasn't conceited and selfish *or* a player."

Sam leaned forward to refill her plastic cup with Coke. "Your mistake with Jerrod was dating a guy who was still trying to get over his ex."

Everything her friends said made sense. In fact, she could see it herself. But hindsight was always twenty-twenty. Spotting all the negatives was a lot harder in the midst of the excitement of a new relationship. What she needed was supernatural wisdom. "I think I need to pray harder."

"Yeah," Holly agreed. "That, too."

She crossed her arms. "You know, I haven't always picked duds. Pierre was a nice guy."

Sam raised her brows. "Are you talking about our senior year of high school? He was a foreign exchange student and went back to France at the end of the school year."

And she'd been heartbroken. He'd promised to come back and continue his studies in America. She'd never heard from him again.

"Sam's right," Holly said. "If they have to move mountains to be with you, while that sounds romantic, it's not really practical."

"Trust me, expecting anything serious to develop between Grant and me isn't practical, either." New York wasn't as far away as France, but it might as well be. His life was there. Tomorrow he'd be flying back. He would make one more short trip. Then she'd never see him again. The emptiness stabbing through her was something she didn't want to admit to herself, much less her friends.

She leaned over Bailey to retrieve a spiral-bound notebook and pen from the coffee table. Time for a change of subject.

"We've got flowers being delivered for Bernie. Anybody have any ideas for Hank?"

She handed the notebook to Samantha, the only one with an empty lap since Morgan had claimed Holly's legs. Sam folded back the cover and wrote *Hank* across the top. "It can't be too mushy."

Jami nodded. Anything Bernie might write to Hank would likely have a touch of sarcasm.

Samantha tapped the end of the pen on the paper several times. "I have an idea." Moments later, she held up the notebook.

Holly read the words aloud. "I can hardly believe no one has snatched you up, a man of few words but great depth, strong yet gentle."

Jami eyed the page with a frown. "That doesn't sound like Bernie."

"How do you know?" Samantha asked. "When have you ever seen Bernie in love?"

"You've got a point." She studied the page some more, then nodded. "It might work. I've got to type it, though. I'd never be able to imitate Bernie's handwriting." Her signature was as unique as Bernie herself, the capital *B* a heavy vertical line with a series of loops and curves extending through the letters that followed, the capital *H* identical except with two vertical lines instead of one.

Holly pursed her lips. "How are we going to get it to Hank?"

"Mail it." Samantha twirled the pen between her fingers. "With just a Murphy postmark and no return address, it could come from anyone."

Holly's brows were creased in thought. Something apparently bothered her about the plan.

Jami frowned. "What's wrong?"

"I don't get it. If neither of them knows who the notes and gifts are from, how is that supposed to put them together?"

"We drop hints," Jami said. "Get Bernie thinking about Hank and Hank thinking about Bernie. The rest will happen. I think it's always been there. Hank's just too shy to pursue it."

Holly leaned forward, eyes sparkling with excitement and a little bit of mischief. "If he thinks she's already interested, it'll help him work up the courage to ask her out on a real date."

"And," Samantha continued, "if Bernie's been anticipating it, she'll be more likely to say yes."

Holly held up both hands, initiating two high fives. "Go, girlfriends. Are we good or what?"

"We're good." Samantha closed the notebook and pushed the pen down into the wire spiral. "So what's up with the boxes? I thought you were done unpacking."

Jami glanced over at the three boxes lined up against the living room wall. "Those aren't mine. They're Grant's."

Sam eyed them with interest. "What are you doing with them?"

"Holding on to them. They're photo albums and things. He wants to throw them away." But she couldn't bring herself to do it. Family was too important to her to throw away years of rich history. And if she let Grant do it, something told her he was going to regret it later. "I'm trying to keep him from making a big mistake."

Holly turned toward her, radiating eagerness. "Are you going to go through them?"

"I don't think he'd appreciate me snooping through his stuff." Although the thought had been there all along, the temptation stronger at some times than others.

"But he's throwing it away," Holly argued. "What would he care?"

"Yeah, but still." As much as she'd like to know what was in those boxes, going through them without his permission didn't sit right with her.

But curiosity had been getting the better of her since she brought them into the house several days earlier. By the time Sam and Holly left, curiosity won out over willpower, and she tore into the first box. Grant would never know. And maybe there would be something she could use for her article.

The photo albums were just as he'd said—pictures of the McAllisters before Gary McAllister was born. The second box was more of the same. The third box was smaller and appeared to be filled with letters, lots of them, all signed by Elizabeth McAllister. She removed the top letter from the stack and began to read.

Dear Gary,

I can't believe you're gone. I keep expecting you to walk through the door, kiss me on the cheek and tell me it was all a big misunderstanding. Then I realize this is it, you're not coming back, and we have to somehow go on without you.

Your father doesn't talk about it much. But he is grieving, too, in his own way. He regrets there was so much conflict between you. You always were a little headstrong, and so is he. That's why the two of you clashed. He tried to stop you from marrying Anna because he wanted what was best for you. Your decision to marry her anyway broke his heart, and he lashed out. But he didn't mean what he

> said, and he'll always live with regret, knowing the last words between you were spoken in anger.

The next several letters were much like the first, a grief-stricken mother pouring out her sorrow over a lost son. Then there was mention of Grant.

> Is it true Anna is carrying your child? I've tried to reach out to her, but she wants nothing to do with me. She blames us for your accident. In time I believe she will soften.

It was signed, *Your loving mother*.

Frowning, Jami looked up from the neat script. Elizabeth McAllister had apparently tried to contact Anna McAllister, and Anna refused. That completely contradicted what Grant believed.

She picked up the next letter and continued to read, page after page. Then the tone changed. It was just one paragraph, inserted into a letter similar to all the others.

> Desmond saw you today. Anna picked you up at the babysitter's house and carried you toward the car. But you wanted to walk and squirmed until she put you down. You're getting so big. I'm so proud of you. Desmond has promised to send me pictures.

Jami laid the letter in her lap. The paragraphs written to Gary blended smoothly into the single one that read as if Grant were the recipient. Maybe it was just a momentary lapse.

She learned the truth long before she reached the bottom of the box. The letters all began *Dear Gary*, but more and more, the line between son and grandson blurred until the only reference to Gary was the salutation itself. Apparently, Elizabeth McAllister had slowly lost her grip on reality. Had Franklin then proceeded to protect the secret, and his wife, in the only way he knew, sealing them off from the rest of the world?

Jami took the last letter from the box and laid it on the coffee table with the others. Beneath were envelopes, the top addressed to Elizabeth McAllister from Anna McAllister. Grant's mother? She probably wrote to ask the McAllisters for help, which, based on what Grant had told her, was denied.

She removed the contents of the envelope, two pages folded separately. When she opened the first, a check fluttered to her lap, and her eyes widened. Ten thousand dollars. Paid to Anna McAllister. But it was never cashed. Instead, *VOID* blazed across the front in angry black print. Why would Elizabeth McAllister write Grant's mother a check and then void it?

Her gaze shifted to the page she'd unfolded. As she read, coldness seeped into her core.

Grant had it all wrong.

It was too late tonight, but come morning, she would be on his doorstep. He would be furious with her for snooping through his things.

But now that she knew the truth, there was no way she could keep it from him.

SIX

Grant slipped his shaving kit into the corner of his suitcase. The gray seal was stuffed in at the other end. Everything was ready to go, including the photo albums and scrapbooks. He would drop the boxes by the post office for shipping. Then he'd have a leisurely breakfast at the Blue Mountain Grill, drive to the airport, return the rental car, and head back to New York.

One week ago, he couldn't wait for his stay in Murphy to end. Now he faced leaving with mixed emotions. His time there hadn't been nearly the drudgery he'd expected when he first arrived. Most of that he owed to one auburn-haired, green-eyed newspaper reporter who wouldn't take no for an answer. She'd turned what should have felt like relentless pursuit into a lighthearted game.

She had a radiance about her, a sense of carefree innocence. Exuberant, quirky and quick to smile, she seemed to carry sunshine with her wherever she went. But she had depth, too, an inner strength, a calm confidence that no matter what happened, everything would be all right. He'd seen it several times, during those glimpses into her serious side. The way she'd put her father's leaving behind her. The encouragement she'd given him when he discovered those suspicious packages. Even her earlier admonition against remaining angry with his grandparents. He hadn't appreciated it at the time, but he had to admit she was right.

He zipped his suitcase and rolled it across the suite. When he swung open the door, Jami stood there, fist poised to knock. His pulse rate kicked up a couple notches, and the start of an involuntary smile tickled his cheeks. As early as he had to leave, he hadn't expected to see her again. He wasn't disappointed.

Then his eyes dipped to the floor. His smile died before it could fully take form. If he hadn't recognized the shape and size of the box sitting at her feet, the word *trash* scrawled across the top would have left no doubt what was inside. She'd promised to throw it away, along with the other two. So what was it doing at his door?

"Grant, please don't be mad."

His chest tightened. Any conversation starting like that couldn't turn out well. "Do I have reason to be?"

"Maybe. But I had to see you. May I come in?"

He crossed his arms and studied her as she shifted her weight and clasped and unclasped her hands. The tightness intensified, spreading into his shoulders and neck.

"Please? I have to show you something."

He let her wait another long moment. There was nothing in that box he cared about. He'd already seen it. Jami apparently had, too. Her offer to take the boxes to the landfill was nothing but a way to get her hands on something belonging to the McAllisters. A pretty deceitful way, considering she'd intentionally misled him. Why was he surprised? She was a reporter, for Pete's sake.

Finally, he stepped aside, jaw tight. She picked up the box and carried it to the table against the wall in the sitting area of the suite. Thick black letters marched across its top, marking it for what it was. It should already be in the landfill by now. Instead, it sat proudly on the table, mocking him with its presence.

"Why do you still have this?"

"I couldn't bring myself to throw everything away without knowing what was there. I was afraid you would regret it later."

"That's my concern, not yours, don't you think?" His tone was hard, and he didn't try to soften it. Whatever warm thoughts he'd had for Jami moments earlier had congealed into a cold lump. She was nothing but a nosy reporter, eager for some juicy tidbit she could use for her story.

She rested her hand on the top of the box. "You need to see these letters."

"I already have. They're written by my grandmother. So they don't interest me in the slightest."

"Did you read all the way to the bottom of the box?"

"I read enough."

"No, you didn't." There was a surprising amount of force behind the words.

He crossed his arms in front of him. "Look, if it bothers you so much, leave the box here. I'll throw it away myself."

Jami popped open its top. She'd tucked the flaps under one another, as he had Saturday. Maybe if he'd taped it shut, she would have stayed out of it. Not likely. *Anything for a story.*

She reached into the box, pulled out a stack of pages and shook them in his face. "Stop being so stubborn. If you're determined to stick your head in the sand, I'll tell you what's in here, because you need to know." She laid the handful of pages on the table and turned to face him. "You saw the first ones, written to your dad. By the end of the box, the letters are still addressed to your father, but everything in them applies to you. It appears your grandmother slowly lost her mind, which might be why they became recluses for the last thirty years of their lives."

He stood staring down at her, arms still crossed, his mood no better than when she'd walked in. Nothing was going to justify her snooping through his things. "So the old woman went nuts. What does that have to do with me?"

In response, she reached into the box and placed a stack of envelopes on the table. After removing the contents from the top one, she handed him a check.

He looked at it before handing it back to her. "My grandmother wrote my mom a check, then voided it. I guess the rare moment of generosity passed before she could get the envelope sealed."

"That's what I thought, until I read this."

He looked down at what she handed him, a sense of dread settling over him. He didn't want to read the letter. Something told him it contained information that would shake his very foundation. For anything less, Jami wouldn't be there, her presence silent testimony she'd violated his trust.

He should hand the letter back and refuse to read it. Then he could keep believing what he had all his life. But that wasn't an option. His eyes seemed to have a mind of their own as they roved back and forth over the note.

> *I am returning your check as well as your letter. My answer is the same as when you tried to pay me to quietly walk out of Gary's life. I don't want your money. I would beg on the streets before I would take anything from you.*

As he read, his mother's voice rang in his head, bitter and shrill, dripping with venom. A single name ended the short paragraph. But the signature wasn't necessary. He knew that heavy, jagged script. Even her handwriting looked angry.

He moved the page aside to view the one behind it. It was his grandmother's letter, begging forgiveness and offering financial assistance. He laid both letters on the table, his mind reeling. Why would his mother tell him the McAllisters wanted nothing to do with him when the opposite was true?

He snatched the other envelopes from the box and, one by one, pulled out their contents. They held letters like the first and one more attempt to send a check. Then there was a single sheet, the letter written by Elizabeth McAllister, and across the bottom, the jagged script he knew so well—*Don't bother trying to write again. Future letters will be returned unopened.* As promised, the last five envelopes were still sealed.

He put everything back into the box and closed the lid, shock still coursing through him. His mother had lied to him. The realization was like a steel-toed boot to the gut. The life she'd built for them was a sham, their struggles brought on by her own pride and bitterness. What else had she lied about?

A hand on his shoulder brought his spinning thoughts to an abrupt stop, and he turned to see Jami staring up at him, eyes filled with pity. Fire shot through his veins, fueled by humiliation. The foundation had been ripped from under him, and she was watching the whole thing. He didn't want her pity. In fact, he didn't want her there at all.

He twisted away from her touch, sweeping her with a disdainful glance. "You sure lucked out." Sarcasm dripped from the words. "You've got all the elements of a sensational story—tragedy, grief, hatred, bitterness, deception, insanity. The high-and-mighty McAllisters, brought to their knees when tragedy strikes. The angry, bitter shrew who denied them their only source of comfort. And the poor schmuck who at age thirty learned his whole life was a lie. Pretty sensational stuff for Murphy."

Jami didn't respond, just continued watching him, except now her eyes were filled with pain. His sarcasm had hurt her. But everything he'd said was true. She was a reporter, and he'd given her quite a story.

"I won't print anything you don't want me to print." Her tone was soft but sincere.

He gave a derisive snort. "What happened to 'A reporter will do anything for a story'?"

"Not this reporter. When I say I won't print something, I won't print it. No matter what." She looked up at him, silently pleading with him to trust her. But trust for him didn't come easily. Every time he tried, it came back to bite him in the rear.

Like when he'd believed Bethany's promise to love and to cherish, forsaking all others. And trusted his best friend to escort her to her events when he'd been too busy to go himself.

"I'm sorry, Grant." Jami's soft words pulled him back to the present. The pity in her eyes was still there. "I had to share this. I couldn't let you go to your grave hating your grandparents."

Instead he would hate his mother.

"You can leave now." His tone was low, with a hard edge. He didn't do angry outbursts. Even when he'd walked in on Bethany and Craig, he'd thrown them out of his bed with an icy calmness that had left them scrambling into their clothes and running for the door. But the calmness had been a facade, a paper-thin wall hiding the storm of emotion swirling inside him, his own silent shouts of denial and the echo of a thousand *what-ifs*.

Jami once again placed a hand on his forearm. "Don't be too hard on your mother. Remember, she's all the family you've got."

His hands tightened into fists. "Get out." He didn't need to hear any more. Dishing out nice-sounding platitudes was easy when life was sunny and the biggest concern on the horizon was what to make for dinner. Yet as soon as the thought passed through his mind, he knew he was being unfair. With an alcoholic father who'd deserted her at a young age and a mother fighting cancer, her life hadn't been easy.

She moved toward the door and, after opening it, cast one pain-filled glance over her shoulder. A cold lump settled in his gut. He was being harder on her than he should. It wasn't her fault he'd been duped.

He pushed the remorse aside. Whatever hurt she felt wouldn't last long. She had what she wanted. All he was to her was a good source for a story. And she was . . . what? A temporary friend, someone who'd made his stay in Murphy a little more enjoyable. Even that was more than he'd been looking for. He wasn't in the market for a romantic fling, and anything long-term was out of the question, regardless of Bernie's wacky schemes. Because no matter how sweet someone seemed, how honest and wholesome, he would eventually find his trust betrayed.

He wheeled his bag to the car, the box Jami had brought propped on one hip. He'd stop at one of the small towns he'd passed on his way up from the Atlanta airport and mail it back to New York with the others. The sooner he could leave Murphy behind, the better.

If he was smart, he'd tell Vanguard to make him an offer on the property with all the furnishings and be done with it. Most of what he wanted was sitting in the backseat. Whatever was left, Vanguard could have. Then he wouldn't even have to come back. He would wrap things up at work, tie up a few loose ends at home and embark on his two months of freedom.

A few minutes later, he cruised down 60, through several miles of nothingness. Woods encroached from both sides, thick underbrush hiding the forest floor. A heavy layer of clouds blanketed the sky. To his left, the sun hovered over the treetops, the only evidence of its presence a section of the horizon not quite as gray. The scene matched his mood—sullen and bleak.

Jami had said to go easy on his mother. But she didn't deserve leniency. What she'd done was unthinkable. For thirty years, she'd saddled him with the yoke of hatred, using him as a pawn in her secret vendetta against the faceless McAllisters. She'd lied to him, kept him from the love of his grandparents and created a life of struggle for both of them. And he wasn't about to let it go.

He reached for the radio dial and resumed the search he'd given up a few days earlier. After a couple of attempts, soft rock filled the car.

It wasn't Rachmaninoff, but it would help dispel some of the sense of isolation. Once he reached the airport, he'd lose himself in a book. He had three, one he'd brought with him and two he'd confiscated from the McAllister library. They were all in his briefcase, along with his iPad and some files he'd carried south.

Up ahead, a sign announced he was about to cross the state line. On 515, he'd have his choice of small towns. He would pick one, eat some breakfast and mail his boxes. Once that was accomplished, he'd head on to Atlanta, where he'd turn in the car and board the plane.

Then he was going to fly home and sever the last intimate connection he had left.

Jami kicked a small rock that had become dislodged from the packed earth around it and watched it tumble down the slope ahead of her. Dusk was still some two hours away, but the temperature in the McAllister woods was quite comfortable, if a little humid. Some distance ahead, both dogs stood with their noses buried in a clump of ferns, tails wagging while they took one of their frequent sniff breaks.

They'd settled in well. Devotion had replaced the sadness in their eyes, and the pathetic whimpering when she left for work each morning had all but ceased. They hadn't even made any messes, other than the one puddle that had sent her flying almost a week ago.

She reached the spot where the latest interesting scent had snagged their attention and clapped her hands. They both looked up, eyes full of eagerness, then trotted off ahead of her. She didn't have them leashed. It wasn't necessary. They never strayed far. They would run ahead, check to make sure she was still following, then stop to see what fun scents they could discover.

It left her free to roam and think. She'd done a lot of that since her encounter with Grant yesterday morning. Thinking, anyway. She'd known he would be angry. But she'd thought she could placate him. She didn't expect him to almost throw her out of the hotel room.

She heaved a sigh. "I should never have gone." If she had kept what she'd learned to herself, Grant wouldn't be mad at her. That hadn't been an option, though. He'd harbored so much anger toward his grandparents she couldn't keep quiet. Of course, in vindicating the elder McAllisters, she'd made his mother the guilty party.

But his mother was still alive. He could mend that relationship. If he was willing. From what little she knew of Grant, it was doubtful. She released a growl of frustration. Over the past twenty-four hours, she'd mentally argued all the pros and cons of her decision until she was ready to scream.

When she wasn't second-guessing herself about giving the box to Grant, she was stressing over the article. She had photos. And she had a few dry facts—the early history of the McAllisters, the condition of the house, where Grant and Anna went after Gary's death, Grant's plans to sell. But to write a really poignant article, she would have to use what was in the box.

She picked up a small branch lying in front of her and tossed it to the side. "I know what Howard would do." The information was public, in a sense. Grant released it to go to the landfill. It was no longer in his possession. "Howard would take it and run with it. And he'd write an exceptional story."

She was talking to herself again, a regular occurrence when alone, especially when she had things to sort out. With Grant back in New York, there was no one to overhear her except the dogs.

Unfortunately, it was going to take more than a conversation with herself to sort this mess out. Because doing what Howard would do somehow felt like betraying Grant. In her case, it would be, because she'd made a promise. She'd given him her word she wouldn't print anything he didn't want her to use. She'd even finished her vow with *no matter what.*

"But Grant would never know." He was eight hundred miles away and not returning to Murphy except for one more short visit. She could publish her story and get her accolades. Then maybe she would stop hearing about what big shoes she had to fill.

No, she couldn't do it. A promise broken was still trust betrayed, even if the person never found out.

She heaved another sigh and cast her eyes heavenward. "Lord, help me to not make a bigger mess of things than I already have."

Her gaze dropped to the two furry bodies bouncing along in front of her. Suddenly they both perked up and shot away, short legs pumping as fast as they could. "Bailey, Morgan," she shouted, "stay!" But they continued their mad pursuit without a break in their stride. She forced her own legs into a run, continuing to call while silently praying she didn't lose either of her dogs. She should have had them on their leashes. But she never dreamed they'd take chase and ignore her commands.

She lost sight of them, but within moments, a chorus of barking reached her from somewhere ahead. They must have cornered whatever animal had sparked their interest. Hopefully it didn't have sharp claws. Or long teeth.

When she broke through the last of the trees into a small clearing, she skidded to a stop. They had something cornered all right. And it didn't have sharp claws or long teeth. A man stood next to a transit atop a tripod. He held up both hands in what she guessed was as nonthreatening of a pose as he could muster.

"I'm so sorry," she called. "They're really harmless." The furiously wagging tails backed up her claims.

"No problem. I heard you calling and knew you couldn't be far behind." He squatted down and offered the back of one hand for them to sniff. Once satisfactory introductions had been made, he scratched both of them on the tops of their heads, then straightened as a second man emerged from the trees at the opposite end of the clearing. He wore the same placket shirt with embroidered script that she could now see read *Adams Surveying*.

Why was Grant having the property surveyed? There was no way his Realtor could have sold it already. She turned to the first man, who still held the attention of both dogs. They looked up at him eagerly, probably hoping for more pats on the head. "Come," she called, clapping her hands twice, and they bounded over to stand at her side.

She turned her attention back to the surveyor. "Were you hired by Grant McAllister?"

"No, Durham Vanguard."

Her heart sank until it wobbled to a stop somewhere between her kneecaps. How could he? He'd sold to Vanguard without even giving the Realtor a chance.

Jami closed her eyes, struggling to compose herself. He knew how important it was to her, how desperately she wanted to preserve the beauty and tranquility of her surroundings.

And maybe that was why he'd done it.

Maybe Grant McAllister wasn't only slow to forgive. Maybe he was vindictive. There was no other explanation. She'd snooped through his possessions and learned things he didn't want anyone to know. Now he was striking out, hitting her where he knew it would hurt.

Had her forthrightness come at a cost higher than his friendship? Was it going to destroy her and her neighbors' peace for years to come?

Oh, Lord, what have I done?

Grant stood in the hallway of the upscale condo complex, cold fury flowing just beneath the surface. He hadn't phoned ahead. He hadn't needed to. The bellman downstairs knew him.

For almost three days, he'd searched for some way to understand why his mother had lied to him all his life. There was none, no explanation, no excuse. If she'd wanted to refuse contact with the McAllisters, that was her prerogative. But forcing that hatred on him was beyond wrong.

He rang the bell, and moments later, the door swung open. Homey scents drifted out and wrapped comforting arms around him. His mother's place always smelled of some food-scented oil or potpourri—hot apple pie, cinnamon rolls, French vanilla roast. This time it was a pleasant spicy-sweet scent, like spice cake ready to come out of the oven. But he didn't even need to step inside to know the kitchen was cold. That tantalizing scent was nothing but an empty promise, a bald-faced lie. Like the tales of hatred and rejection she'd spoon-fed him all his life.

"You lied to me."

Concern flashed across her features, but it didn't last long. Whatever faults his mother possessed, she was always composed. "That's no way to greet your mother after a trip. Come on in, and let me get you a soda."

He followed her into the almost-new two-bedroom condo and waited while she hurried to the kitchen for the promised drink. The money to purchase the place had been his, but the décor choices were all hers and had nothing to do with location or heritage. Terra-cotta tile flowed throughout, set off by pale stucco walls. Area rugs stood vigil at strategic places around the unit, their russet and sage-green geometric patterns striking against a background of warm beige. Metal wall art and various Native American–themed accessories added a Southwest flavor to the setting—Santa Fe in the middle of New York City. Not his style, but it was what she'd wanted.

The clink of ice against glass sounded in the kitchen, followed by the pop and hiss of two sodas being opened. Moments later she returned to press a cold glass into his hand.

"Can I get you anything else?"

He shook his head. No more delays. "I had a very interesting trip, learned a lot."

"Have a seat, dear."

"No, I think I'll stand." Or maybe pace. He crossed the room to where a long, narrow table stood against a wall of glass. The lights of Manhattan stretched out before him, congested streets some fifteen stories below. He took a long swig of his drink, then dropped his gaze to the table, which held a display of candleholders, vases and figurines. For several moments he fingered the rim of the hand-painted clay vase in the center. Three colorful geckos chased one another around its circumference, lighthearted and fun. The scene was out of place in a room so thick with tension.

He dropped his hand and turned to face his mother. "I found out my grandmother, who was too high and mighty to have anything to do with either of us, tried to make contact . . . several times."

His mother settled into one of the two leather recliners and took a long sip of her drink. "You can't believe everything you hear. Rumors fly around these small towns like swarms of locusts."

"That may be. But seeing the proof for yourself is pretty convincing."

He studied her closely, especially her eyes. Blue with underlying hints of aqua, like his own. Except hers were filled with concern. "What are you talking about?"

"Packages, three of them, addressed to me. My grandparents sent me two birthday gifts and a Christmas gift, all of which you refused."

Her gaze darted from one object to another until it came to rest on a watercolor on the opposite wall. It was one of her own, saguaro cacti against the flaming backdrop of an Arizona sunset. But judging from the tension lining her face, she wasn't admiring her work. "I never saw any packages. They were probably sent to the wrong address." She motioned toward the other recliner. "Have a seat, Grant. You're a bundle of nerves. You need to relax."

"No, I don't need to relax." She needed to own up to what she'd done. "The address was right. I had it investigated. But that wasn't the only thing I found." He crossed the room and stood in front of her, willing her to look at him. "I found letters. Lots of them. Even a couple of voided checks."

She drew in a shaky breath but still kept her eyes averted. When she lifted her drink to her mouth, the ice cubes rattled against the glass, and she steadied it with her other hand. Finally, her eyes met his. They held insecurity and a whole lot of regret. "I wanted to tell you."

"Tell me what—that you'd lied to me all my life?"

She lowered her gaze to stare at her drink. "For a long time, I was angry. I blamed them for your father's death. I didn't want you to meet them. I told myself that I was trying to protect you, to spare you the rejection that I'd received."

Heat swept through him, centering in his chest. "You weren't trying to protect me. You had nothing in mind but your own private vendetta."

"I know that now. But by the time I was ready to admit that to myself, you were a teenager. I knew I needed to talk to you, but I didn't know where to begin."

"A good starting point might have been the truth." Hardness underlay the words, but he didn't try to soften them. The apology in her eyes wasn't moving him. Neither were the pitiful excuses.

"I should have told you. But the longer I let you believe the lie, the harder it became to tell you the truth. I knew you'd be angry, and I was so afraid of losing you."

"Knowing I was headed to Murphy, don't you think that would have been an ideal time to come clean? Odds were good that I'd find something in that house that would expose your lies."

She released a heavy sigh, and her shoulders slumped. "Believe me, I worried about that the entire time you were gone."

"And you left me to find out on my own." In front of Jami. A reporter, of all people. "You had no right to lie to me all those years." He slashed his hand through the air to underscore his point, and she flinched as if he'd struck her. "Whether or not I met my grandparents should have been my choice."

"I know, and I'm so sorry."

"Thirty years of lies aren't fixed by a simple apology." He put his almost-full glass on the end table and stalked toward the door.

"Grant? Where are you going?" Panic laced her tone. The rustle of leather told him she'd gotten out of the chair.

"Home."

She closed the gap between them and grasped his arm. "Please don't be angry. You're all I have."

He hesitated. The words were so eerily reminiscent of Jami's.

"Grant, please talk to me."

Without turning around, he shrugged loose from her hold and opened the door. Maybe Jami could shut off the anger and offer instant forgiveness. But he wasn't Jami.

One final plea followed him down the hall. When he reached the elevator, he pressed the button, then cast a glance back. His mother stood leaning against the doorjamb, shoulders stooped. The anguish rolling off her reached out to him, and a sense of tenderness tried to nudge its way into his heart. Jami was right. They were each the only family the other had left. He would forgive her eventually. Just not tonight.

The elevator doors opened, and he stepped on. He'd taken a cab on the way over. Now he would just catch the subway. For the stretch of city between his place and his mother's, either mode of transportation was easier than taking his car.

He stepped from the building and turned right, headed toward the nearest subway station, eight or ten blocks away. The walk would do him good. It might even help work out some of the agitation boomeranging through him.

The woman who'd voided the checks and penned the notes to Elizabeth McAllister had been filled with bitterness. Maybe his mother wasn't that person anymore. Or maybe she was and had simply decided it was wrong to impose those feelings on an innocent child.

But it was too late. The damage was already done. Her cold anger had left its mark on him. His attitude toward his grandparents. The resentment he felt toward Bethany that colored his view of every other woman. The way he stuffed in his feelings and closed off his heart. He was a master at hiding what he felt behind a facade of cool control.

An image intruded into his thoughts—soft features molded into an expression of perfect contentment, beautiful green eyes that could see past a multitude of faults and a smile so open and warm it could melt the polar ice caps. His complete opposite. Jami had something, something that was lacking in his own life. If he didn't take the time to explore what that something was, he was going to regret it later.

Next week, he had to get things wrapped up at the firm. But come Friday, he would be on a plane headed south. He had to make the final trip back to Murphy.

When Jami had shown up at his motel room with that box of letters, she'd knocked his world off its axis. But taking out his anger and embarrassment on her was uncalled for. He had to beg her forgiveness.

He turned the corner, a smile curving his lips. Knowing Jami, begging wouldn't be necessary. Her words circled through his mind—*Life's a lot better when you let it go.*

He understood that now.

He just wasn't sure how to get there.

SEVEN

"That Hank Dorchester is going to be the death of me." Bernie flung up her hands and plopped into the chair at her desk. She was on the warpath, which, for Bernie, just meant a little more volume.

Jami looked up from her work. "What did Hank do this time?"

"It's his ad. Every week he has a whole bucketload of changes. And when I make one teensy-weensy mistake, I can't even finish breakfast and get out of the Grind without him raking me over the coals." She heaved a sigh. "One extra little number, and he acts like it's the end of the world."

"What kind of extra number?"

"Wayne's Wednesday special. They're offering ten percent off all feed."

"And?"

"Weeellllll," Bernie began, cocking her head to the side and hoisting both shoulders, "I sort of got two zeros instead of one."

Jami nodded. "So according to Hank's ad, Wayne's Feed Store is letting all their feed go at a hundred percent off. Bernie, that's free."

"I know. And Hank's afraid people are going to come in to get their free feed and be mad when they have to pay for it. I told him people in this town have enough sense to know it's a misprint. He told me I'm getting old and senile and too much red dye has gone to my brain."

Jami stifled the smile that almost erupted. Knowing Hank and knowing Bernie, that insult came only after she'd slung a few of her own.

Bernie pulled one ankle onto the opposite knee and sat back in the chair. "Well, you know what? I'm gonna fix his fat little fanny. Hank Dorchester ain't smart enough to get one up on me. Wait till you see next week's ad."

Jami shook her head. "Bernie, you're going to get yourself in trouble."

"Nah, I know just how far I can push Hank. Been doing it for years."

That was an understatement. Bernie and Hank had been swapping jibes for as long as she could remember. The only thing Bernie seemed to enjoy more was plotting another matchmaking scheme.

Bernie slid smoothly into her other favorite topic. "So have you heard from Grant?"

"Not a word."

"I'm sure he'll get in touch with you as soon as he gets back."

"Probably not." She heaved a sigh. "I know you always have high hopes for your matches, but if you think this one's going anywhere, you're wishing for the impossible." Disappointment underscored every word, which was ridiculous. It wasn't like she'd expected things to turn out any differently. Held out some sliver of hope, maybe. And let herself dream dreams that she had no business dreaming. But she hadn't expected a thing.

"My, aren't we pessimistic today."

"Not *pes*simistic. *Real*istic." She heaved another sigh, this one heavier than the last. "Grant's mad at me." Actually *mad* didn't begin to describe it. He was selling to Vanguard.

Bernie's eyebrows went up, but the rest of her face fell. "Why?"

A weight bore down on her chest. She'd told Holly and Sam about going through the boxes but hadn't mentioned it to anyone else. At the time, it had seemed okay. Now it just felt wrong, like eavesdropping on a private conversation or hacking into someone's computer.

"Grant gave me some boxes to throw away, told me they had photo albums in them. I couldn't do it. I was afraid he'd regret it later. I finally got into them, thinking there might be something in there I could use for my story."

Bernie nodded slowly. "And Grant found out."

"I told him."

"What'd you do that for?"

"There was information in there that he needed to hear."

Bernie leaned forward, her eyes sparkling with curiosity. "What kind of information?"

"I'm not saying." She hadn't told Sam and Holly, either. That was Grant's family secret, and no one was going to hear it from her.

"Don't give up hope. I'll think of something." For several moments, Bernie sat with her lips pursed, features set in determination.

Jami shook her head and turned her attention back to her computer. She had a story to work on. A real one, not a fairy tale. And she needed to get busy. It was going to be a short afternoon. At four o'clock, everyone was going to head up to the conference room to celebrate Bernie's birthday. The cake wasn't going to be a surprise, but a certain flower delivery was.

Jami smiled in spite of herself. So what if her own love life was a mess? That wasn't going to stop her from enjoying Bernie's.

"Happy birthday to youuuuu." The last off-pitch note lingered in the air for several moments before laughter replaced it. A German chocolate cake sat beneath thirteen flickering candles in the middle of the *Scout*'s conference room table upstairs.

Bernie made an exaggerated grimace. "That was a pretty memorable rendition of 'Happy Birthday.' I don't think I've ever heard one like it."

Matthew, the *Scout*'s editor, pointed at the cake. "How come there are only thirteen candles? We all know Bernie's old as dirt."

She snorted. "I might be old as dirt, but I'm well preserved."

Jami laughed. "I couldn't fit fifty-eight candles, so I did five and eight."

"Good thing, or we would have been joined by the Murphy Fire Department."

A female voice called from downstairs, interrupting their banter. "Yoo-hoo, anyone home?"

A minute later, Josie from Peachtree Florist appeared at the top of the stairs holding a colorful display of carnations, daisies, lilies and baby's breath. "I have a delivery for Bernie." She placed the flowers on the table and had just started to walk from the room when she turned back. "Jami, I almost forgot. Greg wanted me to tell you to give him a call."

"About what?"

"The flowers for your wedding."

Oh, she was so going to kill Robert. Fortunately, he was halfway across the world and wouldn't be back for another week. So he was safe for the time being. "Please let him know there isn't going to be a wedding."

Several heads snapped around, and Donna's brows shot up. "There isn't? Since when?"

Bernie jumped in, and Jami breathed a sigh of relief. She was getting tired of explaining.

"There never was going to be one. Robert made lots of wedding plans. He just forgot to get an answer from the bride."

Her explanation drew laughter from everyone gathered, and Josie held up a hand in farewell. "I'll let Greg know."

"Now to read this card." Bernie pulled the mini envelope from the plastic clip and looked at the faces around her. "You guys are going to make this old lady cry."

When she removed the card, her eyes widened, and she jammed it back into the small envelope.

"What does it say?" Christy asked.

Bernie pressed the envelope into the plastic holder and raised her chin. "I'm not telling. It's private."

A knowing grin spread across David's face. "I think Bernie's got a boyfriend."

"No, I don't." She stood with arms crossed and chin stuck out, daring anyone to argue. Gradually, her features softened, and curiosity overcame embarrassment. "I don't know who it is. It just says, 'From someone who thinks you're one special lady.' And it's not signed."

Jami leaned back in her chair, assuming a relaxed pose. "It shouldn't be too hard to figure out. You only know a couple dozen single men. And I think we can eliminate anyone under the age of forty."

Charlene's face lit up. "DJ's single."

Bernie gave her *the look*. "DJ's eighty-five."

"No, eighty-three."

"He has no teeth."

"He has 'em; he just forgets to put 'em in."

Bernie looked at her askance. "How about if we eliminate anyone over the age of eighty also?"

"What about Hank?" Dwight said. "He's single and not that far from your age."

Way to go, Dwight. And he wasn't even in on their scheme.

Bernie wrinkled her nose. "Hank Dorchester? That crotchety old man? His only interest in me is giving me a hard time. And the feeling's mutual."

Jami laughed again. "This could take a while. Meanwhile we've got candles melting into the icing. Make a wish."

Bernie took a deep breath and blew out every one of the candles. Judging from the dreaminess that had filled her eyes, her wish had something to do with receiving those flowers.

Once everyone dispersed, it was quitting time—actually a little past. Jami retrieved her purse from her bottom desk drawer and turned as a familiar figure opened the front door and stepped inside.

Her stomach quivered, and her heart jumped to double time. She heaved a sigh. She couldn't let him affect her like that. She was nothing to him but a pesky reporter. And he was mad at her.

For the past week, she'd alternated between kicking herself for showing him the letters and trying to convince herself she'd done the right thing. She'd known he wouldn't be pleased with her. But she'd never dreamed he'd be angry enough to call Vanguard.

Bernie rushed around the counter and through the small swinging doors into the lobby. "It's good to see you, Grant. Are you here to see Jami?"

Jami groaned. Bernie was so obvious.

"Only if she's done working."

"She is. Why don't you walk her to her car?"

Jami closed her desk drawer, shaking her head. Bernie was a mess. She wasn't going to give up until Grant was long gone, off on whatever adventure caught his fancy.

She hooked her purse over her shoulder and made her way to the lobby while Bernie scurried out the door. By the time she reached Grant's side, Bernie was already getting into her car.

Grant held the door open for her, and she stepped into the late-afternoon sunshine. He didn't speak until they'd reached her Sunbird.

"I came here to apologize for last Thursday. I was rude, and I'm sorry."

Heat washed through her, leaving everything mushy inside. Good-looking, witty *and* humble enough to admit when he'd made a mistake. The kind of guy that could make a girl swoon. She leaned against the metal railing separating the parking area from the sheer drop-off beyond. "You're forgiven. I know the stuff I gave you was hard to read. I also knew you wouldn't be happy with me for snooping through your boxes. But I didn't mean any harm."

"I know. And now I'm glad you gave me the box. Do you still have the others?"

"I do. You can pick them up anytime." He nodded, and she continued. "What about your mom? Have you talked to her?"

"I have."

"Everything all right?"

"Not yet, but it will be."

"I guess you decided to sell to Vanguard." She didn't even try to keep the disappointment out of her voice. "I ran into the surveyors while walking the dogs."

Grant's brows drew together. "I didn't order a survey."

"Vanguard did. I asked."

His jaw sagged. "Talk about overconfident. You'd think he'd wait for a final answer from me first."

Her heart skipped a beat. "You haven't signed a contract?"

"I haven't talked to him since the first meeting. I told him then I'd make a decision by the end of next week."

She released a huge sigh of relief. He hadn't sold to Vanguard. At least not yet. And if she had anything to say about it, he wouldn't. Before the week's end, she would somehow convince him that what Vanguard planned to do to the land wasn't worth any amount of money. She faced him fully, one arm still resting on the handrail. "How long are you here?"

"Two weeks, maybe longer. Why?"

"I have a proposition for you."

"I'm listening."

"Put him off. Give me those two weeks to show you around and let you experience the beauty we have here. Then if you still want to sell to Vanguard, I won't say another word."

Her pulse pounded in her ears while he considered her offer. Finally, he stretched out his hand. "Deal."

As she accepted the handshake, her heart continued its erratic rhythm. So much was resting on her abilities of persuasion. If she failed, Vanguard would move in and her quiet, peaceful haven would never be the same.

But that wasn't the only thing at stake. For the next two weeks, she was going to spend time with Grant in a fun, relaxed, nonprofessional setting.

Somehow she would have to keep from losing her heart.

Grant stepped onto the wooden porch that stretched across the cedar home and inhaled deeply. Jami had told him her mother was a good cook. Judging from the aroma emanating from somewhere inside the house, she'd learned a thing or two herself. Which was good, since she'd decided to begin her two-week promotional effort by making him breakfast.

Dual barks answered his knock. The door swung inward, and Jami stood in the opening, two little black balls of fur flanking her feet.

An unexpected pang of loneliness hit him. "You have dogs."

"As of my trip to the Humane Society two weeks ago, yes."

He stepped inside, then squatted, offering his hands for them to smell. They both skipped the introductory sniff and nuzzled him, demanding rubs.

Jami continued. "I went to look at a puppy, the operative words being *look* and *a*, as in *one*."

He smiled up at her. "A little impulsive, are we?"

"That's what I've been told, more than once. But one look at those sad brown eyes, and I was toast. Nobody wanted them, and I couldn't walk away. So here I am, owner of two dogs instead of one. But nobody ever accused me of being practical." She smiled down at him, but something told him whatever had been said about her lack of practicality had been in criticism rather than good-natured teasing.

He straightened to his full height. "Who says it's not practical?"

"It just isn't. I've never had a dog before, and now I have two. I don't even know what I'm doing. Although I did stop by the library." She pointed toward the end table, where a book sported the face of a basset hound under the words *Welcoming the New Member of the Family*. Two other books were underneath it, approximately the same size, maybe the same topic. The words *Call Alpine Vet Hospital* were scrawled across a neon-orange Post-it. Jami obviously took her new duties as pet owner seriously.

He swung his gaze back to her face. "It doesn't look like they're suffering any. They've still got all their fur, they're not limping and I haven't noticed any odd tics. I guess I wouldn't be able to see if their ribs were showing under the long hair, but I didn't feel any ribs. So I'd say you're doing all right."

Jami laughed but continued her argument. "I'm gone all day, so I have to keep running home at lunchtime to let them out."

"Which from anywhere in Murphy takes how long?"

"About thirty minutes." She gave him a sheepish grin, then led him into the kitchen, the source of the delicious aroma that had found its way outside.

"Breakfast smells good. What are we having?"

"Breakfast casserole. You know, eggs, sausage, potatoes, cheese."

"So you're trying to con me with food."

"Hey, whatever works." She flashed him one of those smiles that lit her eyes. It seemed to make them a shade richer—the color of grass after a good summer rain. "I thought I would start this get-to-know-Murphy tour right in my own backyard, since that's where Vanguard's equipment would be doing its destruction." She finished the sentence with a wink.

He gave her a mock grimace. "If you can't bribe me with food, you'll guilt me into it."

"As I said, whatever works."

He helped her carry the casserole, juice and coffee to the wrought iron table out back. She already had the places set, with cream, sugar, salt and pepper in the center. She settled onto one of the cushioned chairs, and he took a seat next to her. After dishing up their plates, he picked up his fork, ready to dig in, but Jami's head was bowed.

He dipped his head but didn't close his eyes. Morgan and Bailey sat on each side of him, staring up at him. Once Jami began to eat, he motioned toward the dogs. "Did you feed them yet? They look like they're starving."

"I fed them fifteen minutes before you got here. They always look like that. I think they'd both eat till they explode."

Grant laughed. It was typical of the species. His dog Allegro had been the same way. He took a bite of the casserole, then moved two pieces of sausage to the edge of his plate. "Is it all right if I give them some?"

"One little bite. If I made a habit of giving in to those pleading eyes, their bellies would rub the floor and they'd have to get around on skateboards."

He lowered the tidbits to the two waiting mouths. When he looked again at Jami, she was smiling.

"You really like dogs, don't you?"

He returned her smile. "I do. Why?"

"I don't know. You don't strike me as the animal-lover type."

"I am. I even like cats. I had cats growing up and got a Lab mix a few years ago, a rescue like yours."

"Do you still have your Lab?"

"I don't. My ex-wife got the dog, along with the house, the car and my right kidney."

She flashed him a sympathetic smile. "Sounds like she cleaned you out."

"You don't know the half of it." She didn't just take his money. She took a piece of his soul.

He lifted his gaze to where Bailey and Morgan, having decided no more treats were forthcoming, lay in the yard a short distance away. The whole scene commanded stillness. The flagstone patio blended with nature rather than intruding on it, its jagged edge holding back a sea of soft green velvet. Cottony clouds drifted overhead, blanketing the sun, and a gentle breeze blew, making the temperature almost perfect. The company wasn't so bad, either.

He returned his attention to Jami and the tasty breakfast she'd prepared. "So what's on the agenda for today?"

"Hiking. But not just hiking. Geocaching."

"Geo what?"

"Geocaching. I take it you've never been."

"Never heard of it."

"It's searching for buried treasure. Well, not treasure, really. People hide caches and put GPS coordinates and clues online."

"Sounds interesting." Like an adventure. And he was decked out for it. Jami had told him in advance what to wear. He already had jeans with him, but the hiking boots she recommended had required a trip to Burlington.

Jami was dressed the same, as far as the jeans and boots, but a Michigan State T-shirt took the place of his polo. She wore the barest hint of makeup and had pulled her hair into a high ponytail, which swished at her neck with each movement. The thick elastic band didn't quite capture all the auburn tresses. Some shorter wisps had escaped and lay softly around her face. She looked fresh, natural and downright beautiful.

When they finished breakfast, she slid her chair away from the table, the scrape of metal on stone jarring against the backdrop of nature. Both dogs bounded toward them, legs pumping and ears bouncing. When they reached the patio, they stopped at his feet and looked up hopefully.

"What, didn't you get enough loving when I got here?" He squatted to scratch the backs of their necks.

"They really like you."

As if in confirmation, Bailey lunged and nailed him right on the mouth, and he fell backward, laughing.

"You have to watch her. Fastest tongue in the West. Western North Carolina, anyway."

He ruffled the fur on her back. "I like puppy kisses, just not on the mouth."

Both dogs stayed on his heels as he followed Jami into the house. Another pang of loneliness shot through him. After Bethany had taken Allegro, he hadn't wanted another dog. But maybe it was time to rethink his decision. Once he finished his sabbatical and settled into a routine, he should consider checking out the local rescues. He could pay a neighbor for lunchtime walks. And he *could* get home at a reasonable time in the afternoon. He didn't *have* to work the hours he did.

For so many years, he'd driven himself to get where he wanted to be. Now that he was there, he was still driving himself, trying to stay a step ahead of the emptiness threatening to engulf him. And he'd burned himself out in the process.

That was why he needed his upcoming trip. The break from structure would pull him out of the funk he'd been in for the past two years. Each new experience would infuse him with excitement and help renew his long-lost zest for life. Two months from now, he'd return home a changed man.

At least that was what he'd been telling himself since he first got this crazy idea. And he would keep telling himself that until it was time to go back home to his regular life. Because always in the back of his mind was a seed of doubt, the niggling suspicion there was no cure for the malaise that had taken over his mind, that he would roam the country for two months, then return home no better off than when he'd left.

While Jami loaded the dishwasher, Grant put away the cream and leftover food. Several colorful sticky notes, like the one he'd seen in the living room, decorated the refrigerator door. A dispenser of them sat in easy reach on the kitchen table, between the napkin holder and salt and pepper shakers. And based on the script filling the small, colorful sheets, she'd rescheduled a dentist appointment, was low on yogurt and tomato sauce and needed to locate a book for Holly.

He moved from the fridge to look out the window over the sink. A six-pointed star hung from a piece of monofilament line in front of it, each ray a different color of the rainbow.

Jami glanced over at him. "I made that during my stained glass phase. You'll probably notice a few other pieces around."

"Stained glass phase? You don't do it anymore?"

"I just finished school, so everything I've done lately has been left-brained." She closed the dishwasher door, then rinsed and dried her hands. "When my mom got sick the last time, I did a lot of stained glass, along with several other creative endeavors. It was how I survived. That and lots of long walks in your woods."

She motioned toward the insulated backpack sitting on the counter behind him. "Lunch. You never know how long these things are going to take, so I packed us some sandwiches, fruit and chips." She flashed him a smile that still held a trace of lingering sadness. "Are you ready for your very first geocache?"

"Lead the way."

He had no idea what geocaching entailed, but as long as Jami was involved, he'd be up for it. Something was awakening inside, something that had been asleep for a long time—excitement, enthusiasm, the desire to experience life.

Maybe his upcoming trip around the country wasn't the remedy to his problems. Maybe all he needed was right here, in the form of one spunky newspaper reporter and the faith that was so much a part of who she was. A little more time spent with Jami, and maybe he would get his head back on straight.

Or maybe he'd lose it altogether.

EIGHT

Jami stepped around a fallen tree and stopped to study her handheld GPS. Grant moved up beside her, the pack strapped to his back and her fold-up camping shovel in one hand. He'd insisted on carrying both.

"This way." She held up an index finger and started walking again.

"So what are we looking for?"

"Usually an ammo box or some other waterproof container."

"And the treasure is inside."

She smiled back at him. "It is. Most caches don't have themes, but this one does. It was buried on Valentine's Day, so everything inside will be related to love or romance."

Not a wise choice where Grant was concerned. She was having a hard enough time steering her thoughts away from romance when he was around. But it was an interesting cache that guaranteed some pretty scenery ending at a waterfall. And that was what she was trying to sell Grant on: the beauty of Murphy and the surrounding area.

"So what do we do with it if we find it?"

"We open it up, sign the log inside and rebury it."

"Is that all? What's the point?"

Though Grant was behind her, she could easily imagine his arched brows. Robert never got into geocaching, either. Said it was a waste of time.

She stopped walking and turned to face him. "There isn't one. It's the fun of the search, seeing who else has found the cache and where they're from. You get to explore lots of neat places you wouldn't otherwise go."

"I can't argue with that. Even if we don't find the cache, the trek is worth it just for the view."

Her heart wobbled, knowing that he noticed and, even more, that he appreciated it. And he was right. The narrow trail they followed was awash with color. Rhododendrons and mountain laurel in full bloom painted the mountainside with splashes of pink and white, and wildflowers sprang up all along the path. Maples, pines and oaks towered overhead, their boughs blocking the late-morning sun.

"If you do take anything, you replace it with something else." She pulled a heart-shaped key chain from her pocket. It was made of some kind of clear resin around a photo of rhododendron blooms. *North Carolina* was painted across the surface in fancy black script. "I picked this up at the Curiosity Shop yesterday to add to the cache. Maybe I'll take something else. Maybe I won't." She slid the item back into her pocket, then circled behind him to pull two water bottles from the backpack.

He took a swig from his and wiped his forehead with the back of his hand. "How will we know where to look once we get there?"

"The GPS is good. It usually gets you within thirty or forty feet of where you need to be, but some of the coordinates come with clues." She pulled a piece of paper from her pocket. "Here's this one: 'Step into the mist of the falls and enter Tolkien's world. Therein lies gold.'"

He frowned down at the words she'd scrawled on the sheet of notebook paper. "That's an obscure clue if there ever was one."

"I know. Some of them are pretty hard to figure out." She refolded the sheet and resumed walking. "But all the caches have ratings, and this one's supposedly easy to moderate on both terrain and how difficult the cache is to find. So we should be okay."

For the next few minutes, the hum of crickets accompanied their footsteps. Leaves rustled in a light breeze, and in the distance, a chickadee warbled out its song.

"What other excursions have you planned for me?"

"Whitewater rafting. Tomorrow afternoon, if you're up for it. Samantha owns Wild River Outfitters and would take good care of us."

"Hmm, whitewater rafting. Another new experience."

"We'd only do class twos and threes, nothing too harrowing." She stopped again to take a swig of water and consult the GPS. "In the morning, I'll be at church. You're welcome to join me."

"I'll pass on that."

The adamant tone surprised her. "What do you have against church?"

He shrugged. "From what I've seen, most people's religion is all for show. They get dressed up and go so everyone will see them and think what good people they are. Then they walk out the door and right past someone who needs help." He crossed his arms and gave a wry laugh. "Christianity would probably be a good thing if anybody ever practiced it."

His words sliced through her. If anybody needed the healing and forgiveness Christ offered, it was Grant. "If you're looking for perfect people, you're not going to find them, in church or otherwise. Jesus was the only perfect man who ever lived. The rest of us are just doing the best we can with His help."

"I'm not looking for perfect people, but there should at least be *some* difference. My grandmother—" He stopped, and one side of his mouth quirked up. "I guess I can't use her as an example of a stingy Christian anymore. But I could name plenty of others." He uncrossed his arms, letting his hands fall to his side. "How about if I say yes to whitewater rafting and 'I'll think about it' to church?"

"Sounds good." It was better than no.

"Next week I'm assuming our tour will have to wait till the weekend since you'll be working during the day. I can't imagine Murphy has a whole lot of nightlife."

"You might be surprised. Thursday night is darts at the Grind, and Friday night is the Murphy Art Walk."

He raised his brows. "Murphy Art Walk?"

"It's the first Friday night of the month from May through October. A bunch of the stores downtown participate. Local artists display their crafts, and there's live music and demonstrations." She grinned. "See? We have all kinds of culture here."

They began to move again, and before long, the *shh* of falling water sounded in the distance, barely audible over the rustle of leaves. During the next several minutes, it grew louder and closer until only a steep incline separated them from a raging river. A rope stretched from an oak at the top to a hemlock near the water's edge. A few yards upriver, water roared down a sheer rock face.

She consulted the GPS once more, then frowned at the steep incline ahead of them. "This might be more adventure than you bargained for."

"I'm game if you are. I'll even go first." He stepped forward, grasped the rope and gave it a couple of firm tugs. "If it handles my weight, it will definitely hold yours." He pivoted on one foot, placing his back to the incline, then half stepped, half slid down the steep slope on the balls of his feet, supplemented by the shovel and the occasional knee.

When he reached the bottom, he turned to call up to her. "See? Handled like a native. Now it's your turn."

She clipped the GPS on one hip, then, taking her cue from him, turned her back and started her descent. But hers wasn't as uneventful as his. Two-thirds of the way down, her feet slipped sideways, and she twisted and slammed her side into the slope. She was never able to regain her footing and slid the rest of the way down, hand over hand on the guide rope.

Grant pulled her to her feet. His touch was warm and firm, his hand big and protective over hers. He released her all too soon.

"That didn't look like fun. Are you okay?"

"Nothing's hurt but my pride. And that's not even hurt too badly. I've always been a bit of a klutz. You should have seen me a few days after I got the dogs, when I stepped in a puddle of piddle. I think I went airborne."

Grant grimaced. "Ouch." He reached up to pull a twig from her ponytail. "So how close are we now?"

She unclipped the GPS from her hip, fortunately not the side she'd landed on when she'd fallen. "Really close." She pointed toward the falls. "I'd say twenty or thirty feet that way."

She moved that direction, then stepped onto a rock at the creek's edge. A fine mist enveloped her, settling like a kiss of dew on her arms and face. "We're on the right side of the creek. The other side is too high above the water to be hit with the mist."

Grant stepped up to stand beside her, so close his arm rested against hers. The size of the rock didn't leave him much choice, and soon the aroma of his cologne mingled with the scents of nature. She closed her eyes and inhaled slowly. He wore some kind of woodsy scent with underlying hints of spice, as natural as their surroundings.

"How about reading me the note again?"

His words jarred her from her daydreams, and she stepped down from the rock to reach into her pocket. This crazy attraction she felt was totally one-sided. He would finish his business in Murphy, then be off to parts unknown.

She pulled the paper from her pocket again. "Step into the mist of the falls and enter Tolkien's world. Therein lies gold."

Grant looked around him. "We're in the mist. And Tolkien's most famous works are *The Hobbit* and *The Lord of the Rings*. Do you think it's something ring shaped?"

She brought a fist to her chin and tapped her cheek with her index finger. They were going with the most obvious interpretation and missing something. "I don't think it's a ring. *The Lord of the Rings* is a trilogy. What are the names of the individual books?"

"The first one is *The Fellowship of the Ring*."

She struggled to visualize the set. All four books were in her library at home, but it had been years since she'd picked them up. She hadn't even seen any of the movies recently.

"Towers," he said. "The second one is something like *Twin Towers*."

His guess wasn't right, but it was enough to prod her memory. "*The Two Towers*."

"So what looks like two towers?" He looked around him, eagerness in his gaze. Maybe there wasn't any long-term purpose in what they were doing. But that didn't seem to be dampening his enthusiasm.

"Trees."

"There." He pointed to twin birches growing about three feet apart near the base of the falls. "Therein lies gold."

He closed the distance at a half jog. After shedding the backpack, he unfolded the shovel and drove it into the ground between the two trees. A couple minutes later, his efforts were met with the ting of metal hitting metal. Once he had the box fully exposed, he pulled it from the shallow hole and removed the lid. A small spiral-bound notebook lay on top, hiding whatever trinkets waited beneath.

Jami turned the notebook on end to reveal a variety of items—a silk rose, a heart-shaped picture frame, a refrigerator magnet with the word *love*. At the bottom of the box was a heavy pewter heart with a definite Celtic flair. A leather tie was strung through a loop on the top. She lifted it from the box and traced the intricate pattern with her thumb. "This is cool."

"Are you going to keep it?"

"Definitely." She reached into her pocket, then dropped the key chain into the box. "Now we have to sign and date the log."

Once that was done and they'd returned the box to its hiding place, Grant shoveled the dirt back into the hole and packed it down with one boot-clad foot. "That was fun."

"I'm glad you enjoyed it. I think you should keep this as a souvenir." She held up the pewter heart. "It's heavy enough for a guy to wear."

"You keep it. You're the one who bought the item to replace it."

"And I'm giving it to you. Don't argue with me." She stepped closer.

"A little bossy, aren't we?"

"Only when we have to be." She reached around his neck to tie the cord. "Every time you look at this, you'll remember your first geocache."

"The reminder won't be necessary. I don't think I'll ever forget this day."

His voice was soft and deep, with an underlying warmth. All coordination left her fingers, and she fumbled with the cord. She couldn't have finished tying the knot if her life depended on it. When she lifted her gaze from the piece resting against his chest, her heart rolled over.

She'd been wrong. The attraction she felt wasn't one-sided.

She needed to take her hands from his neck. Standing so close to him had been a mistake, because now he was thinking of kissing her. It was there in his eyes. She needed to back away. She wasn't into short flings, and Grant wasn't a permanent kind of guy. Anything more than friendship would be a huge mistake.

He drew in a tension-filled breath and lifted his arms. But instead of wrapping them around her, he slid his hands over hers and took both ends of the cord from her shaking fingers.

She spun away and strode to a nearby tree, where he'd left the backpack. "What do you say we have some lunch?"

"Lunch sounds good."

She cast a glance over her shoulder. He'd finished tying the cord and stood with his hands in his pockets. Was his voice a little huskier than it had been a few minutes ago?

She unzipped the pack and removed their sandwiches and a bag of chips. Two weeks. That was what she'd asked for and what he'd promised. She could handle it. She was a tour guide, showing him the sights, letting him experience Murphy as a native. It was going to be fun. A piece of cake.

All she had to do was keep herself from doing something stupid.

Like falling in love.

—⁂—

Jami approached the front doors of MountainView Community Church a little earlier than her usual on-the-dot arrival time, but not by much. Music drifted from the sanctuary. Pastor Chris and the worship band were playing a well-known chorus in anticipation of the start of the service. Pastor Jeff would be seated in the front row, ready to step forward to give the opening prayer.

She'd arrived early and waited outside, just in case Grant showed up. As far as any commitment to attend church, he'd left her last night with a definite *maybe*. That had been after a Bojangles' supper and a stroll through downtown. And a concentrated effort to keep thoughts from straying outside the bounds of friendship. At least on her end. And she'd almost been successful.

She reached for the door and swung it open. After standing in the parking lot for ten minutes, she'd given up hope of seeing Grant before noon. Church was a tougher sell than whitewater rafting. He'd experienced too many wrongs, whether intended or not, and had built up too many years of resentment. Unfortunately, he'd probably be gone before she could have any real impact on him. The thought left her with a heaviness in her chest.

Just inside the foyer doors, Dean Reinhardt stood ready with a vigorous handshake and the weekly bulletin. "Good morning, Jami. I heard congratulations are in order. I bet you're excited."

"Thanks." She accepted both the handshake and the bulletin. "I've wanted to be a reporter since I was a kid, so working for the *Scout* is like a dream come true."

"Oh, yeah, I heard you had gone to work for them. Congratulations on that, too. But I was talking about your wedding."

She held up both hands. "No, I'm not getting married. That was a misunderstanding." Why did Robert have to open his big mouth before having her answer? And to Beulah of all people. It was amazing he hadn't posted an engagement announcement in the *Scout* with all the details, right down to what flavor miniquiches would be on the buffet table. She was ready to post an announcement herself, a nonengagement one: *Jami Carlisle is pleased to announce she will NOT be marrying Robert Demming this September.* Otherwise, damage control could take months.

She stepped into the right-hand aisle and scanned those seated until her gaze fell on Sam's dark ponytail sticking through the hole in the back of her cap. Holly and Samantha were never hard to find. Ever since the three of them were old enough to behave themselves without parental supervision, they'd sat together halfway up on the right.

When she reached their row, Holly motioned toward her watch and grinned.

"I know," she whispered. "I'm early. I've been here for the past ten minutes, pulled in as you guys were heading into the building." She slid into the empty seat next to Samantha. "I was watching for Grant. I invited him, but he didn't make any promises." She bent to set her purse on the floor at her feet. "We *are* going whitewater rafting, though. I called yesterday and made reservations for one thirty this afternoon."

Holly perked up. "Add one more. I wanna go."

Jami looked at Sam. "Are you available to be our guide?"

"You bet." She led rafting tours, but five or six other guides helped her out, especially on weekends. "I'll trade groups if I have to. There's no way I'd miss this outing with you and your new boyfriend."

Jami cast an uneasy glance toward the back of the church, afraid Grant might materialize and walk in on the conversation. Her heart leaped, and her stomach followed its path, making a funny little flip. He'd come after all. He stood in the back, looking about as comfortable as a stuffy Washington politician at a southern hoedown. When his gaze met hers, relief flashed across his features, and he started up the aisle.

She turned back to Samantha and Holly, speaking in a hushed tone. "He's not my boyfriend, he's my neighbor. So don't embarrass me." The mischievous sparkle in their eyes did nothing to put her mind at ease.

She flashed him a friendly smile. "You made it."

Grant took a seat, and a hatted figure three rows ahead turned in her chair. Beulah Fines always sat near the front, evidently unconcerned that she obstructed the view of at least a dozen parishioners. Jami frowned. It should be a church rule—big, ugly hats confined to the back row. But if there was one thing Beulah liked as well as being heard, it was being seen. Beulah scanned the rows behind her, the squint even more pronounced with the effort of twisting in her seat.

Then her gaze fell on Grant. Her brows shot upward to disappear under the brim of the gaudy hat. Fortunately, Pastor Jeff grabbed a microphone, signaling the start of the service, and Beulah turned back around in her seat. She would have to hold on to her eager questions for the next hour and a half. Knowing Beulah, it wouldn't be easy.

When Pastor Jeff turned the service back over to the worship team, Jami drew her attention to the words on the screen. The song was one of her favorites. She lifted her voice with the other worshippers, then stole a self-conscious glance at Grant. Sam and Holly were used to her joyful noise, but he wasn't. He met her gaze with a crooked grin, and she leaned toward him. "I warned you."

His grin widened, and he turned his attention back to the front. When she looked at him a few moments later, he wasn't singing, but his eyes were on the song lyrics, and he looked more comfortable than he had when he first entered. He was dressed in black pants and a striped cotton shirt, which his shoulders filled out quite nicely. The heart they'd taken from the cache the prior day rested against his chest, and the spicy-woodsy scent he wore was every bit as appealing in church as it had been on their hike yesterday.

Lyrics to a new song flashed up on the screen, and she tried to corral her wayward thoughts. With Grant standing so close, it was no easy task. She wasn't complaining, though. She'd had to twist his arm, but he was here. Maybe he would come to realize whatever he hoped to find on his travels was no further away than a heartfelt prayer. If only he were staying longer.

As soon as the service was over, she nudged him into the aisle. If they hurried, they might avoid being waylaid by Beulah. They were on a tight schedule—an hour and a half to let the dogs out, change clothes, grab lunch and be on the water. But Beulah could part a crowd as effectively as God split the Red Sea. Most of Murphy ran for cover when they saw her coming or sighed in relief once they realized her squinting gaze was focused on someone else.

Within moments, she was beside them. "Hello, girls. Who's your friend?"

Grant held out a hand before Jami could answer. "Grant McAllister, Elizabeth McAllister's grandson."

Beulah's eager gray eyes went from Holly to Sam, then returned to Grant. Knowing Beulah, she was hoping to piece together a juicy story. "How do you kids know each other?"

Jami stifled a smile. Grant probably hadn't been called a *kid* in over a decade.

"Jami and I are neighbors, at least temporarily, and she's doing a feature article on my grandparents' place."

Beulah expelled a disappointed "Oh" and shook his hand. As soon as she walked away, Jami grinned up at Grant.

"You know you just dashed her hopes."

"How?"

Holly flashed him a bright smile. "You were supposed to say you'd fallen madly in love with one of us and the wedding will be in two weeks. That lame answer about a newspaper story doesn't give her anything to work with."

Samantha laughed. "You know how every small town has a notorious gossip? Ours is Beulah Fines. And she wears the label as proudly as she wears those awful hats."

Jami pursed her lips. Maybe she should put the older woman's big mouth to good use. If she told Beulah about the breakup, she wouldn't have to worry about damage control. Beulah would handle it for her. One side of her said she should leave it to Robert to decide what he told his aunt. Another side said if he hadn't blurted everything to Beulah, she wouldn't be in this mess to begin with.

Yeah, she'd go ahead and talk to Beulah. But not at church, when she was in a hurry and everyone was standing around. She'd call her later.

After they'd stepped out into the sunlight, Jami turned toward Grant. "All right, we're running home to change clothes, and I've got to take the dogs out. We'll pick you up at the Holiday Inn in forty minutes."

"I'll be ready. And what about lunch?"

"Bubba's Burger Barn, right next to Wild River Outfitters. It's more of a concession stand than a restaurant, but it's fast, and that's what we need. So it'll be burgers and fries."

"The lunch of champions." He held up a hand in farewell. "Forty minutes."

NINE

"Around this next bend is our first rapids, class two." Sam sat in the back of the large rubber raft, steering and calling out instructions. Two more people had joined them, tourists from Florida. Each rowed on command, decked out in padded fluorescent life jackets and helmets.

"Great." Grant forced a playful frown. "This is the point where we lose the city slicker from New York."

Jami threw a glance over her shoulder and laughed. She was sitting right in front of him, hair pulled into a high ponytail. Its tip swished against her life vest with every movement of the raft. So far they were all dry. That probably wasn't going to last long.

"Sam knows what she's doing. And there won't be anything rougher than class three. So it'll be quite manageable, even for a city slicker."

In spite of her reassuring words, when they rounded the bend, his heart began to pound. Just ahead was a long stretch of churning, frothing water roaring down a series of drops. Yep, they were getting ready to get quite wet.

A minute later, the raft surged forward and bounced downward amid whoops and hollers and frantic paddling. A wall of icy water slammed into him, sucking the breath from his lungs, and the raft bucked and reared like a bronco determined to throw its rider. He dug his paddle into the churning water and thrust with fast, furious strokes, not fully understanding how that was supposed to help keep everyone in the boat.

Finally, the pitch leveled out and the angry torrent settled. He brushed wet tendrils of hair off his forehead and dissolved into laughter, joined by Jami and the others. He hadn't laughed like that in . . . well, he couldn't remember ever laughing like that. There was nothing quite like the adrenaline rush of being propelled down a raging river with nothing between safety and disaster except a rubber raft and a few paddles.

Jami turned toward him, face flushed with excitement. Water dripped from her ponytail and bangs, and not one square inch of her appeared dry. Even her back was soaked. "So what do you think?"

"This is a blast!" Several more rapids followed, broken by periods of calm. He leaned toward Jami. "I don't know what else you have planned for me, but this'll be hard to top."

"I may not be able to *top* this, but by the time I get done showing you all we have to offer, you won't want to leave."

That was what he was afraid of. He was only two days into her two-week tour, but time was passing too quickly. The activities themselves were pleasurable. But doing them with Jami made them outstanding. He was enjoying every minute he spent with her. Maybe too much.

Yesterday, he'd almost kissed her. She'd stood so close, her arms looped around his neck, the lavender scent of her shampoo teasing his senses. It had been innocent on her part. She had simply tried to secure the cord around his neck.

Fortunately, he'd regained his sanity before he did something they'd both regret. He'd agreed to hang around for two weeks and let her show him the sights. Having some romantic fling while he was here wasn't part of the bargain. And if he started anything with Jami, that was all it would be. In two weeks, he'd pack his bags and be gone.

He dipped his paddle beneath the now-calm surface and rowed in time with the others. With each stroke, the raft made short forward surges. It was hard to believe they were on the same river that had given them such a roller-coaster ride a few minutes earlier. But the tranquil scene was deceiving. The distant roar of raging water was a constant reminder any reprieves were temporary.

Jami stopped paddling to twist on the inflatable seat. "Your upcoming itinerary includes the art walk, Fields of the Wood, the Salty Dog and the Murphy River Walk."

"Sounds like you've got everything well planned out. You're organized."

"Ha! I've never been accused of that before."

He studied her for a moment. Who told her she was disorganized? Probably the same person who'd said she wasn't practical.

"So what's the Salty Dog? It sounds like a bar."

Her grin widened, and he couldn't help but smile back. Jami found pleasure in little things. He'd probably been like that at one point in his life, but he couldn't remember that far back.

"The Salty Dog Gem Mine. Ever been gem mining before?"

"Nope. Another new experience to enrich my life."

Enrich his life. A good choice of words as far as Jami was concerned, because that was exactly what her presence seemed to do. The instant Bethany had left, his zest for life disappeared, as if she'd bundled it up with her personal belongings and taken it with her. Maybe he was about to find it again.

"I think it's about time for *me* to treat *you*. How about if I take you to dinner tomorrow night? Or I could cook for you. The kitchen is fully stocked, right down to my grandmother's china, crystal and linen tablecloths."

He clamped his mouth shut, but the words had already escaped. What on earth was he thinking? Long ago, he'd entertained regularly—friends, business associates, members of the orchestra. But he hadn't cooked in over two years, even for himself. If a restaurant offered quality takeout and was anywhere near his office, the menu was stowed in his top desk drawer. *Rusty* didn't begin to describe his cooking skills.

But it was too late. A dazzling smile climbed up her cheeks and settled in her eyes. "I'd love that."

"I'll see what nice restaurants I can find, too." He had to leave himself an out, in case dinner was a total disaster.

"Okay, everyone." Sam again addressed the group from the back of the raft. "Coming up is our second class three. It's a little rougher than the other one, with a small waterfall at the end. So stay sharp and paddle hard."

The stretch of white water grew more ominous the closer they got. Feet wedged under the inflatable seat in front of him, Grant tightened his grip on the paddle and dug in with strong, smooth strokes, trying to anticipate the raft's movement. The wild current grabbed the rubber boat and tossed it around like a beach ball. When it jerked sideways and spun ninety degrees, he threw his weight into the movement and barely stayed in the raft.

Jami wasn't so lucky. The sudden shift propelled her upward and sideways, and before he could even reach for her, she was sailing face-first toward the churning water. He made a belated, desperate lunge as she plunged beneath the surface.

His heart pounded, and panic spiraled through him. He had to do something.

"Everyone stay in the boat." Samantha's commanding tone brought him up short. "She's got her life vest and helmet."

He waited for her head to break the surface, but there was nothing behind them except angry white water. A giant fist clamped down on his heart and squeezed. Maybe only seconds had passed, but it seemed like an eternity. Jami was in trouble, and nothing else mattered. He threw the paddle onto the floor of the raft and thrust himself over the side, Sam's scolding words echoing in his ears.

Then the icy water engulfed him, and he didn't hear anything else.

Jami fought the panic pounding up her spine. Icy water churned around her, sucking her downward and toppling her head over heels until she no longer knew which way was up. She kicked her feet and flailed her arms, helpless against a current determined to keep her under. Suddenly a strong arm tightened around her waist, pulling her to the surface and molding her against a hard body.

She wrapped an arm around the neck of her rescuer, then gave in to a coughing spasm. Submerged rocks continued to buffet her body, and she kicked her feet, trying to get purchase on anything that would bring her upright and stop her mad descent downriver. When she wiped the water from her face, incredible blue eyes stared back at her, filled with concern.

"Grant."

He winced as the current slammed him against a rock but didn't loosen his grip. "Let's work our way to the edge."

When they reached calmer water, she tried to stand, but her knees buckled. Grant's hold on her tightened. "Whoa, easy."

She kept her arm around his neck. Even soaking wet, his warmth radiated into her, his muscular arms offering strength and protection. A shiver shook her, and she laid her head against his chest, drawing his heat into her body. The current moved against them, gentle now, the water waist deep. The raft was somewhere downstream, the bends in the river hiding it from view.

"I'm sorry you got thrown out, too." She drew in a quivery breath. Hopefully he wouldn't regret going. "It doesn't happen often, I promise."

"I didn't exactly fall out. I saw you go overboard and went in after you."

Her stomach settled into a doughy lump. His first time on the river, and he'd dived in after her. She tilted her head back, heartfelt thanks on the tip of her tongue, but her breath caught in her throat.

All the concern that had shone from his eyes earlier was still there. But so was something else: longing, a silent plea her heart was responding to of its own accord.

"I'd do it all over again."

His voice was low but rich, mesmerizing. It wove a web around her, silken strands holding her motionless. He lifted one hand to cup her face, and she pressed her cheek into his palm. She needed to say something, to disperse this strange energy passing between them. Her mouth opened, but nothing came out.

His gaze dropped to her lips, and he leaned forward ever so slowly. "No regrets." His breath was hot against her mouth, sending shivers all the way to her toes. This time they had nothing to do with the temperature of the water.

She still had time to back away, to stop them from doing something they'd both regret. But her mind and body didn't seem to communicate. At that moment, she couldn't have moved if her life depended on it.

His lips brushed hers, his touch the merest whisper. Strength drained from her limbs, carried away with the gentle current. She tightened her grip on his neck to keep from sinking back into the water, and he took the cue. His mouth slanted across hers, no longer gentle, but possessive and demanding. A tidal wave of emotion swept through her, as if every yearning she'd ever experienced had pointed to this very moment. If she had ever wondered whether a simple kiss could make her pulse race, her knees weak and her head spin, she would never wonder again. Because this one did all that and more. Suddenly, those flowery descriptions in romance novels didn't seem so exaggerated.

Then, just like that, it was over. He broke the kiss and held her away from him. "I'm sorry. I shouldn't have done that."

She let her arms fall from his neck and shivered at the sudden loss of his warmth. "You're probably right." No, he was *definitely* right. It was going to be a long time before she fully recovered from the experience. She brought her fingers to her lips and drew in a steadying breath. "It's one of the rules of journalism, you know—no kissing interview subjects. We learned that in school." She flashed him a crooked grin, trying to convince herself as much as him that their kiss hadn't affected her the way it had. Hopefully she was fooling him, because she wasn't fooling herself.

"We need to get you out of this cold water."

Keeping a tight grip on her hand, he led her toward the bank, the stones beneath their feet slick and uneven. Shouts reached them from a short distance upriver, another raft on its way through the stretch of rapids that had landed her in the water. Right after they stepped onto solid ground, it came into view. Several heads turned their direction. Grant released her, and they both waved.

"So what now? Is Sam going to come back and get us?"

"No. They'll wait for us, but we've got to go to them."

For the next several minutes, they made their way along the river's edge, alternating between wading and making the trek by land, whichever was the easier route.

Grant stepped onto a rock and helped her up. "You, Samantha and Holly seem close."

"Yeah. We're as different as night and day, but we've been best friends pretty much all our lives. Sam and I were together in school, and Holly was a year behind us. Sam was the tomboy. Usually you could find her hanging with the boys, climbing trees or building a fort. Holly was the opposite, a girly girl all the way, frilly dresses and all."

Grant nodded. "I can see that. So what happened to Samantha?"

"When she was sixteen, she ran into a burning barn to save her horses. A flaming beam fell on her."

"It doesn't seem to have slowed her down any."

She bent to pass under a low branch, then smiled back at him. "There's not much that can hold Sam back."

"So she was the tomboy, and Holly was the girly girl. What about you?"

"I was the dreamer, always had my head in the clouds. Some people say I still do." At least one person did.

"Hey, that's not a bad thing." He nudged her with his elbow. "Without the dreamers we wouldn't have any inventions or books or art or technology. We'd still be walking around with our clubs and spears and hunting woolly mammoths."

He lowered himself back into the river, then extended his arm. The bank had become a sheer rock face, leaving them no other route. When she took his hand, it was cool, but warm in comparison to hers, which was slowly turning to ice. The specks of sunshine peeking through the dense growth at the river's edge did nothing to warm her. The water around her legs was so cold it hurt, and her shorts and shirt clung to her skin, wet and stiff.

"I'm having fantasies right now about a hot shower and dry clothes. I'm so cold my goose bumps have goose bumps."

Grant laughed. "You *are* starting to look like a Popsicle. Your lips are turning blue."

They moved around a sharp bend, and as they waded, the large raft came into view, held in place by a downed tree.

When they reached the others, Sam cast them both a scolding glance. "You're supposed to enjoy the Nantahala from *inside* the raft."

Jami shook her head. "I don't even know what happened. One minute I was paddling furiously, and the next I was flying face-first toward the water. Now I'm freezing my rear off." As if to prove her point, another violent shiver shook her body. "At least this happened toward the end of the trip. Dry clothes are only twenty minutes away."

Her estimate was right. Twenty minutes later, she stood with Sam and Holly at a series of lockers, retrieving wallets, towels, clothing and shoes. By the time they emerged from the restroom, Grant was already waiting, wet hair combed back away from his face.

He smiled when he saw her. "Feel better now?"

"A hundred percent."

"Good. Before we leave, I need something to drink. Can I get you ladies anything?"

Jami watched him walk away, a darkened semicircle forming where his wet hair touched the collar of his shirt. If the way to a man's heart was through his stomach, the way to a woman's heart was with selfless acts of chivalry. She sighed and turned to see both Samantha and Holly staring at her with conspiratorial grins. "What?"

Samantha turned to Holly. "Jami's in love."

Holly nodded. "I think you're right. She's positively glowing."

"I don't think she ever glowed with Robert, do you?"

Holly shook her head. "Never."

Jami cleared her throat. "Hello. I'm right here. And no, I'm not in love."

"Uh-huh." Her friends responded in unison.

"I'm not."

Of course she wasn't. Sure, she liked him and enjoyed spending time with him. There was no denying the attraction between them. That kiss had pretty well turned her world upside down.

But falling in love with him? That would be stupid. Their lives were hundreds of miles apart. Even if he decided to keep the McAllister estate and relocate to Murphy, it wouldn't matter. Nothing could ever develop between them. He wouldn't let it.

But her heart wasn't listening. Grant made her feel special. He respected their differences instead of trying to change her. And he could make her pulse race just by walking into a room. She'd finally found it, the stuff of fairy tales, the spark that was always absent with Robert. It was there every time Grant looked at her, every time he smiled.

But in one crucial way, he was no different from the other men in her life. Soon he was going to walk away, and she'd never see him again.

TEN

Jami stepped up onto the McAllister porch, savoring the mouthwatering aromas. After whitewater rafting yesterday, Grant had headed right to the estate, claiming he had a dinner date to get ready for. So she'd spent the evening alone with the dogs, thinking of him, alternating between telling herself a kiss like that had better not happen again and hoping with everything in her that it would.

At least she'd gotten one unpleasant task out of the way. She'd made the phone call to Beulah. That had been twenty-four hours ago, plenty of time for her to spread the word to everyone in Murphy, including Missy's twins. Robert was due back Friday night. He still hadn't tried to contact her. She wasn't complaining.

She reached up to ring the bell, and moments later, the door swung open. Grant stood in the foyer, his clothing protected by a stiff, new apron. A reddish dribble had blazed a trail down one pocket.

She scanned the length of him. "You really look the part."

"I guess I do. I picked this up when I went shopping for the food. If you're not wearing at least a splatter or two by the end of meal preparation, you're not getting into your cooking."

He closed the door behind her, and she drew in another deep breath. Grant was apparently a superb cook. And it was obvious he enjoyed it. Pleasure rolled off him, infectious enthusiasm. If he was passionate about anything, this was it.

As he led her toward the kitchen, she glanced around her. Sometime since yesterday, he'd had the place cleaned. The wood floor was swept, mopped and polished, the layers of dust that had covered the surfaces gone.

"Wow, everything looks good."

"Yeah, I thought we might want to sit somewhere after dinner without having to battle dust bunnies. Besides that, I got a call from Brenda, my Realtor, and she's bringing someone by to look at the place tomorrow."

Disappointment shot through her, and she scolded herself. He wasn't keeping the place. She'd known that from the start. Besides, if Brenda found a buyer, Jami wouldn't have to worry about Vanguard's heavy machinery in her backyard.

Grant continued. "Bernie recommended I hire Andrea Jenkins, who jumped at the chance to earn some money during her summer break. She did an awesome job."

"Andrea's really conscientious. Of course, she's my cousin, so I'm a little partial."

He stopped in the doorway of the kitchen and cocked an eyebrow at her. "Are you related to everybody in Murphy?"

"No, it just seems that way. Aunt Lily had eight children, and all but the youngest two have children of their own now. So that gives me lots of cousins. And the number keeps growing. Andrea's the daughter of Jerry, Aunt Lily's oldest."

"She was worth her weight in gold today."

He turned, and she followed him into the kitchen, where she stopped short. Everything had been cleaned and polished to a brilliant shine, but it was the nook that drew her attention. White linen covered the table, elegantly set with china, crystal and silver, no doubt his grandmother's. Candles burned atop three brass candlesticks in the center. It was a setting fit for a fairy-tale princess. The only thing missing was the string quartet, but the orchestral music drifting in from somewhere else in the house was a good substitute.

She tilted her head toward the nook. "So was that you or Andrea?"

"Andrea washed the windows." He pointed at the large bay, where outside ever-lengthening shadows stretched toward the woods. A patch of wildflowers grew among the downed limbs and underbrush, delicate beauty in the midst of chaos.

"And the table?"

"That was my doing."

"I'm impressed." Actually, she was more than impressed. White linen, fine china, good music and candlelight. And he'd done it for her. Warmth filled her chest, and her insides went all quivery. How was she supposed to *not* fall for him?

He pulled out a chair for her to sit, then laid a linen napkin across her lap. After hanging the apron on a hook, he took two bowls from the table and returned them filled with tomato bisque.

"I feel like I'm in a swanky restaurant." She brought the first spoonful to her mouth and, eyes closed, savored it, rich and smooth against her tongue. She could get used to this. But she wouldn't have the opportunity. Everything with Grant was temporary, as fleeting as the first snowfall, melting as soon as it hit the ground.

Unless she could convince him to stay.

She almost laughed at the ridiculous thought. Maybe he'd use some of his upcoming vacation and spend a little extra time in Murphy. But once that was over, he'd be gone. He'd been burned too badly to commit to anything more serious than friendship. He'd pretty well said as much. No, there was no future for them, no matter how much Bernie wanted otherwise. Unfortunately, Bernie wasn't the only one with hopes.

"So tell me what you've got planned for this weekend. What's Fields of the Wood?"

"It's a Bible park."

One side of his mouth lifted in a half smile. "Church, then a Bible park. What are you trying to do, convert me?"

If only. "You'll enjoy Fields of the Wood. There's Ten Commandments Mountain, where they have the Ten Commandments spelled out in huge concrete letters on the side of it. You can drive up the back, but it's more fun to climb the stairs in the front. I counted them once. If I remember right, there are three hundred thirty-six of them if you go all the way to the lookout at the top. After that, we can climb Prayer Mountain. That one has over three hundred steps, too."

"You're determined to get me in shape."

Her eyes dipped to his muscled chest and arms. There was no *getting* necessary. He was already there. "The other exhibits aren't so strenuous. There's a duck pond and some nature trails, too."

"Sounds like a nice place."

"It is. I thought we could go Sunday afternoon, start with a picnic lunch. Of course, the morning is church."

"I was planning on it."

She gave him a crooked smile. "That was easy."

"I know. I figured while I'm having all these new experiences, I'd go all out." He grew serious. "Actually, since meeting you and your friends, I'm thinking I should reassess my opinions about the church and who goes there."

"I'm glad to hear it." God was working on him. Already he seemed a little more at peace, less cynical.

She tipped her bowl to spoon the last of the bisque into her mouth, not willing to waste a single drop. When she looked back up at Grant, he was watching her. She pointed downward with her spoon. "Delicious."

"Thanks." He took their empty bowls to the sink and returned with two plates of salad he'd retrieved from the refrigerator. "Course number two. I hope you brought your appetite."

"I never leave home without it. That and my handy-dandy spiral notebook. But I left it in the car. I do have my pack of Post-its, though. Those stay in my purse."

"Yeah, I've noticed your preoccupation with neon-colored notes."

She stabbed a bite of salad—tomatoes and cucumbers on a bed of mixed greens, decorated with three whole Kalamata olives and a generous sprinkling of pine nuts. "An idea pops into my head and I don't want to lose it, so I grab the nearest thing to write on. Since I've got them in every room of the house, that's usually a Post-it."

She put the bite in her mouth. Grant had made some kind of citrus vinaigrette dressing. At least she assumed he'd made it, because it didn't taste like anything store-bought. It was heavenly.

"My system's not as disorganized as it sounds." She stabbed some more salad. She would probably drive an ordered, methodical person like Grant crazy. "Every few days, I collect up all the Post-its and put story ideas in one stack, grocery items in another, stuff to go on the calendar in another, et cetera, et cetera. Then I take care of one stack at a time."

"Hey, whatever works."

She hesitated, waiting for the *but*—*but it would be easier to . . . but it would be better if . . .* The *but* never came. A tension she hadn't even noticed drained from her, and she smiled. "Most of the time it works great. But sometimes a Post-it disappears, and I find it stuck to the back of something a month later."

She took a swig of her iced tea and continued. "But don't worry. Tonight the Post-its are staying in my purse. No jotting down story ideas and no interview questions. Everything is off the record." Not that it would matter to Grant. He probably wasn't planning to share any earth-shattering family secrets.

"How long have you wanted to be a journalist?"

"Since I was about ten. But I've always loved to write. When I was in fourth grade, I decided I was going to pen the next great American novel and filled two spiral-bound notebooks before I ran out of steam." She grinned over at him. "Years later I came across them, saw how bad the writing was and ran every page through my mom's shredder. I didn't want to give anyone fuel for blackmail later on."

Grant laughed. "I bet the writing wasn't half bad for a fourth grader."

"I guess it wasn't."

"So was that your last attempt at novel writing?"

She gave him a sheepish smile. "I'm afraid not. I've got a few more started." Seven, to be exact. Although she wasn't ready to own up to that many failed attempts. "I've always dreamed of writing a book, but I guess I'm not very good at seeing things through to completion." Especially with someone pooh-poohing what she was doing every step of the way.

"What's stopping you?"

"From finishing one?" She shrugged. "It's not very practical. I mean, thousands of novels get written every year, and only a small fraction of a percent ever get published."

"Dreams aren't supposed to be practical. If what you wanted was practical and easy, you would walk out and do it. Then it wouldn't be a dream."

His eyes met hers over the dancing flames of the candles, the encouragement there resonating with something deep inside her. Why did he have to be so perfect? Well, not perfect, but someone who understood and appreciated her eccentricities, who encouraged her to fly rather than trying to clip her wings.

She laid her fork across her now-empty plate and sighed, pushing aside the wistful thoughts. "You have to admit, if it never gets published, that's a lot of hours wasted."

"Do you enjoy writing?"

"I love it."

"Then it's not a waste of time, even if you never get published."

She sat for several moments, letting his words sink in. She had another longtime dream. But it was even less practical than writing a novel. Opening a bed and breakfast took money and resources she simply didn't have.

But Grant was right. If she wanted to write a novel, it didn't matter how much time she spent at it. For so many years, Robert had imposed his opinions on her, his ideas for what was best. But it wasn't overt. He didn't push and demand that she change, just slipped in the back way with his disparaging comments. She was only now recognizing that friendship for what it was—toxic.

Grant reached across the table to lay his hand over hers. "Hang on to your dreams, Jami. Don't ever let anyone try to talk you out of them."

She nodded, not trusting herself to speak. What would it be like to have a man like Grant? A man who supported her endeavors? Who encouraged her to reach for the stars?

He squeezed her hand. "Promise me you'll get out one of those incomplete novels and try to finish it."

She swallowed, then drew in a deep breath. "Yes, I'll do that."

"Good. I'm going to hold you to it." He stood and walked away with their salad plates, leaving her sitting alone.

She'd made a promise. She was going to finish one of her books. Knowing Grant, he would hold her accountable. That was okay. Because pretty soon, her evenings were going to be her own. Once Grant left, she would have all the time in the world to write.

It wasn't a thought she relished.

Grant returned to the table with the main course—chicken cordon bleu, potatoes au gratin, and steamed asparagus, complete with parsley sprigs and lemon wedges for garnish. He always took pride in preparing tasty dishes, but tonight, he'd taken extra care with presentation. He'd wanted Jami to feel special.

She sampled each item, savoring every bite. "Mmm, this is wonderful. The whole meal has been amazing. You can cook for me anytime."

Contentment swelled inside him. It was more than just her compliment. It was everything. From the moment he spread out ingredients on the island's butcher-block countertop, he'd felt as if he'd suddenly come to life. When he finished his sabbatical and went back to New York, maybe he would start entertaining again. Maybe he would even pick up his French horn and join a community orchestra. After two long years, he was finally awakening from the dead.

And he owed it all to Jami. Guilt pricked him. He should go ahead and give her permission to use what she needed for her article. If she hadn't used it already. When he returned to Murphy last Friday, he'd been gone a week. She may have turned the piece in during that time. It may have even run by now.

"How is your feature going?"

"Oh, it's going. I tried Flora again, but the number is no longer in service."

"Yeah, I discovered that, too. I tried it a couple days after you gave it to me. She apparently had it disconnected right after you called her." He flashed her a teasing smile. "You must have made quite an impression."

She frowned. "I didn't have the opportunity to make much of an impression. As soon as she found out I was a reporter, she said what she did and hung up the phone."

"And changed her number."

She grinned. "That, too. Anyhow, I spent some time at the library last week, poring over old newspaper articles. And I talked to Hilda some more."

"Did you learn anything?"

"I got a few interesting tidbits to use for my article. Nothing as good as what was in the box, though. So if you change your mind . . ."

So she hadn't included his mother's deceitfulness in her article. Evidently she was keeping her promise. If he didn't give her the go-ahead, would she continue to keep that promise? Or would she print what she wanted once he was gone? Probably so. She would have no reason not to. Other than her word.

Her gaze locked with his. "Just so you know, I'm not the type of reporter who likes to dig up dirt on people for the sake of being sensational. If I were to include what we found, it would be tastefully done. I wouldn't paint your mother in a bad light." She gave him a sad smile. "Her part in this is more tragic than devious."

He nodded, but couldn't bring himself to give in to her request. He wanted her to prove him wrong, to show him she could be trusted, to once again restore his faith in people.

She cut off a piece of chicken and put it into her mouth. "Why did you stop cooking?"

Her question jarred him from his thoughts. She'd asked it before, and he'd told her he'd been too busy. "Lost interest, I guess."

"The same time you lost interest in your music?" Based on her tone, she didn't buy that answer any more than she had the other one.

"Something like that." He motioned toward her half-empty glass. "Are you ready for a refill on tea?"

"My tea's fine." She studied him, lips turned downward in a frown.

He lowered his gaze to his plate and picked at the slivered-almond-and-tomato mixture topping his asparagus. Anything to avoid looking at her. Because if he did, she would be able to see right past the indifference he tried to project.

"You just changed the subject."

"No one wants to hear my hard-luck story." And he didn't want to tell it.

"If I didn't want to hear it, I wouldn't have asked."

Several moments passed while he deliberated. When the pain was still raw and fresh, he had confided in his friends. But soon he found himself distanced from them. Craig's and his mutual friends didn't want to take sides. His married friends no longer seemed comfortable around him, and his single friends felt he was a drag. He couldn't blame them. He *was* a drag.

So for two long years, he'd bottled up the pain and anger, not opening up to anyone. How could he even consider that level of sharing with Jami after just two and a half weeks? He drew in a labored breath and once again met her eyes. And the understanding he saw there shattered the last of his reservations.

"I came home one day and found my wife in bed with my best friend." He released a heavy sigh. "I didn't have a clue. I could read my witnesses better than I could read my own wife." Disgust laced his tone. The majority of it was aimed inward. He'd never forgiven her, but he'd never forgiven himself, either.

She reached across the table to put her hand over his, which maintained a death grip on his fork. "Your ex-wife was an idiot."

He stifled a snort. "Well, she had me fooled, so I'd say *I* was the idiot."

"You're not the first man to be snookered by sweet words and a pretty face."

He didn't comment, just released the fork and turned his hand over to squeeze hers. Some strange kind of energy flowed between them, connecting them in a way he hadn't felt with anyone, not even Bethany.

"She told me if I had given her what she needed, she would never have turned to Craig." He looked down at his plate. "I was working long hours. She didn't understand what it took to climb the ladder of success. And I didn't understand that there's more than one way to define success." He again met her eyes. "I climbed that ladder, made it all the way to the top. But after Bethany left, I wondered if it was leaning against the wrong wall. I'm still not sure."

She squeezed his hand. "We've all let things get in the way of our relationships. The best thing is to learn from our mistakes and try not to be too weighed down with regret."

He gave her a small nod, then released her hand to stab some of the asparagus he'd played with earlier. "That's when I stopped creating gourmet meals and gave up the horn. I poured myself into work, taking on more and more cases. I figured if I could keep busy, I'd stay ahead of the emptiness always chewing at my heels."

"Did it help?"

"Yes and no. Everything was fine while I was working. But no matter how hard I drove myself, eventually I had to come home to an empty apartment." He released a sigh filled with regret. When he continued, his thoughts were no longer in the past. "That's when it's always the worst, in the wee hours of the morning, with nothing to distract me from what a fool I've been."

She flashed him a sympathetic smile. "Stop beating yourself up. Everyone's entitled to a mistake or two, even if they're doozies." She speared her last piece of chicken. "So what about now? Now that you've jumped back into cooking again, at least for one night, what's your next step?"

"Nothing for the time being. I'll be on the road for the next two months." Unless he spent the time in Murphy. Which he might do. None of his travel plans sounded like fun anymore if they didn't involve Jami.

He stood to clear away their dishes. "Are you ready for dessert?"

She put her hand against her stomach and groaned. "I'm stuffed. But I've got to at least have a taste."

He returned with two plates, each holding crepes drizzled with a strawberry glaze and topped with a dollop of whipped cream.

She cut off a generous bite. "A perfect end to a perfect meal."

"You're just easy to please."

"I am, but that's beside the point." She grinned over at him. "So what dreams do *you* have?"

"I'm not much of a dreamer."

"Come on, you must have something. Tell me."

Yeah, he had a dream, and he'd given it up before finishing high school. He shook his head and crossed his arms. "Uh-uh. It's stupid."

"No dreams are stupid. Tell me. I told you mine." Eagerness shone from her eyes, making her look very much the nosy reporter.

"This is off the record, right?"

"Scout's honor." She gave him a mock salute.

"I've always wanted to own a fine restaurant."

Her features went slack. "That's it? That's not a stupid dream."

"I guess it wasn't originally. When I was in high school, I wanted to be head chef in a fancy restaurant. But with my GPA and SAT scores, my mom and my guidance counselors pushed me toward law school. So that dream got tossed aside."

"It's not stupid now, either. Based on what you fed me tonight, you could do it. New York's finest chefs wouldn't have anything on you."

Or Murphy's. The thought came from nowhere. He shook his head again. "It would be totally impractical. I went to school for seven years to be a lawyer. I can't walk away from my law practice."

"Dreams aren't supposed to be practical or easy. You said so yourself. Does cooking make you happy?"

"Totally."

"Do you get the same happiness from practicing law?"

"Frankly, no."

"And could you live on what you've put back until you started turning a profit?"

"I could." Especially with everything he'd inherited from his grandmother.

"So what's stopping you?"

He shrugged and began to clear away their empty dessert plates. "My life has taken another direction. I can't change it now."

"If you're still breathing, you can change the path you're on."

She stood and followed him toward the sink. Once they'd rinsed and put all the dishes in the dishwasher, he squirted some liquid soap into the compartment and closed the door. When he straightened, she was leaning back against the counter a couple feet away, watching him.

"Thank you for dinner. I'm glad you invited me."

He stepped closer. "I'm glad I did, too. This has been . . . good."

She reached up to tuck a stray wisp of hair behind her ear. A fresh, clean fragrance drifted past, a subtle hint of lavender. And a memory that had plagued him since yesterday afternoon crashed forward—the distant roar of the river, her arms around his neck, her warmth pressed into him, his lips on hers. And although he told himself he shouldn't, he wanted nothing more than to relive the experience. Again and again.

He moved closer. Now he was right in front of her, her back still against the counter. His gaze dropped to her mouth. He couldn't help it. There was something mesmerizing about the shape of her lips, touched with peach-colored gloss. He tilted his head down, testing her. He'd said it was a mistake. She had agreed.

Nothing in her expression hinted at those doubts now. Her eyes drifted shut, and he pressed his mouth to hers. Her arms circled his neck, pulling him closer, and he gladly complied. Heat flowed through him, thawing those areas long frozen over and sending life coursing through his veins.

He tightened his embrace. She was firm yet soft, so willing and responsive. The walls he'd kept around his heart for so long crumbled, joining the rubble of the reservations he'd carried all the way from New York.

When he finally pulled away, she opened her eyes and drew in a shaky breath. "And was *that* kiss a mistake?"

"What do *you* think?"

"I wouldn't be a good judge of that right now."

Actually, he wouldn't, either. At that moment, he wouldn't recognize a mistake if it slapped him in the face. Maybe the whole thing was a mistake—the kiss, dinner, his coming back to Murphy. But it didn't feel like one. Something deep within whispered this was where he belonged, right here in Murphy.

Over the past couple of weeks, he'd begun looking at the place through eyes less jaded. The quaint little town had grown on him. Its laid-back atmosphere that forced him to take life a little more slowly. The friendly people who made him feel like a long-lost friend who'd finally returned home. And one quirky newspaper reporter who had the potential to upend his entire existence.

Now he didn't want to leave. Not next week. Not in two months. Not ever.

But Jami was the kind of girl who would require commitment. A lifetime promise. Was he ready to strip himself of every last protective defense, to let down his guard so completely there would be nothing left between bliss and total heartbreak?

He wasn't sure. The only thing he knew was that after just two and a half weeks and two exquisite kisses, he was dangerously close to doing something he'd sworn he would never do again—fall in love.

ELEVEN

Grant cruised down 64, headed toward the old house. With Andrea's cleaning job yesterday, on top of the packing he'd accomplished before heading back to New York, the place was starting to feel like a home. Not enough to consider giving up his comfy room at the Holiday Inn, but he was making progress. Today he'd tackle some more of the mess.

The light ahead turned yellow, and he eased to a stop. Hot Spot sat to the right, a gas station and convenience store. He had frequented it a few times. It was a great place to pick up needed items without having to drive all the way to town.

While he waited, a white van pulled away from one of the pumps, giving him a clear view of the parking spaces in front of the store . . . and a familiar red Sunbird. He glanced at the gas gauge. Five-eighths of a tank. He could top it off. It would give him an excuse to see Jami before she headed in to work.

The light changed, and instead of continuing down 64, he turned in to Hot Spot and pulled up to the pump opposite a faded blue pickup. An overall-clad figure stepped from the cab, and Hank turned and nodded a greeting.

"Are you enjoying your stay in Murphy?"

"I am." More than Hank would ever know.

The older man pocketed his credit card and began to pump his gas. "It's a great place, with some of the world's best people."

Yeah, one person in particular. He swiped his card and put the nozzle into the tank. While he waited for it to authorize, he let his gaze shift toward the building. Jami was inside, standing at the counter, talking to the clerk. She threw back her head and laughed, and though the sound didn't reach him through the thick glass, her sparkling laughter wove through his thoughts, infusing him with warmth and contentment.

When it was time to go back to his regular life, maybe Jami would come back with him. There were papers in New York, a lot of them. He even had an acquaintance who worked for the *New York Times*. Justin probably wouldn't mind putting in a good word for her. If not the *Times*, one of the smaller papers. With her vibrant personality, she would have no problem landing a job.

Even as he contemplated the possibilities, doubt cast its shadow over his optimism. Jami had lived her life in nature, surrounded by mountains and woods and streams. Would she be willing to give up the clean air and open spaces for smog and traffic and skyscrapers?

If so, he'd make it up to her. He'd do whatever he had to do to make her feel at home, to feed her creative side. He'd take her to museums and Broadway shows and parks. And he'd take her to church, as much for his own benefit as hers. Sitting with her at MountainView Sunday had stirred something in him, awakening a longing he didn't even know he had.

When he turned back to the pump, Hank's eyes were on him.

"Are you checking out Jami Carlisle?"

Was he that obvious? Yeah, he probably had it written all over his face, like a lovesick teenager. He put a hand to the pewter heart resting against his chest. Other than when she'd taken him whitewater rafting, he hadn't removed it since she gave it to him. "She's a special lady." No sense denying what he felt.

Hank nodded. "She sure is. But don't be getting any ideas."

A vise clamped down on his chest. "Why not?"

"She's already spoken for."

The vise squeezed harder, and he struggled to take in a shallow breath. "What do you mean?"

"Robert Demming. He and Jami have been sweethearts off and on for years. Now that Jami's finished with school, they're finally tying the knot. It's going to be a September wedding, if I heard right." He turned off the pump and replaced the gas nozzle.

"Jami's engaged?" She couldn't be. There had to be some mistake. She couldn't be that deceitful.

"Yep, she's engaged all right. The official announcement was made about a month ago, but everyone knew it was coming." Hank's eyes dipped to the nozzle protruding from the tank of the Mercedes. "Are you gonna pump your gas?"

Grant lowered his gaze. The fingers gripping the handle seemed to be attached to someone else's body. Jami was engaged. How could he have not known?

The same way he hadn't known about Bethany and Craig. During his orchestra concerts, Craig had sat in the audience with Bethany, and he had been a regular guest at the dinner parties they hosted. Grant had even come home a few times to find his friend there alone with his wife and had never questioned it. He'd been stupid and naïve.

And now he'd done it again. He'd been taken in by a pretty face.

Shame washed through him, pushed along by self-loathing. While he and Jami had shared meals and stories and adventures and quiet moments in nature, she'd been playing him. The genuine air that had intrigued him from the start was all a facade. She was engaged.

Engaged. The word echoed in his mind, taunting him for his naïveté. His fingers tightened, sending gas flowing into the tank. If Jami was engaged, where had the elusive fiancé been for the past week and a half?

He turned back to Hank, who was now getting into his truck. "I've never seen her with anyone. Does he live somewhere else?"

"He lives here in Murphy. But he's been gone the past week or so. Had a wedding to go to up north, then was going on a trip to Europe." He slid into the seat and cranked the truck. "See you around."

As Hank drove away, the pump clicked off, and Hot Spot's glass door swung open. Jami stepped into the early morning sunshine, and a dazzling smile spread across her face. Except now it didn't warm his heart. It sickened him. Because it wasn't real.

Nothing about her was real.

He hung up the nozzle, and when he turned again, she was hurrying toward him. His jaw tightened. Five minutes earlier, and he'd have been down the road. But if he'd been five minutes earlier, he might have missed Hank.

What was she trying to pull? He hadn't jumped to conclusions, reading more into their relationship than he should. She'd kissed him, for Pete's sake. They'd spent time together and shared their joys and hurts and dreams. They'd bonded. At least he thought they had.

He needed to give her a chance to come clean. Maybe things were rocky between her and her fiancé and she was planning to call off the engagement. But even then, she should have told him. Being engaged was a pretty important detail to omit, even with imminent plans to break it off.

Just before she reached him, she skidded to a stop, and her smile faded. "Are you all right?"

"Not really. Is there something you think you should tell me?"

She met his gaze, her own unwavering. She didn't blink or look away or show any of the other signs of deceit. In fact, her eyes held only confusion. She was good.

She tilted her head and tried to force a smile. "You're going to have to give me a hint. My crystal ball's broken."

He swung open the car door. "Never mind." He should have known she was too good to be true.

She grasped his arm, her grip surprisingly strong. "Grant, wait. Tell me what's wrong."

"Let's just say honesty is nonnegotiable."

"O-kay." She stretched out the word, the confusion on her face deepening. "It is for me, too. What, you think I've lied to you?"

"Sometimes lies are told in the things we *don't* say." He slid into the driver's seat but couldn't close the door, because she had stepped into the opening.

"What haven't I said? Ask me anything. I'll tell you." She lifted both hands in a gesture of openness. "I cry over sappy movies. My first term of college, I almost flunked algebra. Holly and I once got in trouble for hiding the teacher's chalk and eraser. What else do you want to know? Let's see. I talk to myself. A lot. They say you're only crazy if you answer yourself. Well, I do that, too."

He cranked the car, shaking his head. She was telling him everything except the one thing he wanted to hear. "Bye, Jami. The game's over."

"What game?"

The one you're playing with my heart. He kept the words to himself. He wouldn't admit to her that she'd duped him. He didn't even want to admit it to himself. He eased off the brake and let the car creep forward. "You're off the hook on the rest of the tour. I'm not selling to Vanguard."

He shut the door and turned toward the highway. As he prepared to pull back onto 64, he cast a glance in his rearview mirror. Jami stood watching him, jaw agape. For the second time, he was leaving her standing in a parking lot, plans thwarted. But this time he was justified.

He turned onto the highway and accelerated. He still had a few more days of work before he could turn everything over to the Realtor. But once he finished the last of his sorting and boxed up the few remaining keepsakes he hadn't yet shipped back to New York, he would be gone.

His hand went to his chest and wrapped around the pewter heart resting there. A few minutes ago, it had held so much meaning. Now it represented nothing but betrayal.

He gave it a hard downward yank. The leather tie snapped, and he threw the once-cherished piece to the passenger floorboard. He didn't need to be reminded of geocaching or any other activity he'd done with Jami.

In fact, he wanted nothing more than to get far, far away—away from Hot Spot, where his newfound hope came crashing down around him, and away from Murphy, where an auburn-haired pixie uncovered his heart, then stepped on it.

―⁂―

Jami swept through the front door of the *Scout*, purse hanging over one shoulder and notebook clutched against her chest. She'd spent the morning working in the field, partly because she couldn't stand the thought of staying cooped up inside, and partly because she hadn't been ready to face Bernie so soon after Grant's terse words.

Actually, she still wasn't ready to face Bernie. But David would probably have something to say if she tried to avoid the office indefinitely. She pushed her way through the swinging doors at the end of the long counter. Bernie was sitting at her desk against the wall, fingers flying over the keyboard, apparently oblivious to the work going on around her.

Jami made her way across the large, open room, offering nods and soft greetings to the three coworkers she passed. As soon as she pulled her chair away from her desk, Bernie looked over at her.

"There you are. I was beginning to wonder if I was going to see you today."

"I spent the morning taking pictures and doing interviews. Now I'm ready to start writing my library article." And maybe Bernie would take the hint and let her work. Not likely, since their paths hadn't crossed since Sunday. But it was worth a shot.

She laid her notebook on her desk and turned back the cover, then opened a blank document on her computer. Bernie watched in silence, then finally leaned forward.

"So tell me how things are progressing with that red-hot grandson." Her voice was a coarse whisper. "The last I knew, you were going whitewater rafting together."

Jami sighed. So much for taking hints. "We did. I got thrown from the raft, and he dove into the raging river to save me."

Bernie put a hand over her heart and slumped sideways in a feigned swoon. "Oh, you're giving me palpitations. How romantic."

"And last night, he made me dinner."

"Handsome, successful, romantic and a good cook, too."

Yeah, she'd been as impressed as Bernie. So impressed she'd pretty much handed him her heart on his grandmother's fine china.

Bernie plopped her foot on the floor and leaned forward, brown eyes sparkling behind her jewel-studded glasses. Bernie was always vibrant. But that vibrancy was most obvious when she was plotting another match. She soaked up every juicy detail, and on those rare occasions when her matchmaking attempts worked out, she could barely contain herself. She plopped her hand down on her desk. "I knew it. Things are moving along even faster than I'd hoped."

"They were till this morning, anyway."

"Oh, no." She sank back in the chair, face crumpling in disappointment. "What happened?"

"I don't know. I ran into him at Hot Spot, and he roped me into a game of twenty questions. Apparently he wasn't happy with my answers. Of course, it's kind of difficult to give good answers when you don't have the questions."

"Jami, girl, you are making no sense whatsoever."

Yeah, that was exactly how she'd felt about Grant that morning. She couldn't begin to guess what had gotten into him. Twelve hours earlier, they'd stood in his kitchen, and he'd kissed her like there was no tomorrow. Thoughts of that kiss still sent a quivery weakness down both legs. Then, literally overnight, he'd grown cold and angry.

"He seems to think I'm keeping something from him. And when I couldn't tell him what it was, he said the game was over."

"What game?"

"That's what I asked him. He didn't answer, just drove away."

Bernie sat in silence for several moments, frowning. She was scheming. Jami could see it in her eyes. Finally, she gave a short nod. "I'll go talk to him, find out what's ailing him."

"If he wouldn't tell me anything, I don't think he's going to tell you. Besides, I don't want him to know I talked to you."

She nodded again. "You've got a good point. Guys don't like it when their women talk about them."

"I'm not Grant's woman." Her tone held more disappointment than denial. Because that was exactly what she wanted to be.

She heaved a sigh. She'd done it again. She'd tumbled into another relationship where the only possible destination was a dead end. Not only were their lives eight hundred miles apart, Grant wasn't about to let down his guard and risk his heart. His refusal to talk to her this morning proved it.

And it left her with an emptiness inside that refused to go away. In time, those days with Grant would be nothing but a pleasant memory. And the ache inside would fade until it disappeared altogether. In the meantime, she would occupy herself any way she could. No more pity parties. She squared her shoulders and picked up the phone.

Bernie's face lit up. "Are you calling him?"

"No, I'm calling Holly." She would see what her two best friends were doing tonight. If they were tied up, she would challenge Bernie to a game of Scrabble. And if Bernie was tied up, she would take the dogs for a long walk in the park. Anything to get her mind off Grant.

Somehow, in less than three weeks, he'd swept her off her feet and made her believe in fairy tales again. She'd been sure she had finally found her prince.

But she'd been wrong. He wasn't a prince. He was a frog like all the others.

And he'd just hopped out of her life.

Grant started down the steps, a box propped on one hip, the other hand resting on the banister. His thoughts were still a massive jumble.

It was hard to believe less than twenty-four hours ago, he'd been with Jami, sitting around a table laden with food, flickering candles in the center, romantic music playing in the background. They'd talked and held hands and shared long-ago experiences. And she'd kissed him. Okay, so he'd initiated that. But she hadn't done anything to discourage him.

And all the while she was engaged. The sweet, innocent air, everything she silently communicated through those expressive eyes, all a facade. He'd been sucker punched, a solid steel-toed boot planted right in his gut.

Thank goodness he hadn't fallen in love with her. He'd come close. He definitely cared for her. And that was bad enough. But the whole situation was a kick in the gut in another sense, too. He'd wanted to believe there was someone out there who was exactly who she claimed to be, without deceit or guile. Someone with true integrity, pure and selfless. He just wanted to believe in some kind of innate goodness in another human being. Like the second grader who knows deep down that chubby men in red suits can't really fit down chimneys or fly in reindeer-led sleighs but isn't quite ready to let go of the hope it might be true.

Well, he had no childlike wonder left. Every last bit of it had been stamped out of him by life—a mother who spun elaborate tales of rejection and fed them to him like candy. A woman who promised to forsake all others but embraced infidelity, professing a love that didn't exist.

And a lady who filled his thoughts with enchantment but belonged to another.

He laid the box on top of two others sitting against the foyer wall and straightened with a sigh. He'd given her the opportunity to come clean, to tell him about Robert. But she'd refused. If she would keep something that important from him, what other secrets would she hold? How could he reconcile her deceitfulness with her claims of being a Christian, all her talk of God and church?

Church. He'd gone as a young child. His grandparents had taken him every Sunday. Sometimes his mother went. Usually she'd stayed home. Then he and his mother had gotten their own place. And other than the two times he'd gone with Bethany before using the excuse he had to work, that was the end of church.

Until Jami.

She'd talked him into trying it. Surprisingly, he'd liked it. God had felt closer there. Of course, God was everywhere. He knew that from his childhood. But Jami seemed to have something he'd never experienced, something he wanted. At least he'd thought she did. Now he knew her faith was all talk.

So where did that leave *him*? He shook his head. God put Himself at a big disadvantage, leaving it to people to be His examples.

As he passed the living room on his way back upstairs, a single bong of the grandfather clock announced the half hour. Five thirty. What was Jami doing, and what was she feeling? Disappointment? Frustration her plans had been thwarted? Relief he'd left before her fiancé was due to return? She was probably on the phone with him at that very moment, whispering sweet nothings, awaiting their reunion.

What kind of game had she been playing? Had she planned to enchant her way past his defenses, then dump him as soon as her boyfriend came back, acquiring yet another name to add to her list of broken hearts? Worse yet, had she been lured by the McAllister fortune and planned to hold on to both him and her boyfriend? Had history been about to repeat itself?

Whatever her plans, they hadn't worked. Thanks to Hank, he'd seen through the beautiful facade and gotten out relatively unscathed, with no damage to his bank account and minimal damage to his heart.

He plodded up the steps toward his grandmother's room. A few more boxes, and he would be ready to leave North Carolina behind and tour the country. He tried to stir up some enthusiasm for what he was about to do. But the whole trip seemed like an empty shell of his Murphy experiences, a poor-quality counterfeit. He longed for more days with Jami, traipsing through the woods, hearing her laughter, feeling her warmth next to him. And the more he thought about it, the more the longing intensified.

Okay, maybe the damage to his heart *wasn't* so minimal.

Frenzied barking announced the presence of guests moments before the doorbell sounded. When Jami swung open the front door, the barking stopped immediately. Samantha and Holly stood on her porch, Samantha holding a frozen lasagna and Holly clutching a spiral-bound notebook.

Holly grinned. "We're here to cheer you up."

"And feed you." Samantha held up the lasagna.

She backed up to let them in, and Holly immediately shed her high-heeled sandals. With nothing more important on the agenda than a covert meeting with her two best friends, she still looked as if she'd just finished a photo shoot. Her black dress jeans molded themselves to her hips, and her blouse screamed Saks Fifth Avenue, although it was more likely outlet mall or discount online clothing store. Holly knew how to look like a million bucks without spending it.

Jami closed the door behind them. She had filled Holly in on the conversation she'd had with Grant that morning, and Holly had likely explained everything to Sam.

"I'm all right. At least I will be. Eventually." She forced an uncomfortable laugh. "I'm a mess. I've known him less than three weeks, and I'm as bummed as I was when Jerrod dumped me." Actually, more so. She'd dated Jerrod through her entire first year of college. Then he'd gone home and hooked back up with his ex.

Grant hadn't hooked up with anyone. He'd just closed himself off and shut her out of his life. When Jerrod left her, she'd at least understood the demise of their relationship. With Grant, she had no clue.

She took the lasagna from Sam. "Nothing says comfort food like Italian, so let's get this show on the road. I refuse to feel sorry for myself tonight."

Sam responded with a fist pump. "That's the attitude."

Jami followed her into the kitchen, with Holly in the rear. Where Holly was sophisticated elegance, Sam was relaxed simplicity. She was dressed in her typical blue jeans, T-shirt and tennis shoes, her dark ponytail pulled through the opening in the back of her ever-present baseball cap. When Sam shed the cap, it was for one of two reasons: to exchange it for safety gear when on the river or to sleep. She collected caps the same way a lot of women accumulated shoes.

Samantha turned on the oven and prepped the lasagna for baking. Finally, she put a sympathetic hand on Jami's arm. "Are you sure you're okay?"

Jami shrugged. "I guess. I mean, it's not like I've never been through this before. This is par for the course. It seems the only men I find interesting are the ones who split before anything gets too sticky. The dependable ones bore me to death."

"You know what I think?" Holly plopped a cutting board down on the counter. As soon as she'd entered the kitchen, she had rooted through the crisper for salad ingredients and now had a nice collection of fresh veggies waiting to be washed. She leaned back against the counter, wearing a smug expression, as if she'd just figured out the answers to all of life's questions. "I think your choice of men is a protective mechanism."

"What do you mean?"

"Your dad walked out on you at the tender age of eight. That made you feel lost and insecure. And even though you're all grown up, those feelings have never left. Deep down, you're afraid of being abandoned. Pierre leaving after you had fallen so hard for him only reinforced those fears. So did Jerrod's dumping you to go back to his girlfriend. Ever since then, you've gone for the men who, for one reason or another, aren't likely to commit. That way there's no chance of a serious relationship developing, and you avoid the possibility of getting hurt."

Jami planted her hands on her hips. "What's this? You've changed your major? Now you're going to be a psychologist?"

"I did take psychology a couple semesters ago. But I don't have to be a psychologist to figure you out. I know you too well. If it were only once or twice, I'd say it was a temporary lapse in judgment. But there's a definite pattern here."

Samantha studied her. "You know, I think Holly's right. You always accuse your exes of being commitment phobic, but maybe you're the one who runs from commitment. Think about it. Women have types of men they're attracted to—certain build, hair color, personality type. But the one thing the guys you've dated all have in common is the unlikelihood that anything serious will ever develop between you."

"All except Robert." Holly picked up a head of romaine lettuce and ran water over it. "He falls into the dependable-but-boring category."

Samantha looked at Jami. "What do *you* think?"

"I think you should both be arrested for practicing psychiatry without a license." She took a plump red tomato from the counter and washed it. Samantha and Holly were wrong. She'd gotten over her father's leaving years ago, the moment when she decided to forgive and let go. That experience was *not* keeping her from finding lasting love as an adult. She just had bad luck with relationships.

But what if Holly were right? "Okay, Dr. Phil, let's say I *do* have abandonment issues. Now that you're done analyzing me, how about telling me what I can do about it?"

Holly made quick work of the tomato, pushing the pieces off the cutting board with the edge of the knife. "Dunno. Psychology 101 didn't cover that."

Samantha pursed her lips. "All I can suggest is to remember life is full of uncertainty. You've got to be willing to take some risks."

"Spoken by someone who battles rapids for a living." Jami smiled wryly. "I think I'll chalk this whole experience up to another one of Bernie's failed matchmaking attempts."

Sam frowned. "Bernie can lay claim to a lot of those." The oven beeped, the signal that preheating was complete, and Sam slid the lasagna in on the top shelf. "I think her all-time worst match for me was Daniel."

Holly groaned. "Thank God his family didn't stay in Murphy long. He even got on *our* nerves."

"I know," Sam said. "If I'd had to endure one more story about how he took down a masked gunman with his bare hands, I would have died. But Bernie thought we were the perfect couple."

Jami laughed. Bernie had been relentless when it came to Sam. "She was determined to get you hitched."

"And all the while I had a terrible crush on Kyle."

Jami looked at her sharply. "You had a crush on Kyle? I thought you guys were just friends."

"The best. But I also had a crush on him, which I did very well keeping to myself."

She sure had—she'd even kept it from her two closest friends.

Holly pulled her lower lip between her teeth. "Bummer. I would have never gone out with him if I'd known. How come you never told us?"

Sam shrugged. "I don't know. Embarrassed, I guess. I mean, Kyle always went after the gorgeous model types, not the tomboys. I almost told him how I felt the night of the fire. Then I was so glad I didn't."

"Really," Holly said, "being he was the creep who set it."

Sam took a carrot from the fridge. "We don't know that for sure."

Holly narrowed her eyes. "You saw him."

"I saw someone. Kyle denied it was him."

Holly huffed out an exasperated sigh. "Of course he denied it."

Sam removed a flat grater from the drawer and set to work on the carrot. "Anyway," she said, both her tone and her glare redirecting the conversation, "if Bernie had tried to match me up with someone like Kyle at the time, I wouldn't have had any complaints. Instead she kept picking losers."

Jami picked up the notebook Holly had laid on the counter. "Speaking of Bernie, we need to strategize the next phase of Operation Bernie Match-Up." She led her friends back into the living room. The oven timer would beep when the lasagna was ready to come out. Meanwhile, they'd put their heads together and scheme.

And that was exactly what she needed, the opportunity to focus on someone else's love life. Because the more she thought about it, the more she was afraid her friends were right.

From the time she'd been old enough to understand fairy tales, Jami had dreamed that Prince Charming would one day ride in on his white horse and carry her away. As she'd gotten older, the dream had matured. The horse had disappeared. The basic premise hadn't.

Through all the frustration and heartbreak, the dream had simmered, lying dormant in the back of her mind. No matter how bleak her prospects, she'd never given up hope that someday that special someone would ride into her life and sweep her off her feet.

But for that to happen, she would have to be willing to let down her guard and risk her heart.

Otherwise, her prince would never be more than a distant, misty dream.

TWELVE

Jami placed her egg burrito and coffee on the table and slid into a chair, ready for her weekly breakfast with her friends. Except both friends had canceled. Samantha had woken up feeling under the weather, and Holly hadn't woken up until five minutes ago.

She cast a glance at the door as Bernie stepped inside, clutching several pieces of paper. Bernie's gaze circled the Grind, then stopped on Jami. Two seconds later, she was beside her. Bernie could move surprisingly fast for her age.

"This is brilliant." She shook the pages she held. "When this hits the stands, everyone's going to rush to the Humane Society to adopt a pet."

"Thanks." She'd given the draft to Bernie yesterday. It was nice having an expert set of eyes on her work before uploading it to the news folder for Matthew to edit.

At least she'd managed one good piece of journalism. Actually, she'd managed several. Only the McAllister article was giving her fits. It wasn't coming together at all.

It wasn't just that she didn't have the information she needed. Or the permission to use what she had. It was much more personal than that. Since the moment Grant drove away yesterday morning, she'd played through every detail of their time together, searching for something she'd said that he could have taken the wrong way, but had come up blank.

That was because she hadn't done anything wrong. Everything had been fine between them when she left him after dinner. Whatever Grant's problem was, it had nothing to do with her. She needed to just forget about him. And she needed to get the article finished, because she'd never be able to put the last two weeks behind her while it was hanging over her head.

Bernie plopped the pages she held down on the table and settled into the chair opposite her. She was beaming, and probably not just from the brilliantly written article.

"You look as if you're about to burst with good news."

"Not much." Bernie shrugged, but the feigned nonchalance didn't hide the excitement bubbling beneath the surface.

"Have you heard from your secret admirer?" She knew the answer without asking. Two days ago, Holly, Samantha and she had set up phony accounts and e-mailed both Bernie and Hank.

Bernie beamed more brightly. "In fact, I have. I've gotten two e-mails from him."

Two? Holly was staying on top of things. "Any idea who it is?"

"Obviously someone who appreciates good taste." She rested both elbows on the table and leaned forward. "He says he's intrigued by everything about me, from my fiery red hair that has as much pizzazz as I do to my colorful wardrobe, which is as unique as its wearer." She raised her chin. "Those are his words, not mine."

"Well, it sounds like you've made quite an impression." She picked up her coffee mug and took a long sip.

"Yup. When we get together, we're going to tour the country on his Harley."

A quick gulp kept Jami from showering coffee all over the table but induced a coughing spasm. *Harley?* Where had that come from?

She'd composed Tuesday night's e-mail herself. And Holly likely didn't mention anything about a motorcycle. "He said that?"

"Well, he didn't come right out and say it, but it's how I picture him, wild and daring with just a touch of bad boy. But gentle and caring, too."

Hank, wild and daring? With a touch of bad boy? At least she got the gentle and caring part right. "You'd better be careful coming up with too many preconceived ideas, or you might be disappointed."

"Whatever he is, I'm sure I won't be disappointed. But enough about me." She sat back in her chair, the radiance instantly fading. "I don't suppose you've heard from Grant."

Before she could respond, Hank appeared beside the table. "Good morning, Jami. Sorry to interrupt." Then he raised a folded sales insert and shook it in Bernie's face. "What in the Sam Hill is this?"

"What in the Sam Hill is what?" Bernie's tone, as well as her expression, was all innocence.

"Wayne's ad."

"Oh, *that*." Bernie gave a dismissive wave of her hand. "You use the same old picture every week. It's always Hank in his overalls, standing in front of the store."

Jami raised her brows. That was because Hank was the store manager and that was what he always wore, even to church.

Hank planted one hand on his hip. "What's wrong with that?"

"It's boring. You have to admit, this replacement photo is a whole lot more interesting."

"I'll be a laughingstock." He shook the paper at Bernie once more. "You went too far this time, Bernadette Hopkins."

With the paper folded, Jami couldn't see what had Hank so riled up. Whatever it was, it was no simple mistake. Bernie had said she was going to fix him, and judging from Hank's reaction, she'd outdone herself.

"Oh, Hank, you're making a mountain out of a molehill."

"This is no molehill. It's slander."

"How do you figure that? Slander is saying something about someone that's not true."

"Well, it's going to make people *think* things about me that ain't true." He opened the paper, then folded it back. "Did you see what she did?"

Before Jami could answer, the newspaper flopped loudly against the table. She slapped her hand over her mouth, but a muffled snort slipped through her fingers anyway. No wonder Hank was fit to be tied.

Bernie had replaced the usual photo that made up the top left-hand corner of Wayne's ad with one that had to have been altered. As usual, Hank was in his overalls. But only the bottom twelve inches of the legs were visible. The rest was hidden beneath a colorful floral-print dress. A pink silk scarf accessorized the look, along with a big, floppy hat that would put Beulah Fines's monstrosities to shame.

Once Jami corralled her urge to giggle, she dropped her hand and looked at Bernie. "Where did you get this?"

Bernie's eyes danced. She was having a lot of fun at Hank's expense. "It's priceless, isn't it? Three or four years ago, we had a harvest party at church. One of the games we played was a relay race, men against women. The women had to pull on men's jeans, a flannel shirt and suspenders, and the guys had to dress in that." She pointed toward the paper. "The women won, by the way."

Hank crossed his arms and glared at Bernie. "You better put the old picture back in and print me an apology, or I'll sue."

"All right, all right." Bernie grinned up at him, obviously not remorseful in the least. "I'll put the old picture back in. But I've got to draw the line at the apology."

"Well, you owe me something."

She sat back in her chair, lips pursed as she appeared to toss options around in her mind. Actually, she'd probably made plans for how she was going to handle the fallout before the print was even dry. Bernie was a pro at long-distance scheming. Finally, she sighed. "I'll tell you what. I'll give you next week's ad at fifty percent off."

"You'll give us next week's ad free. Because you've already got the money for this one, and we're not paying for an ad that's got me in a dress."

"All right. Free it is. You drive a hard bargain, Hank Dorchester."

"So no bill next week. Don't forget."

"I won't forget. Now go on. Jami and I have important business." She made a shooing motion with both hands. "Where were we? Oh, yeah. I can't believe he just shut you down like that."

Jami sighed. "I can. Any relationship with him was doomed from the start, for a lot of reasons."

Hank had gotten as far as the next table before he turned back around, confusion written all over his face. "Who are you talking about?"

Bernie looked up at Hank. "Grant McAllister. He and Jami had been seeing a lot of each other, and things were really heating up. He even kissed her."

"Bernie!"

"Well, did he?"

"That's not important."

"I knew it!" She turned back to Hank wearing a knowing grin. "Then yesterday morning, out of the blue, he turned cold."

Hank looked back and forth between the two of them, deepening furrows lining his brow. "But you're engaged to Robert."

Jami sighed in exasperation. "No, I'm not. I never was." Couldn't someone throw a wrench into the gears of the Murphy rumor mill?

Hank's jaw dropped as understanding swept away his confusion. "Uh-oh."

Bernie looked at him sharply. "Uh-oh what?"

"I told Grant Jami's engaged."

Jami slumped in the chair, her gut filling with lead. The lie Grant had accused her of. The secret he'd tried to get her to confess. Now it all made sense. Apparently Beulah's latest bit of gossip had made it to everyone except Hank. Now Grant believed she had duped him, just like his ex-wife. *Oh, Lord, please give me a chance to make this right.*

Bernie's reaction wasn't nearly as calm. Her eyes lit with fire, and she jumped from her chair. "You did *what*? You big clod!"

She snatched the sales paper from the table, probably because it was the nearest thing she could grab that wouldn't result in a battery charge, and proceeded to beat him with it.

He raised an arm in defense. "I didn't do it on purpose. I ran into him at Hot Spot. Jami was there, and he was looking at her with puppy-dog eyes." He emitted a small groan. "Oh, man. I messed up."

"You sure did." Bernie wrapped one wiry hand around his wrist and forced him into the chair next to her. "We've gotta fix this."

"We?"

"You bet your bonnie blue britches *we*. You're the one who messed this up, and you're gonna help me fix it."

He looked at her across the table. "I'm sorry, Jami."

"Don't apologize, Hank. There's nothing to fix. Grant and I are just friends." That kiss had affected her way more than it had him. Otherwise, he would have talked to her and tried to clear up the misunderstanding.

Bernie pulled a smartphone from the purse on the table, and Jami's jaw dropped. "What are you doing with my phone?"

"Calling Grant." Her fingers worked over the screen. "Here he is." She sank into the chair next to Hank. "But I'm going to call him from my phone. He probably won't take calls from yours since this bozo messed everything up." She emphasized the last few words with a glare cast his way.

Jami shook her head. She would let Bernie go ahead and make the call, partly because she really wanted Grant to know the truth and partly because trying to dissuade Bernie would be a lost cause. When one of her matches was at stake, she was a mama pit bull.

Bernie put the number into her own phone, then pressed it to her ear. "Grant? Bernie Hopkins here. I'm calling to clear up a big misunderstanding." She glared at Hank. "*Someone* was disseminating bad information. Jami's not engaged." She was talking fast, probably trying to get all the words out before Grant hung up on her. "Robert and Jami have been friends all their lives, even dated some. And in Murphy, all it takes is two dates, and the news flies from one end of town to the other—you're getting married and planning to have eight children." She laughed at her exaggeration, then continued. "Robert's been trying to get Jami to marry him, but she kept putting him off. She told him a final no around the time you came into town."

Several seconds of silence passed before Bernie spoke again. "You don't have to take my word for it. I've got Hank here with me." She passed the phone to Hank.

"Hi, Grant. Bernie's right." He continued in his low, slow drawl. "For years, everybody's been saying Jami and Robert are getting married. And I didn't know any different."

Bernie leaned toward the phone. "Hank's a bit of a doofus."

He jerked away from her. "No, I'm not. Unlike a certain nosy newspaper reporter, I got more important things to do than keep up with everybody's personal lives."

"Well, if you're not gonna bother to keep up, then don't perpetuate false rumors."

"I wasn't perpetuating anything."

Jami stifled a laugh. If those two didn't have something to bicker about, they wouldn't have anything to say to each other.

Bernie took the phone back from Hank. "So do you believe me now?" After a short pause, she spoke again. "Good. I'm glad we got it straightened out." She swiped the screen and laid the phone on the table. "Damage control accomplished. The romance of the century is back on."

Jami shook her head. "Forget it, Bernie. I can't be with someone who will walk away at the drop of a hat."

Bernie reached across the table to pat her arm. "Don't be too hasty, dear."

"Let's face it. This match was nothing but one big mistake." One of a long list of mistakes. Bernie needed to stick with the newspaper business and give up matchmaking.

Jami sighed. And she would stick with caring for two lovable fur balls and give up fanciful dreams of fairy-tale endings.

—⁂—

Grant pulled into the parking lot of the *Cherokee Scout* and stopped next to the red Sunbird. Jami was still there, but at a few minutes till five, she should be coming out any minute.

He drew in a deep breath and lifted his hand to the heavy metal heart resting against his chest. After the call from Bernie, he'd retrieved it from the floorboard. The pewter heart represented more than just his first geocache. All Jami meant to him was symbolized in its beautiful, complex pattern.

She wasn't engaged. She hadn't lied to him. His mouth lifted in a relieved smile. But guilt and regret tempered the unfettered joy he should have felt. He'd made a huge mistake. Instead of openly communicating with her, he'd offered her vague hints and expected her to read his mind. When she failed, he'd bid her farewell. He'd hurt her again. For the second time, he owed her a huge apology.

The front door of the *Scout* swung open, and two women walked out, neither of them Jami. But the next time it opened, Bernie came through, Jami behind her. His pulse kicked into overdrive, and he stepped from the car.

The instant Jami's eyes met his, something flashed across her features. She was happy to see him. Or maybe it was surprise. He circled the Mercedes and met her at the rear quarter panel of her own car. Whatever he'd seen at first was gone now, and the air between them crackled with tension.

He shifted his gaze to the side, where Bernie had reached her green Bug but didn't make any move to get in.

Okay, he could do this with an audience. "I'm sorry about the way I acted yesterday. I thought you'd lied to me, or intentionally led me astray. You can probably tell lying is a big sore spot with me."

She gave him a stiff nod. "I understand. Apology accepted."

He shifted his weight to the other foot. Her guard was up, the warmth in her eyes missing. It was gone from her voice, too.

"Will taking you to dinner make up for my jumping to the wrong conclusion?"

"That won't be necessary. You're forgiven." She returned his smile, but it wasn't the relaxed, easy smile he was used to.

He cast another glance in Bernie's direction. She still stood there, watching them. She wasn't even trying to be inconspicuous. She probably wanted to view her success, or failure, firsthand.

He turned his attention back to Jami. "How about letting me take you out for all the nice stuff you did for me?"

"That's what dinner at your place was for."

"No, that was in exchange for you taking me whitewater rafting. What about the geocaching?"

She stepped around him to open the driver door. "Trust me, your cooking made up for both."

He sighed. Had he really messed things up so badly she didn't want to see him again? The thought left a hollow emptiness inside.

"I still want to take you to dinner tomorrow night." He gave her another tentative smile. "To quote a pretty newspaper reporter I know, 'I'm not beyond begging.'"

Her lips quirked up, and some of the tension between them evaporated. "I can't. I've got plans for the evening."

Bernie hurried around the car and joined the conversation. "No, you don't." She turned her back on Jami. "Dinner sounds great. Tomorrow night, you say?"

He eyed her with raised brows. She was bold. And she obviously had an agenda. Before he could formulate an answer, Jami cut in, a touch of annoyance in her tone.

"Since when are you my appointment secretary?"

"Since you've gotten it in your head to be stubborn."

"I'm not stubborn, just busy."

Bernie leaned against the Sunbird and crossed her arms. "You're not as busy as you think you are. Tomorrow night's free."

"No, it's not. You invited me over for Scrabble, remember?"

"Well, I'm afraid I'm going to have to uninvite you. Something's come up."

Grant stifled a chuckle. Whatever put Bernie in his corner, he would thank her later.

Jami shot her a warning glance.

"All right, all right." Bernie winked and scurried back around to the Bug, then got inside and backed from the parking space.

Grant watched her leave, unable to hide his amusement. "I don't think I've ever met anyone like Bernie."

Jami grinned, and this time, the gesture seemed to touch her eyes. "Believe me, no one else has, either. God broke the mold after he made her. But I have to say it's been nice having her here. I feel like I have my own personal mentor."

"I'm sure it makes settling in a lot easier."

"It does."

"So when is the McAllister article coming out?"

"Week after next. Next week the Humane Society one is running. It'll of course feature Bailey and Morgan."

"Two of my favorite furry friends."

Her smile broadened, chasing away the last of the tension. "That one was easy to write. The McAllister feature is turning out to be a lot harder. So let me know when you change your mind."

So now it was *when* instead of *if*.

But she was right. As much as he wanted to see if she would keep her promise, when it came down to it, he wouldn't be able to tell her no much longer.

Dinner, a walk in the park and a few more kisses, and he would end up giving her anything she asked for.

—⚭—

Jami put her key into the lock, and immediately dual barks sounded from inside the house. When she opened the door, Morgan and Bailey stood looking up at her, bodies wiggling in excitement. She squatted to pet them, and they both rolled onto their backs for tummy rubs.

"I'm so glad Bernie talked me into that trip to the Humane Society."

Tails wagged in response. When she moved farther into the room to lay her purse on the coffee table, they pranced after her. She smiled down at them. At least Bernie had done something right. Bringing home two dogs was a lot more practical than trying to build any kind of relationship with her temporary neighbor.

The last thing she'd expected was for him to show up at the *Scout* yesterday afternoon. She couldn't say she was angry with him. Although she didn't excuse him for refusing to talk to her, she wasn't blind to her own part in the misunderstanding. Even though she'd called off the engagement before she ever met Grant, she should have told him about Robert. Robert was gone, thousands of miles away, so there'd been no chance of them running into one another. But with all the rumors flying about, there was too much chance that Grant would have a conversation with someone ill informed. She should have considered the possibility, because that was exactly what had happened.

She took the two leashes from the hook by the door and, after connecting them to both dogs, stepped out into the front yard. The whole incident had upset her too much. In fact, it had almost devastated her. Which was nuts. Number one, she hadn't known him that long. Number two, Grant wasn't going to be a permanent fixture in Murphy. From the moment she first laid eyes on him in the Holiday Inn parking lot, she'd known his stay would be brief. But what her brain acknowledged, her heart refused to heed.

Now she'd been hooked into dinner, thanks to one scheming, meddling matchmaker.

Bernie loved trying to bring people together. But she didn't consider the fallout—the broken hearts left behind when things didn't work out.

It had been easier when Jami thought Grant wasn't attracted to her. At first, he hadn't even seemed to like her. And although they'd gotten past that bumpy start, she'd been sure he felt nothing more than friendship for her. But the almost kiss at the waterfall had put a big dent in that theory. And the two actual kisses blew it apart. There was a definite attraction, and it wasn't one-sided.

But it didn't matter. She'd been through enough of that type of relationship, where the signs *Start Here* and *Dead End* shared the same post.

She gave the leashes a small tug and led two reluctant dogs toward the house. They'd both finished their business and now seemed engaged in nothing more than a sniffing expedition. Grant was going to be there in thirty minutes, and she wanted to freshen up her makeup and change clothes before he arrived. She didn't know where he planned to take her, but he'd said to dress casual.

When she answered the door a short time later, Grant stood there wearing a polo shirt, a pair of khaki pants and a smile that turned all her defenses to mush.

"How about we bring the dogs?"

She raised a brow. "I don't know of any pet-friendly restaurants in Murphy."

"We won't need one. I have something different planned for tonight."

His *something different* was a picnic at Koneheta Park. As he removed containers from a large cloth-lined basket, pleasant aromas mixed with the scents of nature.

"I know how much you love the outdoors. I thought this would be a good alternative to a night out at a restaurant."

Warmth infused her, and she released a sigh filled with longing. Why did he have to be everything she'd ever dreamed of, a real-life Prince Charming? She closed her eyes and let the rustle of leaves and the hum of cicadas weave through her, adding peace to the blanket of contentment already swaddling her.

She needed nature as much as she needed food and water. It was where she refreshed and recharged and drew her inspiration. And it was where she connected with God. And the fact that Grant understood that after just two short weeks endeared him to her even more. "This is perfect."

He laid out place settings, then uncovered the bowls. Everything matched.

"Did your grandmother have this picnic set?"

"No. I made a Walmart run this morning."

She stabbed a piece of baked chicken, then spooned potato salad and green bean casserole onto her plate. "And the food?"

"All homemade. I gave up my room at the Holiday Inn today and moved into the house. It makes things much easier."

After silently blessing the food and including thanks for the unexpected addition of a certain man in her life, however temporary, she opened her eyes to find him breaking off some bites of chicken and slipping them under the table.

"They already ate, you know."

"They always look hungry. But I know you have to keep them from getting fat. If this becomes a regular thing, I'll have to curb my urges to spoil them."

If? Was there even the remotest chance dinners together could become a regular thing? No, and she refused to get her hopes up. She was a dreamer, not delusional.

They each finished their dinner with a leash around one wrist and dogs between their feet. When their plates were empty, Grant took a final container from the picnic basket.

"I hope you like banana pudding."

He removed the lid, and she looked into the bowl. The dessert had whipped cream topping and vanilla wafers lining the edge. "Mmm, looks delicious."

He plopped a generous serving into each bowl, then took a bite. "What else do you have planned for me?"

"What do you mean?"

"We've still got one week left on this get-to-know-Murphy tour."

"I thought that was off. You already agreed to not sell to Vanguard."

"I guess I did. But I've decided to still hold you to the tour."

"Alrighty then. I guess we're back on for the art walk tomorrow night, the Salty Dog Saturday and Fields of the Wood Sunday."

He grinned. "I still say Salty Dog sounds like a pub. Maybe even a biker bar. Are you sure we're not going to get there and have to make our way around a bunch of Harleys?"

She giggled. "I'm positive. I've been there. No Harleys, unless it's the mode of transportation for one of the miners."

When their dishes were empty, Grant stacked everything and put it back into the basket. "Will this be okay here unattended? I'd like to take the dogs for a walk along the river. You, too." He held out a hand to help her up.

"I don't think anyone will mess with it." They'd left the Mercedes in the parking area of the recreational center, and it was a bit of a hike back.

Even though she was on her feet, he didn't release her. But she didn't mind. Walking hand in hand with Grant as the sun sank toward the horizon somehow felt right.

He dropped her hand to drape an arm across her shoulders. "Thank you for agreeing to this, in spite of my stupidity."

"Yeah, for someone smart enough to graduate from law school, that was a pretty dumb move."

He gave her a playful shake. "You didn't have to agree so readily."

"It's okay. Everybody's an idiot at one point or another."

"Does this mean you've forgiven me?"

"I'm not one to hold grudges."

He drew to a stop and turned her to face him. "I've seen that. And it's one of the things I love about you."

Love? No, silly. He'd just used the word in the same sense that one talks about loving hiking or Mustangs or broccoli.

He tilted his head downward and pulled her closer. As the distance between them dissolved, an image flashed into her consciousness—that diamond-shaped yellow sign with bold black letters—*Dead End.* A nanosecond later, his lips met hers, and the image was gone, sucked into a tornado of sensation that threatened to carry her away, too.

In the back of her mind, a small sliver of something still rational flashed a warning. There was a precipice ahead, and she was running straight for it.

But that distant little voice wasn't nearly as persuasive as the pressure of his mouth on hers or the waterfall of emotion flowing through her. Maybe it was stupid. But she was going to grab hold of her dream with both hands.

She would deal with the consequences later.

THIRTEEN

The rapid click of computer keys filled the large, open space of the *Cherokee Scout* office, and the air hummed with a focused, productive energy. Fridays were always busy, with everyone trying to wrap things up to go to press the following week. At least *someone* was getting something accomplished.

Jami tapped her pen on her desk and frowned at the pages in front of her. The writing wasn't bad, but it wasn't good, either. She had tried to make it snappier, tried to inject some emotion into the story. All four pages bled red ink, testimony of her failed attempts—words changed, sentences added, then deleted. Sure, it wasn't the final draft. But even her rough drafts usually had more life than what she was holding.

If Grant would just give her the go-ahead to use what she'd learned from those letters, she could wrap it up in no time. And she'd have a great article. He seemed close to giving in. Right on the verge, actually. But something was holding him back. He was testing her, seeing if he could trust her to keep her word. She was sure of it.

She wrinkled her nose at the pages on her desk and crossed her arms with a frustrated sigh. Maybe she should set it aside and work on something else. She still had another week to get it together. She worked better under pressure, anyway. Nothing like a deadline to force creativity out of a lazy slumber.

She slipped the pages into a neon-green file folder marked *McAllister* and sat back in her chair, eyes closed. With her fingers at her temples, she made several slow circular motions, easing stress and soothing the frustration brought on by the not-so-productive morning.

At least her assignments for next week's edition were already finished and edited. In the meantime, if she couldn't manage any coherent writing, maybe she could jot down some ideas. She picked up a pen and held it poised over the legal pad on her desk. How about "Money-Saving Day Trips"? Or maybe a "Things to Do in and around Murphy" series. She'd have to get the idea approved, but she could run with that.

She picked up the phone and dialed a familiar number. "Hey, Jordan. Is Samantha off the river yet?"

After a few moments of silence, Samantha came on. "Just finished my morning run. What's up?"

"How about a feature article on Wild River Outfitters?"

"I never turn down free publicity."

"Once I get the okay, I'll be out for pictures." She dropped her voice to just above a whisper. "Guess who showed back up Wednesday afternoon."

"Grant?" The hope in Sam's tone was obvious.

"We had a picnic in the park last night. Tonight we're doing the Murphy Art Walk. Even though he's promised not to sell to Vanguard, he's holding me to my offer to give him the deluxe two-week tour."

"Good."

"I don't know how good it is, but Bernie didn't leave me any choice. On dinner, anyway. She pretty much accepted the invitation for me."

"I'm not surprised. Speaking of Bernie . . ." The line fell silent a moment. "Is she sitting next to you?"

"No, she left for a while."

"Good. I have news to report. I stopped by Wayne's Feed Store today, and Hank was bebopping around like a teenager. He was even whistling."

Jami laughed. *Hank* and *bebop* didn't belong in the same sentence. The e-mails were getting the response they wanted. So had the plant they'd had delivered to the store for Hank's birthday the prior week. Now if they could just get Hank and Bernie thinking about each other.

"We need to change our tactics," Jami said. "We're trying to get Bernie sweet on Hank, and she's fantasizing about some tattooed Harley rider with a ponytail."

"Uh-oh, that's not good." Sam's tone was somber, but there was a definite smile underneath. "What do you have in mind?"

"Stronger hints. You know, something pointing Hank to Bernie and Bernie to Hank."

"Hmm, they both have May birthdays."

She was right. They were the last week of the month, five days apart. "What do you have in mind?"

"What if we say something about it in the e-mails?"

"Good idea. That would eliminate eleven-twelfths of the prospects."

"How about this?" The exaggerated clearing of her throat told Jami whatever Samantha came up with wasn't going to be serious. "My love for you is immeasurable, my friend, my companion, my soul mate. Now we share a birth month. Soon we'll share so much more."

Jami giggled and rolled her eyes. "Leave off the cornball sentence at the beginning, and you might have something we can work with."

"How about this?" This time Sam sounded serious. "Did you know we share a birth month? Soon I hope we'll share so much more."

Jami frowned, still not convinced. "You don't think it's too suggestive?"

"Not unless your mind's in the gutter. I say we use it. For both of them."

"All right. I'll e-mail Hank from Bernie's dummy address, and you can e-mail Bernie." A satisfied smile crept up her face. It was going to take a lot of creative thinking, but if they were successful, Murphy's most notorious matchmaker might find her own happily ever after.

They ended their conversation in the nick of time. Jami had just hung up the phone when Bernie stepped through the front door, the monster handbag she always carried over one shoulder and her cell phone in her hand. A minute later, she plopped the oversize purse on her desk and held up the phone.

"Things are smoking between me and Mr. Wonderful." Bernie pulled a tape recorder and legal pad from the bag and dropped her phone inside. "We've been burning up the Internet, sending those e-mails back and forth."

She wasn't exaggerating. It was a good thing Holly didn't take a summer job between school terms, because it was all they could do to answer them all. Hank was keeping them busy, too, but he wasn't nearly as prolific as Bernie. "That sounds encouraging. Any idea who it is?"

"Not a clue. I told him I wanted to meet him, but he wants to woo me a little longer."

"A true romantic."

"I know. Isn't he wonderful? Just like your Grant." She released a sigh. "Dinner out, kisses in the moonlight. Someday you'll thank me."

"Or kill you."

"Not this time. I'm breaking my losing streak with this one. I feel it in my bones." With that, she removed some earbuds from her top desk drawer, opened a new Word document and set about transcribing what she'd recorded.

Jami sighed and turned back to her own work. If only *her Grant* would let her use the information she needed for her article. She opened the green file folder and looked at the papers inside, all stained in red. Next week probably wouldn't yield anything more usable than what she already had.

Unless . . . Her eyes flared as a new idea settled in her mind.

For the next two hours, she pounded the keyboard, fingers flying as sentences, then paragraphs, filled the screen. Once finished, she proofread what she'd written, then sat back with a satisfied smile. Oh, yes. It was good.

The next task would be to choose pictures. She'd already scanned some great ones from the photo albums. And her camera's memory card held dozens more. By the time she finished, it was after three. She did a final save, then printed what she'd done.

Bernie glanced over at her. "You've been pretty intent there for a while."

"I've finally got an article on the McAllisters that I'm happy with."

She gave Bernie a broad smile and slipped the pages into the green folder. It was time to leave for her dentist appointment, so final edits would have to wait until next week. Once she was confident the article was the best it could be, she would show everything to Grant.

He would see how tastefully she'd handled it and would give her the go-ahead.

She was sure of it.

Grant stabbed two small cubes of cheese with a toothpick and put them on a plate next to the crackers and cantaloupe already there. His plan had been to finish the art walk, then take Jami to one of the local restaurants for dinner. But after being encouraged to sample the snacks at most of the places they visited, he was beginning to rethink the remainder of their evening.

Jami moved to the side to admire an amber-and-blue-beaded necklace. Matching earrings were affixed to a card in its center. She ran a finger over one of the shiny beads. "My mom used to make stuff like this."

He stepped up next to her. "My mom has never made jewelry, but she picked up watercolor a few years ago. She's pretty good."

"I tried it for a while. One of my paintings is hanging in my office at home."

"I didn't know you were an artist."

"Neither does anyone else." She grinned at him. "I didn't say I was any good at it." She turned and made her way back toward the door, scanning the pieces displayed as she passed. "My painting stage was about six years ago. That would have been after scrapbooking and before stained glass."

"Wow, a jack of all trades."

"And master of none. Before I could get really proficient at anything, something else would always catch my attention."

As he headed down the sidewalk, bluegrass music drifted to him from the prior block, one of the local bands performing for those who had come out to enjoy the evening's activities. Besides the music, food and variety of art on display, the event had offered demonstrations of painting, weaving and sculpting. He'd been impressed with the level of skill.

He led her into the next store. "What about your novel writing? Have you pulled one out and dusted it off?"

"Not yet, but I will."

He gave her a look that was playfully stern. "Remember, you promised. I'm holding you to it."

"I know. I've been busy."

"That was my excuse." He gave her a nudge. "You'll have to think up one of your own."

"So I guess 'lost interest' is off the table, too." Her smile faded, and her gaze grew wistful. "No matter what my next craze was, my mom was always my biggest supporter. It didn't matter that in six months I'd probably lose interest and be on to something else." She shook her head. "She was awesome."

"I can tell you miss her."

"A lot. You're lucky you still have yours."

She stopped in front of a watercolor of two deer frolicking in a meadow. Though her gaze was on the painting, the faraway look in her eyes told him her thoughts were elsewhere. She finally turned to face him.

"Have you talked to her?"

"Not since the night I confronted her." It was something he needed to do. She was probably going half crazy, wondering if her lies had cost her the relationship with her only son. She had friends, and she had her painting. Other than that, she had him. He really should call her. And he was going to. When he was no longer angry and could think about her without his insides drawing into a knot.

That time hadn't come.

And it wasn't because he hadn't made an effort. He'd tried to let go of the resentment, to put it all behind him and start fresh. How had Jami done it so easily? How had she been able to forgive her father for all the wrong he'd done? Actually, it hadn't been easy. She'd told him that. It had taken years. And lots of prayer.

Whatever she'd done, it had worked. She didn't have a bitter bone in her body. That open, loving attitude radiated from her, pouring over onto everyone she met. If only he could find some for himself and bottle it up. Unfortunately, it wasn't for sale in any store.

But maybe what Jami had found was offered 100 percent free.

Maybe if he let her God work on him the same way He had her, he wouldn't have to try so hard.

Morgan and Bailey lay stretched out on the living room floor, eyes closed, and the mellow tones of Kenny G's sax came from the stereo, giving the atmosphere in the house the air of a lazy Saturday morning.

Jami swiped a cloth across the coffee table, removing that week's accumulation of dust, along with a couple of stray popcorn kernels. Grant was taking care of business at his place and wouldn't be picking her up until after lunch, which was giving her the perfect opportunity to get all her weekend chores done.

She moved to the bookcase and reached up to dust the front edge of the top shelf. The one below it held two somewhat lopsided vases and a variety of bowls that she'd made at a pottery class sometime back. After ensuring that shelf was dust-free, she moved to the next. Halfway across, she hesitated. A burgundy-colored binder stood in the midst of the how-to books occupying the shelf. It wasn't labeled, but even though months had passed since she'd last opened it, she knew what was inside.

She pulled the binder from the shelf, carried it to the couch and folded back the cover. Seven index tabs poked out from the pages inside, each bearing handwritten letters. She touched the first tab. *Jasmine novel.* All of her stories were assigned titles based on the name of her heroine. She hadn't gotten far enough on any of them to come up with creative titles.

She moved to the second tab. *Bethany novel.* Okay, maybe she should change the name on that one. She continued flipping pages. One section was thicker than the others. The Dani novel was her favorite, the one she'd gotten the furthest on. She began to read the typed words. Not bad. Could she pick up where she'd left off and see the story through to completion?

Yes, she could do it. She'd made a promise to Grant. Maybe it was time to work on fulfilling that promise. She picked up a pen from the end table next to her. First she would read through what she'd done, making notes. The story was too old to be on her laptop. But there was a flash drive somewhere. If she could find it, she'd save herself having to retype it.

By the time she finished reading, handwritten notes filled the margins on several of the pages. Thanks to a couple of creative-writing electives she'd taken in college, she knew more now than when she'd penned the words.

She glanced at the clock, then leaned forward to place the binder on the coffee table. Grant would be picking her up in less than an hour to go gem mining, and she needed to fix herself some lunch and take the dogs out before he arrived.

As soon as she stood, Bailey and Morgan perked up, their eyes following her. When she walked into the kitchen, they were right behind her.

"No second breakfast."

She moved toward the refrigerator, and her gaze fell on the calendar hanging adjacent to it. Robert was due back late last night. But she didn't need the calendar to know that. He'd left on his three-week trip the day she met Grant, and yesterday marked the three-week anniversary of that meeting.

She heaved a sigh, guilt chewing at her insides. Seeing her with someone else so soon after their breakup would devastate Robert. He didn't need to run into the two of them together in town or get the information through the rumor mill.

Putting her planned ham-and-cheese sandwich on hold, she bypassed the refrigerator and retrieved her phone from the living room end table. She paced the floor while Robert's phone rang one, two, three times. Midway through the fourth ring, a sleepy voice answered.

"I'm sorry, did I wake you up?"

"No. I was thinking about not answering it."

She closed her eyes. That wasn't sleepiness she'd heard in his voice. It was sadness. "I'm so sorry. I never intended to hurt you." And now she was getting ready to rub salt in the wound she'd inflicted three weeks ago.

"Better now than after we were married."

She pulled her lower lip between her teeth. At least he could see that. She drew in a deep breath. "I met someone."

"Already?" It was just a single word, but the pain behind it sent shards of glass through her heart.

"I know it's sudden. And it may not even work out." In fact, chances were good it wouldn't last any longer than Grant's extended vacation, that when it was time for him to resume his old life, they'd part ways with little more than a friendly farewell. "But I wanted you to hear it from me."

"I can't say I'm surprised. I should have known I'd never be able to hold on to your heart." His tone didn't hold criticism or bitterness, just a sort of somber resignation. He released a heavy sigh. "I don't know what you're looking for, but I hope you find it."

She swallowed a sudden lump in her throat. "So do I."

After a stiff good-bye, on both ends, she laid the phone back on the end table and headed for the kitchen. Except now she wasn't hungry. Anger she could handle. Knowing she'd hurt someone always crushed her spirit. She knew how it felt. She'd been in his shoes too many times.

And it probably wasn't over. Sometime soon, they'd be in the same boat—both with broken hearts.

Why did love have to hurt so much?

Grant shook hands with the elderly man standing just inside the door of MountainView Community Church. He was a whole lot more comfortable walking in this time than he'd been a week earlier. What a difference seven days could make. Actually, it wasn't just the time. It was the fact that he was spending it with Jami.

He'd dropped her off at home last night after an afternoon and evening out. Gem mining had been especially enjoyable. They'd bought a couple of what the mine called "rock-hound bags" and some gold ore pay dirt. The gold panning yielded several gold flecks, which they'd each stored in a vial provided by the mine. Jami's gem bag contained three tiny semiprecious stones. When he'd washed all the dirt and mud from his own, a decent-sized emerald lay against the screen. At least that was what the mine operator had said it was. Only its slight greenish tint distinguished it from any other dull, rough rock. He planned to have it tumbled and set into a necklace, then surprise Jami with it.

He moved into the sanctuary and scanned those sitting in the chairs, waiting for the service to begin. He found Holly and Sam immediately. The wavy blonde hair and the dark ponytail pulled through the ball cap were dead giveaways. Beulah Fines sat two rows up, adorned in another gaudy hat, this one covered in purple, orange and green flowers. Was Jami's ex there somewhere?

Last night, she'd told him about the guy. He'd been back in Murphy for two days. She'd called him yesterday to warn him about them. After all the criticism she'd taken from Robert over the years, Grant would rather she not talk to him at all. But the fact she'd felt the need to make that phone call said a lot. A lightness swept over him, and his mouth curved into an easy smile. Maybe there was a chance of something deeper between them than a brief friendship.

He moved down the aisle toward Holly and Sam. Jami hadn't arrived yet. Holly saw him first, and her face lit up. She slid down one chair and motioned Sam to do the same, leaving two empty seats on the end.

Sam looked at her watch. "It's five minutes till time to start, so you'll see Jami walk in in about four minutes."

Sam's estimate was right. Jami slid in next to him and flashed him a brilliant smile. About a half minute later, the pastor picked up the microphone to welcome everyone there, then moved into the opening prayer. Grant slid a sideways glance at Jami. She and her friends reflected the apparently broad range of acceptable attire at MountainView's services. Jami wore dark pants and a silky blouse with green, black and white swirl patterns. On his other side, Sam was dressed in jeans and a *God's Got My Back* T-shirt in the same shade of blue as her ball cap, and Holly wore a knee-length dress.

The same way attendees' clothing projected a *come as you are* sentiment, there seemed to be no wrong or right way to participate in the music. The worship band began the first song, and almost everyone rose to their feet. As the song progressed, some clapped, some raised their hands and some sang along with a sense of reverence. Nothing about the service reflected the rigid stuffiness he'd always associated with church. Of course, his perceptions were 10 percent experience, 90 percent conjecture.

As the lyrics to the second song displayed on the screen, he tried to sing along. It was a peppy, upbeat number with a catchy tune. A couple songs later, the tempo slowed and the tone grew worshipful. "Great I Am" displayed on the screen. The next song carried the same theme—the greatness and majesty of God.

When he looked over at Jami, her eyes were closed, and her face radiated contentment and peace. He felt it, too. But while Jami's joy came from within her, what he longed for seemed to hover just out of his reach. She had something he didn't. And he was only now becoming aware of the void. Or maybe he'd known it all along. Maybe that void was at the root of the malaise that had overtaken him.

As the voices rose all around him, something stirred inside, a sense of awe and wonder. He lifted his own voice, softly at first, then with more passion. God was here. He could feel His presence. What would it take to truly connect with Him? Was he even ready? When the last strains faded, he still couldn't answer either question.

As everyone eased into their seats, the title of the sermon flashed up on the screen—*God Is Bigger than Our Problems*. He couldn't argue with that. He'd always believed in the greatness of God. But believing with the mind was different from experiencing with the heart. Sure, God was bigger than anything going on with man. But how could that knowledge be applied on a personal level? How could he find reconciliation with his mother? How could he rediscover his enthusiasm for life?

The answers to his questions were somewhere, maybe even within these four walls. Somehow, some way, he was going to find them.

Even if it meant staying in Murphy until he did.

FOURTEEN

Grant leaned back in the wrought iron patio chair and breathed in the tranquility of nature. A soft breeze rustled the trees, and the hum of cicadas rose and fell. The sun had dipped below the horizon some time ago. But he was pleasantly full from the meal Jami had prepared and not in any hurry to go home. The dogs didn't look interested in moving, either. Both were stretched out on the flagstone patio, one on either side of him, eyes closed.

He reached for Jami's hand. "I want to take you somewhere special tomorrow night."

Of course, everywhere they'd been was special. Jami made it that way. She'd capped off an enjoyable weekend with a picnic and tour at Fields of the Wood. Even last night's stroll with the dogs along the Murphy River Walk had been more fun than anything he'd done in New York recently.

She smiled over at him. "And where might that be?"

"The Crest Mountain Dinner Show in Asheville. I know it's quite a drive, but their website promises elevated entertainment, fine food and spectacular views."

"That sounds awesome. When should I be ready?"

"Between four and four thirty. Earlier in the afternoon, Brenda's bringing back the people who looked at the property. They want to see the place again and have some questions for me."

"That sounds promising." The words were upbeat, but her tone held thinly disguised disappointment.

And he had his own reservations. He was no longer sure he wanted to sell. With all her talk on pursuing dreams, Jami had gotten him thinking. What had started as a small seed during dinner at his place had sprouted into a whole slew of *what-ifs*. He'd pondered the scenarios, run the figures and looked at the plan from every angle until his brain had protested from sheer fatigue. But he wasn't one to make decisions impulsively.

Jami released a soft sigh beside him. She sat bathed in the soft glow of the patio light, her face pensive. What was she thinking about? Was she considering the possibility of something permanent between them? Did she have as many regrets as he did, as many walls to break through to find the freedom to love again?

She tipped her head back, and he followed her gaze upward. A half-moon rested on the tips of the trees, cast against a backdrop of inky black. The sky was cloudless, awash with thousands of tiny points of light. If it weren't for the soft glow coming from the bulb behind him, he would see thousands more.

Jami drew in a deep breath. "How can anyone look at all this and deny God exists?"

"I don't know. I've never denied He exists. No matter what has happened, I've always known He's there." He just hadn't felt very close.

Jami put an elbow on the table and rested her chin in her hand. "You're right. He's always there. But He's not just out there. If you let Him in, He's right here." She put a fist to her chest.

Yes, he'd memorized those Bible verses and sang those songs as a kid. It was all so simple then. That was when he was young and idealistic, before life had kicked him around a few times.

Was any of what he'd learned even relevant in a grown-up world, facing the stark reality of adult-size problems? From what he'd seen, there was a lot of going through the motions without ever letting Jesus's words touch the heart. A lot of people's faith seemed to be nothing more than a platform from which to judge the rest of the world. If having a relationship with God didn't make any difference, why bother?

But it made a difference in Jami's life. Something drew him to her in a way he found irresistible. And that something had faith at its core. It colored everything she did and was the source behind the sense of peace and contentment she radiated.

But he was too cynical for that kind of blind trust, too jaded. Life wasn't that simple. Of course, Jami had had her own issues to work through. But she'd succeeded. Was there hope for him, a chance he could experience some of that peace and contentment himself? Was there something he could grasp hold of that would bring joy and meaning to his life?

He stood, then offered her his hand. "It's getting late. I'd better go so you can get some sleep."

He helped her to her feet, then pulled her into his arms. After a lingering good-night kiss, he still didn't release her. The problem was he didn't want to go home. The more time he spent with her, the harder it was to say good-bye, even overnight. He'd put his travel plans on indefinite hold. And when his sabbatical was over and it was time to return to his life in New York . . . He didn't even want to think about that.

After a final kiss, he released her and made his way to his car. Less than five minutes later, he drew to a stop next to the defunct fountain. The lights flanking both sides of the double front doors cast a soft glow over the entry area. The huge, old place was growing on him. Sometime in the past couple of weeks, it had begun to feel less like an inconvenience and more like home. His roots were here. His father had played in these rooms.

But it was more than that. Murphy was where he'd found himself again, where he'd rediscovered his joy. It was the place where a beautiful, sweet young lady had sent life coursing through a heart that had turned to stone.

And he didn't want to leave.

But if he worked up the courage to take the leap he was considering, maybe he wouldn't have to.

The following afternoon, Grant watched Brenda escort the well-dressed couple down the sidewalk toward her SUV, then closed the front door. He hadn't been there the first time she'd brought them. He should have made himself scarce this time also.

The guy was all right. The woman hadn't taken her nose out of the air the entire time she was there. Even though it was clear in the listing that the place was being sold "as is," she'd come up with a whole list of demands, repairs she expected to be made before closing, at the expense of the seller. He'd politely let her know she could look elsewhere.

Grant smiled. His only prospect for a sale had gone up in smoke, but he was actually relieved.

Because now he knew for sure. He was going to do it. It was so impractical, so out of character for him. He didn't make life-altering decisions without weeks of consideration. But nothing had ever felt more right. Excitement coursed through him at the thought. In two more hours, he'd pick up Jami, and over dinner, he'd tell her.

He moved to the entry table, where the *Scout* waited for him, untouched since he'd picked it up in town this morning. This was the week Jami's Humane Society article would run, featuring Morgan and Bailey, two rescue success stories. He headed toward the parlor with the paper.

Once he had settled onto the couch, he thumbed through the pages, searching for the story. But instead of dark eyes looking out from brown-and-black faces, a familiar young couple smiled from the page. What were his grandparents doing where Jami's article was supposed to be?

Other photos occupied the page, interspersed among the text. He recognized them. Some came from the photo albums he'd cast aside. Others Jami had taken. He read the headline and drew his brows together in confusion. *The McAllister Legacy: A Tale of Triumph and Tragedy.* She'd said the McAllister feature wouldn't run until next week. Did she lie about it?

He scanned the article, impressed with the quality of the writing. But his positive thoughts didn't last long. She'd written a poignant piece, all right. Lots of emotion. Descriptive settings. Amazingly in-depth reporting. But everything she'd promised not to print was there, every last detail.

He sat motionless, mind reeling. He needed to talk to her. There had to be some misunderstanding. Just like when he'd thought she was engaged.

No, this was no misunderstanding. She'd promised she wouldn't use anything she found in the box without his permission. Yet, here it was, in black and white. Pain shot through him, that white-hot streak of betrayal. Did she think he wouldn't find out? Or did she believe she would have him so enamored by the time he did that he wouldn't care?

Well, she was wrong. Trust was everything. It didn't matter how hard he'd fallen for her. If he couldn't trust her in this, he wouldn't be able to trust her in anything. If she professed her love, like Bethany once had, he'd never know if she was sincere.

Grant pushed himself to his feet, decision made. He would move ahead with his original plans, the ones he'd made weeks ago. Plans that didn't include Jami. A vise clamped down on his chest. Walking away would be the hardest thing he'd ever done. But she was leaving him with no choice. Whatever they'd shared, it was over.

Because without trust, they had nothing.

—⚬—

Jami moved to the front window and once again glanced at her watch. It was four fifty, so Grant was only twenty minutes late. Not *that* late, at least by her standards. They could still get there on time. Asheville was only two hours away in good weather. Unfortunately, what bore down on them now looked more ominous than good. Thunder rumbled in the distance, and heavy gray clouds rolled in, blanketing the landscape in premature dusk.

She turned away from the window and checked her reflection in the large oak-framed mirror hanging over the living room couch. This was the first time she'd dressed up for him. For over half an hour, she'd fussed with her hair, trying it up, down, pulled to one side, adorned with various jeweled clips and pins. It was a good thing she'd started getting ready an hour earlier than what she thought she needed, because she'd used every minute of the extra time.

And she was happy with the result. Her hair looked as if she'd just come from Precision Cut & Color. She'd swept the reddish-brown locks into an elegant French twist, leaving two spiral curls to frame her jaw. And she'd spent almost as much time with her makeup. It was tastefully done, but much more than her usual quick swipe of blusher, lip gloss and eye shadow.

She stepped away from the mirror and once again glanced at her watch. Now it was almost five. She tried to ignore the uneasiness swirling in her gut, the little voice warning her something was wrong.

But it couldn't be. When they'd parted last night, everything had been perfect. He probably had a good reason for being late. But he should have contacted her.

She marched to her purse and pulled out her phone. There was no need to work herself into a tizzy when a simple call would put her mind at ease. But Grant didn't answer. What was going on? Had he taken a nap and overslept? That had to be it. Nothing could have happened between now and when he left her house last night.

Of course, that was what she'd thought the last time. She closed her eyes and tried to silence that persistent little voice. But as time passed, the whispers grew to shouts, too loud to ignore.

"Okay, I'm going to his house." Once she saw his car sitting in the driveway, she could put her silly insecurities to rest.

She grabbed her keys and headed out the door. As she made her way up the kudzu-bordered drive, lightning danced across the sky. A long rumble followed. She rounded the bend, and her heart fell. The driveway was deserted, the house dark.

Grant was gone.

She shifted into park and sat motionless for several minutes, engine idling. Without his presence, the house seemed cold and lifeless. As she sat in the grayness of the dreary afternoon, it projected that emptiness right into her heart.

Grant was gone, had disappeared without warning. The whole situation thrust her back to the other time in her life when someone had left in a similar way. *He* hadn't said good-bye, either. She'd just gotten up one morning, and he'd been gone.

But Grant wasn't her father. And she wasn't an eight-year-old girl anymore.

She circled the fountain and drove slowly back down the drive. Once home, she plopped onto the couch with a heavy sigh. Bailey and Morgan jumped up to crowd onto her lap. Wet, pink tongues offered sympathy, slurping noisily up each cheek, wreaking havoc with the makeup she'd applied with such care.

She pulled them close and stared out the front window. Thunder echoed off the mountains, creating a constant rumble that rose and fell but never completely gave way to silence. The storm was closer, threatening to come through with all it had promised and then some. But it didn't matter. She was going to stay locked inside, safe and dry.

And alone.

Bailey and Morgan snuggled closer, alternating between nuzzling her hands with their noses and staring up at her with huge brown eyes full of concern. She had no answers for their questions, because she had no answers for her own. How could he do it? How could he make those unspoken promises, then walk out without even saying good-bye? Why did the most important people in her life just walk away?

The first heavy raindrops slapped against the window, driven by the gusts riding the front of the storm. She slouched forward to hug both dogs to her chest, an overwhelming sense of loneliness engulfing her. Her mother had left her, but she'd had no choice. She'd fought long and hard, giving up only when she'd had no more strength left to fight.

Her father had had a choice. He'd walked away without a second thought while an eight-year-old girl had cried herself to sleep and asked God why her daddy didn't love her. And while a nine-year-old girl had checked the mailbox, praying for a card or letter, he'd moved on with his life and written off the family who loved him. And while he'd done whatever it was that men like him did, a ten-year-old girl had closed off her heart and simply stopped loving.

Suddenly she was once again that little girl, lost and alone. And the tears she'd sworn to never shed again escaped their restraints and rushed to the surface. No matter how hard she fought to hold them back, they kept coming. There were too many, flowing from a bottomless well that had burst open after being sealed for so many years.

Outside, the sky split apart with a flash and a deafening crash, spilling its own grief and rage in a torrent likely to continue into the night. Both dogs tried to crowd onto her lap, little black bodies quivering in fear. She buried her face in their fur.

How could he do it? How could a father walk away from his eight-year-old child without a backward glance? Had he really been able to blot her from his memory as if she'd never existed? Or did she sometimes slip unexpectedly into his thoughts, stirring at least a smidgen of regret? Fifteen years later, did he even remember her?

She slid her hands down both dogs' backs, wet with her tears. When they looked up at her, those big brown eyes seemed to hold sympathy, a silent show of understanding. Someone had cast them aside, too. After seven years of being a part of someone's family, something had happened that had landed them in the shelter. She cupped Morgan's face in her hands, then Bailey's. "He at least owed me a good-bye." The complaint applied to Grant as much as her father.

Well, she had learned her lesson. Grant had disappeared from her life not once but twice. The first time, he'd just clammed up and shut her out. The second time, he'd physically left. Though she could overlook a multitude of wrongs, being abandoned wasn't one of them. So what if he could make her pulse race by walking into a room? It didn't matter that his kisses left her breathless, that simply being with him gave wings to her dreams and made her heart soar.

Even if he did come back, she wasn't interested.

Jami sat on the couch, a book open in her lap and a quivering ball of fur attached to each hip. Almost an hour had passed since her meltdown, but the heavens still waged war outside, with no cease-fire in sight. Crashes of thunder punctuated the roar of rain, the accompanying flashes casting the landscape in virtual daylight.

At least she'd washed her face, so she was no longer wearing mascara from her eyelashes to her chin. And she'd had some supper—reheated tuna casserole. It likely didn't compare to the fare at Crest Mountain, but it was all she could muster up. She didn't even bother trying to feed Morgan and Bailey. During storms, they were too uptight to eat.

She flipped the book over, then ran a hand down each of the dogs' backs. Tension tightened their bodies, and their heads raised simultaneously. Then both dogs flew off the couch and ran, barking, to the front door. An instant later, the bell rang.

She drew her brows together. Who would venture out in weather like this?

When she peered through the panes of glass making up the top of her door, a familiar figure stood on the front porch, clad in a dripping yellow rain slicker. *Jerry.* What was her cousin doing there?

"It's okay, girls." She gave each dog a pat, then reached for the lock.

Her next thought sent panic shooting up her spine. Something had happened to Aunt Lily. Why else would Jerry come out in weather like this? She threw the lock and swung open the door, her heart pounding in her chest.

A hand came up and pushed back the rubber hood, revealing brown hair tinged with gray and dark eyes in a lined face. This wasn't her cousin.

Her fingers tightened on the doorknob as a sense of familiarity nibbled at the edges of her mind. "Can I help you?"

"Jami?"

It was a single word, but enough to confirm the recognition she'd been trying to deny. Cold crept through her, and her brain shut down. Thunder rumbled, and the downpour continued unabated, a tension-filled backdrop to the heavy silence stretching between them. The vinyl-clad visitor shifted his weight from one foot to the other. Rain slanted in under the porch roof, pelting him and spattering the hardwood floor inside the house.

She swallowed hard and tried to kick her mind back into gear. The floor was getting soaked, and so was he. She could towel the floor dry later. But she couldn't care less about her unwanted visitor. No one had asked him to come, especially on a night like this.

He finally spoke the words she knew were coming.

"Jami, I'm your father."

She nodded—she hadn't yet found her voice—and another heavy silence passed. Long ago, he'd walked out of her life. Back then, she would have given anything for a visit, even a phone call. Now she wanted neither.

He cleared his throat and dipped his head, seemingly as much at a loss for words as she was. And she had no intention of making it any easier for him, even if she'd been able. There was no excuse for what he'd done, nothing he could ever do to make it right.

He shifted his weight once more and began. "I'm here to beg your forgiveness. I'm not asking to be part of your life. If you say you hate me and never want to see me again, it's what I deserve. I let alcohol control me, and I'll always regret the decisions I made because of it."

So he felt regret. When had that started? Not early enough to have come back and been a father to her.

"I'm different now," he continued. "I haven't had a drink in over two years. I even team lead an AA group. But part of healing is making amends to those you've wronged. And there's no one I've wronged more than you and your mother."

At the mention of her mother, Jami's already-frayed nerves unraveled even further. Year after year, her mother had held on to her faith, never giving up hope her wayward husband would one day straighten out and return to the family he'd abandoned. Well, she'd finally gotten her dream. Too bad she hadn't lived long enough to see it.

Jami sucked in a shaky breath. "You're too late."

He heaved a sigh, his shoulders slumping with the motion. "I don't expect you to be able to set aside everything that happened in the past. I only hope that over time you'll find it in your hearts to forgive me. I wronged you both, and I'm so sorry. I'd do anything to make it up to you."

Realization trickled through her, and her jaw sagged. He didn't know. "You came back too late. Mom died a year ago."

His eyes widened, deepening the creases in his brow, and the color leeched from his face. "Beth is . . . gone?"

He turned away, face toward the rain, and stuffed both hands into the pockets of his jacket. Soon his shoulders jerked with silent sobs. A pang of tenderness tried to nudge its way into her heart, but she slapped it aside. He didn't deserve her sympathy. He'd walked out and stayed away fifteen years.

It was a year too long.

Her mother would have offered the forgiveness he sought. There wasn't a bitter bone in her body.

"The breast cancer came back." Of course, he wouldn't have known about the first time, either. Her mother had fought both battles with the support of her sister and friends while he'd drowned himself in a bottle.

He turned back around to face her, his features drawn and his posture stooped, grief now piled on top of the regret he'd carried for so many years. He started to reach for her, then dropped his arm. "I'm so sorry."

She didn't respond. The past hung between them, dark and ugly, too many wrongs on the one side and too many hurts on the other.

"Can I take you to breakfast?"

Jami shook her head. "You've already said your piece, and I have nothing I want to say to you." She turned, offering him a cold shoulder. He'd come back because they told him in AA he needed to make amends. Tough. She had no intention of making his little exercise in assuaging his guilt successful. Regret for the choices he'd made should hang over him until the day he died.

Some guilt of her own swept through her, and her chest tightened. The thoughts bouncing through her mind went against everything she'd been taught. And everything she'd said to Grant about forgiveness. But at the moment, practicing what she preached was beyond her human capabilities. And divine help didn't seem to be forthcoming, either, if the cold knot of anger in her stomach was any indication. It was in check, but she couldn't say for how long.

The old man finally sucked in a deep breath. "I'm staying at the Mountain Vista Inn in town, room one twelve. If you want to talk, even if it's to yell at me and tell me you hate me and wish I were dead, I'll be there through the weekend." He attempted a shaky smile. "It would probably do you good to get it all out. Bitterness can ruin your life if you let it. When the Bible says we're to forgive our enemies, it's for our own good."

The tenuous hold on her self-control snapped, and she whirled to face him. "Don't go quoting the Bible to me."

Week after week her mother had taken her to services, and during that whole time, he'd never darkened the door of a church. Who was he to tell her what the Bible said about anything?

His gaze dropped to his feet. "Very well. If you change your mind, you know where to find me. Monday I'll be heading back to Greensboro."

She nodded and closed the door. No, she wouldn't change her mind. At ten years old, she'd accepted his leaving and closed off that part of her heart. And it didn't need to be reopened. Not now. Not ever.

She trudged back to the couch and picked up her book. Bailey and Morgan settled in next to her, slightly calmer after the distraction of a visitor. She dropped her gaze to the page, and a recent conversation flashed through her mind. She had encouraged Grant to let go of the bitterness toward his grandmother and, more recently, his mother. Offering that advice had been easy when she thought she didn't have any bitterness herself. Now she felt like a hypocrite.

Lord, help me work through this. I don't know what to do.

Because no matter how convinced she'd been that she had buried the past and held no grudges, her stomach twisted at the thought of letting her father walk back in and pick up where he'd left off. He didn't deserve any second chances, not after staying away so long. He just needed to go back to where he'd been for the last decade and a half—out of her life.

FIFTEEN

Grant walked through the front door and wheeled his suitcase toward his bedroom. It had been a long day. Actually, he was into the next one, since midnight had passed two hours ago. He couldn't get a direct flight on such short notice, and his best option involved a two-hour layover. But now he was home, ready to get a good night's sleep, throw his packed bags in his car and head out. This was the day he'd looked forward to for the past three months.

Except now, the idea didn't hold any appeal. Touring the country alone. What was the use? What pleasure was there in trying new things with no one to share the experience with? Of seeing new sights with no one to tell?

But he had to give it a try. There had to be a remedy for the malaise that had descended on him over the past several months. What had started as vague restlessness had evolved into complete dissatisfaction with life. Nothing spurred his interest anymore.

And his trip to Murphy had only made it worse. It was supposed to be nothing more than a little hiccup in his plans, a slight delay in his anticipated trip. Instead, what he found was a small taste of the unknown something that made life complete, the elusive ingredient that at times seemed so close but tantalizingly out of reach.

He strode to the bedroom and kicked off his shoes, disturbing the perfectly kept atmosphere of the room. The bed was made, its brushed-nickel headboard reflecting the crisp white light. Tile ran wall to wall, a sea of marble beneath black laminate dressers, nightstands and an entertainment center.

Everything cold and sterile, like his life.

For a brief moment, Jami had brought warmth to his soul. But everything about her was a farce. Maybe she cared for him. But it wasn't enough. He couldn't commit his life to someone who would throw away a promise to advance her career. That one decision showed him where he ranked in her life—somewhere below her goals as a reporter. Her career came first.

Realization slammed into him. That was what he'd done to Bethany. How many times had she begged him to take her to one of her social events and he'd offered excuses? There was always that new client to take to dinner, the next big trial to prepare for. Eventually, she'd stopped asking.

He shook his head. He was finally on the receiving end of what he'd so many times dished out. *What goes around comes around.* Some inner voice told him he deserved it. Maybe it was karma. Whatever it was, it wasn't pleasant.

Leaving the suitcase near the door, he carried his shoes to the large walk-in closet. A long-neglected black case waited in the back corner, untouched for so long he'd almost forgotten it was there. For several moments, he stood, shoes in hand, staring at the oddly shaped object. He hadn't picked up his French horn in years—two, to be exact.

Now the forgotten black case seemed to beckon him. He slid the shoes into the same wooden cubby he'd removed them from almost two weeks earlier and hauled the case to the bed, where he unfastened the two silver latches. Polished brass glinted golden under the overhead lights, and he ran his hand over the smooth rim of the bell.

He loved the French horn, its rich mellow tones and soothing melodies. But when he inserted the mouthpiece and raised it to his lips, the sound that came out was neither rich nor soothing. It was a sickly bellow, the cry of an elephant in mourning. He depressed the valves in rapid succession, then pursed his lips again. That attempt wasn't much better than the first one.

How could he have stayed away so long? How could he have just ceased to live for two whole years?

He placed the horn back in its case and walked from the room. When he reached the kitchen, he headed straight for the fridge without flipping the switch. Stark white light from inside chased away the shadows in the room, and he took a bottle of sparkling water from the top shelf. He'd eaten on the way home from the airport, which was a good thing, based on the contents of his fridge. Except for the other four bottles of water and a half gallon of milk five days past its expiration, the clear plastic shelves were empty. The state of his fridge summed up his life about as well as his décor did.

He sank onto a bar stool, and his gaze fell on the clock over the sink, its black metallic hands backlit by an eerie green glow. He should go to bed. He needed to get some quality sleep, or he wouldn't be safe to drive. But sleep was likely to elude him tonight.

He picked up the water bottle and took a long swig. A hint of raspberry brushed past his senses, so subtle it was nothing more than a brief aftertaste. Come morning, he would head out. Maybe he would take 95 and make his way down the coast. There were a lot of interesting beach towns along the Atlantic.

But no matter how he tried, he couldn't inspire any enthusiasm for his trip. He needed to snap out of it. This was the reason he'd rearranged his schedule at the firm and dumped his entire caseload on his partners.

He'd promised them that after his trip, he'd come back renewed and refreshed.

But what if it didn't work? What if the only place he could find what he needed was a little mountain town in southwestern North Carolina?

And the only one who could make him whole again was the sassy, quirky newspaper reporter who'd stolen his heart?

—⚉—

Grant zipped the suitcase closed and lifted it from his bed. It was jammed full of clothes. His iPad was stuffed into the front pouch, along with a couple of books. Another smaller piece of luggage held his shower bag, shoes, belts and other miscellaneous items. He was now packed, ready to leave.

He pressed a hand to the side of his head and closed his eyes. The ibuprofen he'd taken upon awakening hadn't kicked in yet. Neither had the cup of coffee he'd washed it down with. The night had been way too short.

He rolled both bags from the room and toward the front door, the rumble of wheels against tile echoing through the penthouse. This was it. The start of his long-awaited trip. He was going to do it. And his travel plans were no more concrete than heading south along the coast and seeing where fancy took him.

But something unsettling darkened the edges of his mind. And it had nothing to do with his lack of preparation. It was the sense that he was leaving unfinished business. He still hadn't spoken with his mother. He'd promised Jami he'd do it when he got back to New York.

Of course, Jami hadn't kept her promise, either. She'd practically sworn an oath that she wouldn't use any of the information she'd found in those boxes. Then she'd done it anyway. She hadn't even given him a heads-up. Instead, she'd let him be blindsided.

But regardless of what promises had been made or broken, he needed to talk to his mother. After all, he was leaving for two months. What if something happened to him while he was gone? What if something happened to her? If his final words to her were spoken in anger, he would spend the rest of his life with regrets.

The same as his grandparents had.

He locked the door, then pulled his bags toward the elevator. Midmorning, the traffic would still be crazy. But he would load his things in the car and drive. Then, once he finished talking to his mother, he could be on his way.

The drive gave him all kinds of time to second-guess his plans, and by the time he reached her front door thirty minutes later, he'd just about changed his mind. What was he going to say to her? He couldn't tell her everything was okay, because it wasn't. And he couldn't say he'd forgiven her, because he hadn't. So what was he even doing there?

No regrets. That was what he was doing there. He didn't know if he could put the past behind him, but he had to try.

He rang the bell, and when the door swung open, several emotions played across her face—shock, then relief, then total joy. But it was her eyes that shot a red-hot arrow through his heart. They were puffy and glistened with moisture. She'd been crying.

"Grant." She reached out to clasp his hand and led him into the condo. "I'm so glad you're here."

His gaze shifted to the coffee table, where a stack of photo albums lay, the top one open.

"I was looking at pictures." She sank onto the couch and motioned for him to sit. When he'd settled in beside her, she picked up the open album. "Remember this?"

He looked at what she held. On the left-hand page was a picture of him at about seven years old, roasting a marshmallow over an open fire. A small dome tent stood in the background. Beneath that photo was one of him and his mother sitting in a canoe, each holding a paddle.

"It was a camping trip." The only one he'd ever been on. He'd forgotten the details, who they were with and why they'd gone. But as he looked at the pictures, he remembered what it had felt like to spend an entire weekend with his mother instead of the babysitter, to go out and do something fun, to have her be relaxed and attentive instead of stressed and exhausted from yet another fourteen-hour day.

She rested her hand on the book. "I was working as a secretary for a construction company. It was just a temporary job, but it was the best I'd ever had. I still waitressed nights and weekends, but this one weekend, they were doing a company camping trip. I asked off at the restaurant those two days, and the contractor I worked for set us up with a tent, air mattresses, sleeping bags and a lantern."

Judging from her wistful tone, the trip had been as special for her as it had for him. They hadn't taken many vacations together. Her work schedule never allowed for more than occasional day trips.

But that was the choice she'd made. If she'd taken help from the McAllisters, she wouldn't have needed the second job. He'd have been raised by his mother instead of an ever-changing parade of babysitters, and *vacation* wouldn't have been a foreign concept.

He pushed the thoughts aside. He was trying to find the path to forgiveness, and focusing on the wrongs wasn't it.

She turned the page, and he dropped his gaze to the book. After several more pictures from that same weekend, the scene shifted to the beach, one of those day trips. Finally, she closed the book and sighed.

"When you left, I was so afraid I was never going to see you again. I shouldn't have lied to you, and I'm sorry."

Yeah, she shouldn't have lied to him. But what about refusing the McAllisters' help out of sheer stubbornness? What about putting her desire for revenge over his happiness? Was she sorry for either of those decisions?

She laid the book aside and took his hand in hers. "Will you please forgive me?"

Forgive her for lying? Or forgive her for everything? Would he be able to do either? Using him, then lying to him about it. Teaching him to hate. What she'd done was so wrong.

An admonition slid through his mind—*He who is without sin cast the first stone.* He'd heard the words quoted several times. They'd been spoken by some great religious teacher, maybe even Jesus.

Grant sighed. He certainly hadn't been perfect. Bethany would vouch for that. How could he not grant his mother the forgiveness she'd asked for when he'd made so many mistakes of his own?

He met her gaze. She stared up at him, her eyes pleading. The sheen he'd noticed on first arriving seemed to be back. His chest tightened. Until this morning, he'd never seen his mother cry. He nodded. "I forgive you."

What he said wasn't entirely true. But was it an outright lie? Maybe not.

Maybe it was what he needed. Because maybe the first step of the forgiveness process was speaking the words.

Jami dragged herself in the front door of the *Cherokee Scout*, clutching a stack of dog-eared pages. She wouldn't feel any worse if she'd caught the flu bug that had kept Bernie out the first three days of the week. She hadn't slept well at all last night. And crying didn't suit her. It left her with a massive headache and an unbecoming puffiness no amount of artfully applied eye makeup would cover.

Grant never contacted her to apologize for standing her up last night. Not that she'd expected him to. It wouldn't have made any difference anyway. She was through with him. She was maybe even through with men in general. At least for the time being.

On the way to her desk, she gave brief hellos to those who'd made it to work before her, which this morning was most of the staff. She'd gotten a late start, then made a couple of stops on her way in.

She plopped the stack of pages she held on her desk. It was both versions of the McAllister article, the dull, lifeless one and the one that sparked with vitality. Yesterday, she'd finished final edits and taken them home. Her plan had been to show Grant both and try to get his permission to print the good one. But if not, she at least had a plan B.

She sank into her chair and reached for the mouse, ready to transfer the plan-B version to the news folder on the server. Even though Grant was gone, it didn't negate the promise she'd made.

Once finished, she picked up a hot-pink folder she'd titled *Things to Do in Murphy*. She'd gotten the go-ahead for the series yesterday. It would span several weeks. The first installment would be Wild River Outfitters. She already had some great pictures. Now she would work on putting together an article that would hopefully drum up some business for Sam.

In spite of the seventh-grade marching band playing against the inside of her head, she made good progress over the next hour and a half. By lunchtime, she'd finished the draft, selected some photos and come up with good cutlines.

The front door swung open, and Bernie's coarse voice cut across her thoughts. After greetings and several proud comments about how even the swine flu was no match for Bernie Hopkins, she reached her desk and sank into the chair.

Jami smiled over at her. "I'm glad you're feeling better."

"Me, too. I've been dying to hear about how things are going with Grant, but until late last night, I was too sick to even feel like picking up the phone. So tell me all about it."

Jami frowned. "Don't get too excited. There's nothing to tell. Grant split."

Bernie's eyes widened. "He left? Why?"

"No idea. Tuesday night, he's telling me to be ready at four because he's taking me to Crest Mountain Dinner Show, and Wednesday afternoon he's gone."

Bernie shook her head. "Something must have happened."

"Between Tuesday night and Wednesday afternoon? Face it, Bernie. This match is just another one of your disasters."

"I bet he'll be back." She set her jaw in determination. When one of her matchmaking schemes was at stake, Bernie didn't give up easily. "Meanwhile, how about letting me take you to Downtown Pizza for lunch? I've got four days of not eating to make up for."

Jami retrieved her purse from the bottom drawer and walked to the front with Bernie. Having company for lunch sounded good. Maybe it would help take her mind off Grant. As they rounded the end of the long counter separating the work area from the lobby, Hank stepped inside, and Bernie approached him.

"What are you doing here so early? You don't usually get your stuff in till midafternoon."

He laid a sheet of paper on the counter. "I figured if I got my ad to you early, you might manage to get it right."

Jami stifled a snort. They were at it again.

Bernie angled her face upward, taking on the air of condescension she always managed just for Hank. "That photo was no mess-up. It was payback. A most brilliant one, I might add."

Hank planted his hands on his hips. "But advertising all our bags of feed free was a mistake."

"You're making a mountain out of a molehill." She waved away his complaint. "How many of the fine people of Murphy have tried to walk out of Wayne's with a free bag of horse feed?"

"That's beside the point. See if you can do it right this time." He pushed the paper toward her, then offered her his back. "Hi, Jami. I wanted to tell you what a good job you did on the story this week."

"Thanks. That one was near and dear to my heart. Makes you want to run right out and adopt a pet, doesn't it?"

Hank's brow folded in confusion. "Adopt a pet? Why?"

"Well, I thought—" she stammered, feeling like the amateur she was. If her article didn't tug at the heartstrings, she didn't do a very good job of getting her point across. Hank was quiet, but he wasn't slow. "Bailey, Morgan, all the homeless cats . . ."

Hank shook his head. "I must have missed the part about dogs and cats. But I'll read it again."

Missed the part about dogs and cats? That was the whole article. Unless . . . A cold lump settled in her gut. She'd printed the draft of the McAllister article on Friday, and Bernie had seen her slip the hard copy into the folder.

"Bernie? My Humane Society article went in, right?" She'd been too busy the past two days to even look at a paper.

Bernie shifted her weight from one foot to the other, barely able to contain her excitement. "After you left for the dentist Friday, I just had to see what you'd done. It was so good. You had some great pics, too. I went ahead and uploaded everything to go in this week. I was planning to tell you on Monday, then got sick. Your Humane Society article will run next week."

Jami groaned and covered her face with her hands, a lead weight filling her stomach. Between the time Grant left her house Tuesday night and when he was supposed to pick her up for dinner the next afternoon, he'd read the article. And he believed her promise to not print his family secrets was nothing but a lie.

"Jami?" A rare hesitancy filled Bernie's tone.

She lowered her hands. "That wasn't supposed to run."

"But you said you were happy with it. And I know why. It was brilliant. David even said so. There was nothing you could have done to improve on it."

"There was information in there Grant didn't want me to use. And I gave him my word I wouldn't. I'd decided to write the article the way I wanted to, sure once he read it, he would be fine with it."

"And what did he say?" The hesitancy was still there, multiplied times ten.

"Nothing. I did a final edit yesterday and was going to show it to him last night." She'd made a promise. And he'd wanted to believe her. She'd seen it in his eyes. Trust didn't come easily for him. His not letting her use the information was a test. And she'd failed it miserably.

Somehow, she had to make things right. Not to salvage lost love. She'd already tossed that aside last night. But she couldn't let him go through his life believing she'd betrayed him. He had to know that, at least once, his trust wasn't misplaced.

"So *now* who's the doofus?" Hank's tone was soft. And instead of the usual mocking glint reserved solely for Bernie, his eyes held nothing but sadness.

Jami unclipped the leashes and hung them on the hook near the front door. As she walked to the kitchen, the dogs bounded ahead of her. They knew the routine. When she got home from work, the first thing on the agenda was taking them out. The immediate second was dinner.

At least someone in the Carlisle household felt like eating tonight. For half the afternoon, the pizza she'd eaten with Bernie had lain in her gut, an indigestible lump. After Grant ran out on her, she hadn't thought things could get any worse. Finding out the McAllister article had run had proven just how wrong she'd been.

Three different times, she'd tried to call Grant, twice from her cell phone and once from the *Scout*. All three times it went to voice mail. The last time, she left a message asking him to call, saying that there'd been a misunderstanding. So far, he was ignoring her message the same way he'd ignored her calls.

After feeding the dogs, she stood in front of the open refrigerator for a good half minute, hoping that something already made would somehow materialize. It didn't. She'd eaten up the last of her leftovers with the prior night's supper of tuna casserole. Finally, she took out ingredients for omelets and closed the door. Breakfast for dinner. It would be convenient, tasty and fast.

Fifteen minutes later, she headed to the living room with her steaming supper, cheese oozing from its curved edge. Tonight would be a good movie night. Instead of sitting at the table and moping over Grant, she would turn on the TV and find something to cheer her up. Or at least occupy her mind for a couple hours. Maybe a good disaster movie—a ginormous asteroid barreling toward earth at a billion miles per hour, or the granddaddy of all earthquakes swallowing California and marching eastward across the United States. Or maybe even one of those alien-invasion movies. Anything but a romance.

She plopped down on the couch, and her gaze fell on the binder lying on the coffee table. The Dani story. Saturday morning, she'd gotten as far as reading what she'd written and making some notes. Since then, after a thorough search of the house, she'd located the flash drive that held the file. That was as far as she'd gotten.

She laid her plate and fork on the table and picked up the binder. Finishing one of her novels was a promise she'd made to Grant. But Grant was gone. He'd taken off and wasn't coming back. She crossed the room to stand in front of the bookcase. When she'd slid the binder halfway into its slot on the shelf, she stopped.

Her promise wasn't just to Grant. It was to herself. Writing was *her* dream. Not *his*. Just because she'd given up on a fairy-tale prince sweeping her off her feet, there was no reason to throw away her dream of writing a novel. Besides, it would be good for her. Therapeutic. Creative endeavors were always therapeutic, the same as being in nature.

She turned from the bookcase and crossed the living room to her office, snatching up her omelet on the way. Forget the disaster movie. She had a book to write. She plopped the binder on her desk and laid the plate next to it, then put the flash drive into the port on her computer. A minute later, she had the file saved to her hard drive and opened, ready to work.

If only she could get a hold of Grant. If he wasn't roaming the countryside, thinking she'd betrayed him, it would be much easier to put the past four weeks behind her. But setting him straight was going to be impossible when he refused to accept any call coming from the 828 area code.

But maybe he wouldn't reject 706, especially with the Georgia location.

Smiling, she hurried to the living room to retrieve her phone. Within moments, she was seated back at her desk, fork in one hand and phone pressed to her other ear. Holly answered on the second ring.

"How about a round of minigolf at the Lilly Pad Village Saturday?"

"Sounds good. But why Blue Ridge when we've got minigolf right here in Murphy?"

"I need to use a pay phone."

"What's wrong with yours?"

"Nothing. I'm on it now." She drew in a deep breath. "I found out why Grant took off."

When she'd filled Holly in on the details, Holly released a low whistle. "Whoa. Bernie really messed up this time. She had a match that actually worked, then ran him off."

"I've got to straighten it out. I can't stand the thought that he thinks I lied to him. I've tried to call him to explain, but he won't accept any calls from this area code."

"But if you call from Blue Ridge . . ."

"That's right. I'm hoping he'll see *Georgia* and not even connect that Blue Ridge is only thirty minutes from Murphy."

"Once he finds out what really happened, he'll be back."

"I don't want him back. I just want to straighten out the confusion."

"Are you sure?"

"Positive." Grant wasn't the type to stick around. At the first hint of trouble, instead of hanging in there and talking it out, he clammed up and took off. She couldn't live like that.

"Well," Holly said, "count me in for minigolf."

"Excellent. I'll get a hold of Sam."

As she disconnected the call, the weight that had been bearing down on her seemed to lighten. If everything went as planned, in another forty-eight hours, it would all be over. Grant would be on his merry way, enjoying the sights, knowing she hadn't betrayed him. And she would be moving forward with her dreams, conscience clear.

Unfortunately, that simplified scenario didn't take into account the time it would take to heal her heart.

SIXTEEN

Waves crashed against the shore a few yards from where Grant walked, sending cool water swirling around his bare feet at regular intervals. He'd left New York shortly before noon, then spent the next several hours speeding down the interstate, trying to outrun the loneliness dogging him. But no matter how he tried, it overtook him anyway. Loneliness had no speed limits to obey.

Except for one brief gas and bathroom stop, he'd driven straight through to Virginia Beach. He'd never been there, but it was a coastal town, as different from Murphy as a place could be. And that was what he needed—something to help him forget his experiences of the past five weeks, not remind him of Jami at every turn.

And that was why he no longer wore the pewter heart. He couldn't bring himself to part with it, though. Not yet, anyway. Instead, he'd tucked it into the bottom of his suitcase. Someday he would get rid of it. Or wait to wear it until it meant nothing more to him than a cold piece of metal.

Three times, Jami had tried to call him, twice from her cell and once from the paper. The third time, she left a message. It was short—"Grant, there's been a terrible misunderstanding. Please call and let me explain." Her tone had held urgency, and an underlying sadness had tugged at his heart. But he wasn't ready to talk to her.

He hadn't wanted to care for her. He'd wanted to wrap everything up and walk away, no attachments, no regrets. But every hour they spent together, she'd wheedled her way further into his heart, right past all his defenses.

And look where it got him.

He stopped walking to face the surf, and a wave sucked sand from under his feet on its return to the ocean. At shortly after nine on a Thursday night, he had the beach to himself. Even the seagulls had settled in for the evening, their raucous calls silenced. A warm sea breeze whipped his clothes against his body, and the roar of the ocean surrounded him, advancing and retreating.

Nothing to remind him of Jami. Yet everything did.

He'd had her pegged so wrong. The sweet, wholesome air was nothing but a ruse, the unwavering honesty that assured him he could finally let down his guard and trust, a bald-faced lie. And he'd fallen for it hook, line and sinker. Jami's burning goal was career advancement, getting the story at any cost. She'd put it above everything else, even her own integrity.

Even his heart.

He pulled his feet from the sand that had molded around them and resumed walking. Yep, he'd been duped. The first time, he'd been young and inexperienced. He hadn't been knocked down enough to realize everyone had an agenda and that agenda came first.

Now he had no excuse. He'd been there, experienced those hard-earned lessons. And he'd still let down his guard and blindly allowed a beautiful woman access to his heart. Stupid, stupid, stupid.

Well, it wouldn't happen again. The temporary facade of happiness wasn't worth the betrayal that followed. Two years ago, that black hole had almost swallowed his soul. He wasn't going back there ever again.

Or maybe he'd never left.

Maybe he was still stuck in the deep abyss, where the darkness was so thick it leeched all joy and meaning from life. He'd been there so long. How would he ever break free?

An image flashed through his mind—an old man, tired and spent. Bank accounts bursting and no one to share them with. His zest for life gone, his soul sucked dry. He moved away from the pounding surf and sank onto the soft sand. He'd just been visited by Dickens's Ghost of Christmas Future.

Jami's advice intruded into his thoughts again—*life's a lot better when you let it go.* She was right, but he was no closer to figuring out how than when she'd first spoken the words. Jami's answer would be a relationship with God. In spite of her faults, she possessed a peace that had eluded him most of his life. And he still didn't know where to find it.

Everything Jami had told him, the things he'd heard at church—it all seemed too simplistic. Faith was for children, starry-eyed innocents who hadn't yet had their idealistic views shattered by reality. He'd outgrown that kind of faith years ago. But was there such a thing as grown-up faith? Faith that was real, that made a difference in the way a person lived? Jami was as close to the real thing as he'd ever found. But she had no qualms about lying to him, or at least breaking a promise.

Maybe he was expecting too much. Jami had said it herself—Jesus was the only perfect man who ever lived. Maybe he should be looking at Jesus's example instead of picking apart His church.

Grant pushed himself to his feet and continued moving in the same direction he'd been walking earlier, taking him yet farther from where he'd started. But it didn't matter. He didn't plan to return until he'd sorted out everything wrong in his life. He would walk all night if he had to.

Sunday morning, it had seemed much clearer. With Jami standing next to him, a chorus of voices raised in song, he'd felt God's presence all around him. It was easy to connect with God in a church filled with prayer and praises. But could He be found on a dark, deserted beach in Virginia?

"God, are you here?"

The wind picked up his words and threw them back at him. He drew in a deep breath and tilted his face heavenward. The stars that had shone so brightly in Jami's sky the other night lay hidden behind a puffy blanket of charcoal. The moon was invisible, too, tucked away in its section of sky.

He lowered his gaze and stuffed his hands into his pockets. God's presence was hidden from him as surely as the stars and the moon. But God was there. He knew it. The same way he knew the moon and stars wouldn't hide forever.

"God, please somehow let me know you hear me and you care."

His own words brought him up short. Even if he received an answer, what would he do? He wasn't ready to make a commitment, because he wasn't sure he could live up to it. What if he made mistakes? What if he became one more reason for others to shun Christianity?

He stopped walking and turned to face the water. Waves washed ashore in the unending rhythm of the ocean. Farther out, the black expanse stretched into infinity, melding with an equally dark sky. He pulled his hands from his pockets and stood motionless, a sense of reverence filling him. The vastness of God's creation never failed to remind him of his own insignificance.

Soft, silver light sifted over him, as if a curtain were being lifted away. Diamond-tipped waves rolled ever closer, and the sand was bathed in a luminescent glow. When he lifted his gaze upward, the clouds had parted, revealing an unobstructed half-moon.

Wonder filled him, and a song welled up inside, a chorus he'd learned just that week. He whispered the words. "How Great Is Our God." The song had moved him when he sang along with the other worshippers in the comfortably furnished church. And it moved him now, standing in God's own sanctuary, a floor of sand, a ceiling of clouds, the moon providing His light, the wind and waves His music.

"How great is our God . . ."

He lifted his voice in praise, and the wind carried the words up and away.

"How great is our God."

And that was his answer. With God's help, he could do whatever He asked of him. For once in his life, he wasn't doing it on his own.

He dropped to his knees in the sand and, as he'd been taught so long ago, surrendered his life to God.

―⁂―

Grant turned the book facedown in his lap and looked out over the beach. The shadow of the hotel marched slowly toward the sea, offering some relief for those tourists wanting to escape the blazing sun. From his vantage point on the fifth-floor balcony, he could see all the activity below without hearing most of the noise. Even the excited squeals of the children were muffled by the time they reached him.

He'd arrived in Myrtle Beach midafternoon with a lightness in his heart that he hadn't experienced in . . . well, ever. A sense of peace had enveloped him from the moment he made his decision on the sand, and he'd slept better last night than he had in months.

After checking in, he'd taken a walk on the beach, then spent the past two hours reading, alternating between the Gideon Bible he'd found in the nightstand and the legal thriller he'd brought from New York.

He hadn't called Jami yet, but he'd forgiven her. Eventually he would talk to her and let her know he harbored no bad feelings. Just not now. The pain was too raw. He'd given her his heart. And he was having a hard time getting it back. Meanwhile, he would take his walks on the beach, read in the shade of the balcony and wait for her hold on him to loosen. He had found peace. Someday he would find healing.

He closed the book and stood. It was time for another walk. He strode from the room and rode the elevator down five floors. But a thousand walks on the beach wouldn't ease the emptiness that filled him every time he thought of life without Jami. She was exactly what he needed, her lightheartedness the perfect complement to his own brooding nature, her spontaneity the balance to his rigidity. She'd awakened something in him, softening his hardened heart and stoking to life embers long since burned out.

He heaved a sigh and started down the beach, flip-flops in his hand. The sand was soft against his bare feet, the warm breeze soothing. A couple strolled toward him, hand in hand, and the crushing emptiness became a stabbing pain that shot through him like an arrow. In time, it would dull. It might take months, but eventually Jami would be nothing more than a bittersweet memory.

He sank onto the sand, then crossed his legs at the ankles and leaned back on his hands. Children frolicked in the surf a short distance away, carefree and happy, and a little farther out, whitecaps glistened in the late-afternoon sun. A pelican swooped down, dipping its head into the waves and emerging with a fish. In another hour, he would be going in search of supper himself. And eating it alone.

Was that what Jami would be doing? Or would she have Samantha and Holly to keep her company? She had probably made it home by now and was taking Morgan and Bailey for a walk.

A twinge of guilt passed through him. He should have called her. Even if he'd told her off for breaking his trust and said he never wanted to see her again, it would have been more considerate than leaving her hanging. Eventually he would apologize for standing her up. Regardless of what she'd done, he owed her that. Then he could move forward, conscience clear and wrongs forgiven.

Or maybe not. Had he truly forgiven her if he refused to have anything to do with her? It was easy to say, "I forgive you," and walk away. But was that really forgiveness?

He pushed himself to his feet and moved back up the beach. Maybe forgiveness required more than words. Maybe it required action.

He broke into a jog, energy surging through him. His decision was made. By the time he arrived in Murphy, it would be well after midnight.

But first thing tomorrow morning, he would be on her doorstep, ready to put legs to his newfound faith.

The upbeat strains of Mandisa's "Overcomer" filled the room, and the early morning sun streamed in through the gaps in the miniblinds. The radio had clicked on twenty minutes ago, but Jami was in no hurry to get up. Holly and Sam wouldn't arrive for their minigolf outing until ten. Once they arrived in Blue Ridge, she'd look for a pay phone, call Grant, and hope and pray he answered.

She stretched her arms skyward, allowing a huge yawn to take over. She couldn't roll onto her side. There was a dog plastered to each hip. Bailey inched upward, belly crawling to her favorite location: within tongue shot of any human face. Morgan, refusing to be outdone, eased up to shower the other cheek with doggy kisses.

A series of knocks shook her from her languidness, and both dogs perked up. The frenzied barking began a moment later, and as soon as she lifted them from the bed to the floor, they took off running for the front door. She shrugged into her robe, and before she even made it out of her room, the doorbell sounded. Whoever her visitor was, he or she was awfully impatient.

She padded barefoot through the living room, tying her robe as she went. The instant she looked through the peephole, her heart rolled over, taking her stomach along for the ride. It was Grant. Now she would have the opportunity to tell him the truth, that she didn't betray him.

That was the only reason she was glad to see him.

She ignored both her stomach and her heart and steeled her mind. Her message said for him to call her. Not show up on her doorstep at seven a.m. No problem. As soon as she set him straight, she would tell him good-bye. Her decision was made, and nothing was going to change it. He'd thought the worst and tried, convicted and sentenced her without giving her an opportunity to defend herself.

She swung open the door and invited him in. "Thanks for coming and giving me a chance to explain."

"I didn't come for an explanation." He squatted to pet the dogs, who were both squealing and wiggling in excitement. Then he straightened and stepped inside, closing the door behind him. "I came back to try to make everything right. You've been telling me life is better when you don't hold grudges, but it took God and me having some long talks on the beach for it to sink in." Peace and contentment underlay the smile he flashed her, relaxing the planes of his face and chasing away the hardness she'd often seen there. His talk with God had obviously made a difference.

He continued before she had a chance to respond. "I'm here to apologize. I'm sorry I stood you up. I was angry and hurt when I discovered you had published the things you promised you wouldn't. But that was no reason for not calling and letting you know what was going on."

"That's what I need to explain." She motioned for him to sit on the couch, and she sank down next to him. "I went through all day Wednesday thinking my Humane Society article had run. I didn't find out the truth until Hank came in Thursday and complimented me on the other one."

Grant looked down at her, one brow cocked in disbelief. "You didn't know?"

"No, I had no clue. I had written a draft of the McAllister article and left it in a folder on my desk. Bernie read it and thought it was so brilliant she decided to swap out the two articles."

"So it ran a week early. Does it really matter?" The accusation she'd expected to hear in his tone wasn't there.

"Yes, it matters a lot. It wasn't supposed to run at all. At least not without your approval." She sighed and sat back on the couch. "I was having such a tough time with the article I decided to write it the way I wanted to write it, do a few edits, then show it to you Wednesday night. I was pretty sure you would like it and give me the go-ahead. But if you didn't, I wasn't going to use it."

He stared at her in silence, as if he were having trouble digesting her words.

She continued, her tone soft. "I didn't betray you, Grant, and I couldn't stand the thought of you going through life thinking I had. I'm so sorry."

He took her hand in his. "You did nothing wrong. Even when I thought you had, I had already forgiven you." He let his head fall back against the couch. "I'm not the same bitter man who drove away from here three days ago."

"I'm glad." There was a hitch in her voice, one she hoped he didn't notice. Whatever he said, she couldn't let it sway her.

"I went to visit my mother. Everything's good between us."

"You're not angry with her anymore?"

"Not really. More disappointed than anything."

She nodded. "I can understand that." Except what she felt toward her father was much darker than disappointment. Grant had forgiven his parent before she'd forgiven hers.

He turned his head toward her and smiled. "Guess what else I did when I was home."

"What?"

"Got out my French horn."

"How did it go?"

He grimaced at the memory. "Pretty bad. I've got to get my embouchure back. French horn is a beautiful instrument when it's played properly. I could listen to it all day. Played poorly, though, it sounds like something that should be put out of its misery."

Jami laughed, some of her tension dissipating. "I heard quite a few of those wails in the junior high band room. That's all the more reason to get back into it before you lose any more."

"I'll take it into consideration, quite seriously, in fact." He nailed her with a look that was playfully stern. "And you're going to pick up one of those novels you've got lying around and finish it."

"I will. In fact, I've already started. I'm reworking what I'd already written, but I should be ready to add new words in a few days."

"Good." He squeezed her hand. "Now that I'm back, I'd like to reschedule the dinner reservation I so stupidly canceled Wednesday night."

She drew in a shaky breath. This was it, the moment she'd known was coming the instant she'd seen him standing on the porch. And saying the words she needed to say was even harder than she'd expected. Because things were different now. He'd let God get a hold of him. And he wasn't just talking the talk. He was backing it up with actions, offering forgiveness without even being asked. Everything had changed.

But really, nothing had. He was still the same man she'd met in the Holiday Inn parking lot, eager to wrap everything up and hit the road. He was here for now. But what about next week? And the week after that?

She shook her head. She couldn't do it. She couldn't keep seeing him and having her heart torn from her chest every time he decided to clam up and take off instead of talking to her.

"No?" His face fell. "I should never have left the way I did. When I came here a month ago, falling in love was the furthest thing from my mind. But somewhere along the way, you captured my heart. Now I can't imagine my life without you." He brought her hand to his mouth and held it there, never breaking eye contact.

If her stomach had flip-flopped before, her whole abdominal cavity settled into a quivering lump now. She pulled her hand free and stood to pace the room. She couldn't let stunning blue eyes sway her. Or soft, warm lips. Grant's waltzing in and out of her life had to end. Now.

"I'm sorry, Grant. I can't be with you. I just can't do it."

He rose, too. "Jami, please give us a chance. We love being together. I can tell you care for me. And I'm crazy about you. We've got to give it a try."

"I can't." Whatever Grant said, chances were good he would eventually walk away. It was a risk she wasn't willing to take.

Grief-stricken eyes locked with hers. "If you give me another chance, I swear I'll never leave like that again."

Hot tears surged forward, but she blinked them back. She had to stay strong. She could no longer let herself be swayed by that smooth baritone voice, the warm smile, those intense eyes. She squared her shoulders, trying to fight the devastating effect he had on her. It was hopeless. Standing there in her robe, her feet bare and hair mussed from sleep, she felt even more vulnerable, if that was possible.

She shook her head and moved to the front door. "I'm sorry, Grant. I just can't do it."

He took her cue, and she closed the door behind him, heart twisting in her chest. She could think of all kinds of reasons for giving in to his plea. She loved every moment she spent with him. He accepted her as she was and didn't think she should change. When he was near, her heart beat with an exhilaration and excitement she hadn't felt in a long time, if ever. No matter how she fought it, she was dangerously close to falling head over heels in love.

And those were the reasons she had said no.

—∞—

Grant closed the door to his room and slid the key into his pocket. After his early morning visit with Jami, he'd gone to the Grind and conversed with people he didn't want to see and choked down a Danish he didn't care to eat. Then he'd tried to return to the house.

But it was too quiet, with nothing to distract him from Jami. Everywhere he went, shadowed images sifted through his mind, and he saw her at every turn. Relaxing in the parlor, sharing a plate of cookies. Walking through the house with a camera strapped around her neck. Sitting in the breakfast nook, oohing and aahing in delight at each of his creations.

So he'd checked back in at the Holiday Inn. It wasn't much better. But at least he had the TV to provide some diversion. Now he was headed to Brother's Restaurant for dinner alone, the first of many such dinners if something didn't change. Hopefully Bernie would think of something. She'd been in his corner since day one. He released a snort. If all he had to hinge his future happiness on was one of Bernie's harebrained schemes, things were bleaker than he'd thought.

He could try praying. Of course, he had been. Just not very earnestly. It somehow didn't seem right, asking God for personal favors when he'd ignored Him since kindergarten. Maybe in a few weeks, when he'd logged in some more church services and prayed some unselfish prayers, he would be entitled to some selfish ones.

No, that was ridiculous. It wasn't a system he had to pay into before being allowed to collect. He remembered that much from his childhood.

Lord, I've made a mess of things. I know I don't deserve it, but I'm asking you to help me win Jami back.

As soon as he stepped out the lobby door, a green VW Bug squealed into the parking lot. Fiery-haired Bernie bolted from the front seat and made a beeline for him.

"I'm glad I caught you. I've been looking for you all morning, ever since I ran into Jami and she told me you're here." She stopped to catch her breath. "We've got to think of something. You're crazy about her, and I know she feels the same way about you." She shook her head. "Your leaving without calling to say good-bye, I'm afraid she took it kind of hard."

"But she knows what happened. I told her how sorry I am and promised it would never happen again. In fact, before I even came back, she tried to call to explain." And he'd been an idiot for not answering.

"She wanted to let you know she didn't betray you. But anything more than that—" Bernie expelled a heavy sigh. "When Jami was eight, her father abandoned her."

Grant sank back against the hood of the Bug, the full weight of the situation slamming into him. She had shared that with him. And Bernie was right. He'd hurt her in the worst way possible. He gave a hopeless lift of his shoulders. "I don't know what to do to win her back."

"I've been racking my brain all afternoon, and I think I might have come up with an idea. We've got to get Jami past her fears."

"I'm here to stay, and I'm willing to do anything to get her to see that."

"Great. Here's my idea." Her eyes lit with cautious hope. "What did you just say?"

"I'm here to stay."

"You're not leaving?"

"I'm not leaving. I've been tossing around the idea of turning the McAllister mansion into a bed and breakfast and opening a restaurant there. I was going to discuss it with Jami when I took her to dinner.

But since arriving this afternoon, I've done a lot more thinking, and I've made my decision. I'm going to do it."

A broad grin spread across Bernie's face. "Well, hot diggetty dog!"

Then the smile faded, and she pursed her lips. Apparently he was going to witness some of that Bernie scheming firsthand.

"So what was your idea?" he asked.

The expression of intense concentration vanished, and the smile returned, lighting her eyes with glee. "Forget my first idea. This one's even better. Jami's going to interview you. She just doesn't know it yet."

"Go on."

"We'll set it up for Tuesday at seven at Doyle's."

He eyed her doubtfully. "She's not going to agree to meet me for dinner."

"She's not going to know."

"How do you intend to accomplish that?"

"I'm going to tell her she has an assignment, an article on a new business coming to Murphy, and I've already contacted the owner and set up an interview. Can you make it?"

He flashed her a conspiratorial grin. "I'll be there with bells on."

"Now that's a scary picture." She turned and took a step toward her car, then spun to face him again. "What's your middle name?"

"Edward, why?"

"Just curious." She headed toward her car, mumbling as she went. And though she was turned away, her words drifted back to him, bringing an amused smile.

"Hot diggetty dog! I'm so good at this I sometimes amaze even myself."

SEVENTEEN

Jami stood in front of the hotel room door, staring at its number. She tightened her fingers around the strap of the purse hanging from her shoulder. She wasn't ready for this. Twice she'd raised her hand to knock, then once again lowered it. As long as the door stayed closed, she didn't have to face the past, didn't risk reopening wounds long since healed.

Since her father showed up on her doorstep four days ago, she'd struggled with indecision. She knew what she needed to do, had known from that first moment of recognition. Learning that Grant had made amends with his mother just increased the pressure to throw away every last thread of bitterness and open herself up to reconciliation. And while everything within her wanted to move on with her life as if he'd never reappeared, that still, small voice wouldn't leave her alone. In fact, it had grown annoyingly persistent.

So here she was, standing in front of door number 112, trying to work up the courage to knock. Besides the Spirit's gentle nudging, she had questions, and this was the only way to get them answered.

She squared her shoulders and raised her hand once more. A stiff breeze swept through the parking lot and past the front of the building, whipping tendrils of hair across her face and plastering her silk blouse against her side. Another summer storm in the works, one more reason to hurry this up. She sucked in a huge gulp of air and gave five firm raps on the door.

It swung open moments later, and her father stood just inside. In the light of the fading afternoon sun, he looked much older than his forty-eight years. His brown hair was laced through with silver, the latter having taken over some time ago. Tiny spider veins crisscrossed his nose, and sunken cheeks lent a gauntness to his features. Years of hard living had embedded themselves into the lines of his face.

He swung the door wider, a cautious smile breaking the solemnness that had been there moments earlier. "Would you like to walk?"

Jami nodded, and he stepped outside, closing the door behind him. As he crossed the parking lot, she walked next to him, her heart aching. No, she wasn't ready for this. And she probably never would be. *Lord, help me to do what I need to do.*

For some time, they strolled along the side of the road, the same stiff silence between them. She had so much to say, but where would she even start? He'd walked out, left her mother to raise her alone, hadn't called or written or come back for a single visit. What could she say that would help her truly let it go? What could *he* say?

She drew in a deep breath, closing her eyes for the brief inhale and exhale. The rustle of branches nearby formed a soothing backdrop to her churning thoughts. Usually the sights and sounds of nature worked wonders to settle her jumbled emotions.

But not today. Her chest grew tighter with every breath, and a golf ball–size lump had taken up residence in her throat. What was she even doing here? Maybe it had been a mistake to come. If she'd waited one more day, he would have been gone.

She turned to look at him. "Why? Why did you do it?"

"Why did I leave?" He met her eyes for a moment before letting his gaze dip to the ground. "Your mother gave me an ultimatum: quit drinking or go. She didn't want you growing up with an alcoholic father.

She was so sure I would just quit. But I knew I couldn't do it." He shook his head, shoulders bowed in regret. "Lord knows I'd tried—several times. And I failed every time. So I left, promising myself as soon as I could stay sober for two years, I'd return. Well, the longer I stayed away, the harder it was to come back."

"But you never called, not even on my birthday." Her voice caught on the last word, and hot tears surged forward, stinging her eyes on their way to the surface. She blinked them back, determined to be strong.

"That was a mistake." He still didn't look at her. "I felt like such a failure. I hated myself and the pathetic man I had become, and I didn't want you to remember me like that. I think I was punishing myself, too. I didn't deserve the wonderful wife and beautiful daughter I'd been given. So I turned my back on you both." He stopped walking, and when his eyes met hers, they were moist. "That is a decision I will regret until the day I die."

"So why now? Why come back after all these years?"

"I finally made my two-year goal. I felt if I could do it for two years, I could do it indefinitely. And I believed with two years of sobriety to prove it, you and your mother would see I had changed." He shook his head and lifted his hands to his face. "I wish to God I had come back sooner."

She blinked back another surge of tears. The breeze picked up, sweeping aside the last traces of sticky heat that had hung like a heavy blanket all afternoon. It now carried the musty scent of rain. The promise of rebirth, the cleansing wash that would leave the air pure and the landscape vibrant. The morning after a heavy rain always felt like a brand-new start. Unfortunately, fresh starts were much easier in nature than in life.

"So what happened? Something must have gotten you where you are today."

He began walking again. "It did. The best thing that ever happened to me—I was beat up, thrown in a ditch and left for dead."

She raised her eyebrows. "That was a good thing?"

"Absolutely. Before that, my life was hell. I was on a destructive downward spiral, with no hope of ever coming out of it. I lost my job and got evicted from my apartment. So I lived in my car. When that got repossessed, I lived under bridges, on park benches and, during the winter, in makeshift shelters of cardboard boxes and discarded lumber—anywhere I could find to help shield me from the weather."

He shook his head, frown lines deepening at the memory.

"God sent some angels, though, beacons of light in the darkness. Twice a week, a ministry in the area served a hot meal and did a church service while we ate. I just came for the food, but all the while, those words were sinking in. I just didn't know it at the time." He smiled, and his green eyes didn't look so tired.

"Anyway, the night I was beat up, a pastor of a small house church found me. He called nine-one-one, and when I got out of the hospital, he took me in. He told me that ten years ago, he was exactly where I was. That was the first glimmer of hope I had that maybe there was a way out. Those people with that mission were angels God brought into my life, but Pastor Joe was the prince of them all. Through everything, all my failures, all the times I fell off the wagon, he never gave up on me."

He smiled, eyes alight with conviction. "You know what was the real turning point? Figuring out I had to stop trying to do it by myself. I now ask God for help every day, every hour if I have to. I've got a church family that supports me and a small group of Christian friends who hold me accountable."

"So you made your two-year goal."

"I did, and I knew it was time to make amends to those I had wronged, you and your mother most of all."

He looked past her, toward the trees lining that part of Terrace Avenue. But judging from the faraway look in his eyes, he wasn't admiring the scenery. Some of the strain had left his face, leaving a softness that wasn't there earlier.

He released a sigh. "Beth was a special lady, gentle, caring, beautiful. I never saw anyone with so much patience and love."

Jami nodded. Love, patience, empathy, forgiveness and too many other good qualities to name. And a calm confidence God was in control, no matter what life threw her way. It was a confidence nothing could shake, not abandonment, not cancer, not even death. If her mother were still alive, she would know just what to say to guide her through this unwanted reunion with her father. And she would have the wisdom to help her put Grant out of her heart and life for good.

Her mom had always been her best friend—a Sam or Holly with an extra three decades of experience. Almost a year had passed, and the empty space she'd left was still as large and painful as ever.

"You know, Mom never gave up hope. She prayed for you until the day she died."

"I put her through so much." His tone was heavy.

She drew in a shaky breath. Their shadows stretched out in front of them, lengthening as the sun sank lower in the sky. Up ahead, the road made a gentle curve to the right, disappearing into the trees encroaching on both sides.

When she looked again at her father, his head was bowed, his shoulders bent, both hands buried deep in his pockets. He spoke without lifting his eyes.

"It's too late for me to make things right with Beth. I'm probably too late for you, too. I hurt you severely, and I can't tell you how sorry I am. I don't expect you to welcome me back into your life. Even forgiveness is too much to ask at this point." His shoulders rose and fell in a prolonged shrug. "I just hope over time, you will come to not hate me."

"I don't hate you," she whispered. "Not anymore."

He stopped walking and turned to face her. Tears were pooled on his lower lashes. "You don't know how happy that makes me. It's much more than I deserve."

And it was all she could give. Eventually she would forgive him—God would require no less—but she just wasn't there yet. And she wouldn't say the words until she meant them. She turned to head back toward the Mountain Vista Inn, and he fell in beside her.

"Will I see you in the morning before I leave?"

She took a deep breath. She needed time, a chance to digest this sudden addition of a father to her life. "I don't know. I have a lot going on."

"Well, let me give you my cell number. Then if you have a spare minute, you can give me a call."

She pulled her phone from her purse, ready to program in the number. At the name field, she hesitated. She didn't even know what to call him. He'd walked out of her life when she was eight. Back then, he was "Daddy." Now, fifteen years later, "Dad" didn't feel right, and neither did "Father." He'd been neither to her. She finally keyed in *Carlisle, B.*

When they reached the parking lot, she turned to face him. "I'm glad you're doing all right." It was a stiff prelude to *farewell*, but it was all she could muster. She couldn't tell him she was glad he'd come back, and she couldn't say she'd missed him. At least not while being totally honest. And a hug was out of the question.

"I hope you stay on the right track."

He gave her a stiff nod. "Thank you for coming."

He turned and headed toward his room. As she opened her car door, he called her name. When she turned around, he stood framed in the open doorway.

"You've grown into a young lady that would make any father proud."

She gave him an almost imperceptible nod, feeling disappointed but not able to put her finger on why. He'd answered her questions. He'd explained why he'd left, shared his struggles, even told her how sorry he was for leaving. But she had come with more than questions. When she'd stood on the stoop, working up the courage to knock, it had been with a heart full of yearning, the hope talking with him would somehow make everything all right.

But it hadn't. The hurt was still there, the damage borne of years of rejection.

She slid into the driver's seat and closed the door. As she reached for her seat belt, her gaze swept the front of the building, past door 112. Her father still stood there, watching her. He was probably holding out as long as he could, not knowing if he'd ever see her again. She didn't know herself. She cranked the car and backed from the space.

Before she even made it out of the parking lot, her cell phone rang. It was Sam. Jami pushed the events of the past half hour to the back of her mind and injected some cheer into her voice.

Sam wasn't fooled. "Are you okay? You sound a little . . . off."

"I just visited my father."

"Oh."

The single word was heavy with unspoken questions. During minigolf yesterday, she'd filled Sam and Holly in on both Grant's return and the visit from her father.

"Things went all right, I guess. I mean, there weren't any cross words. He told me how sorry he was for everything, and he explained a lot of things I didn't understand before."

"So it went well, all things considered. But you sound disappointed."

She pressed the "Speaker" icon and dropped her phone into the cup holder. "I don't know." She pulled out of the parking lot to head for home. "I think I somehow expected more. I mean, it took me four days to work up the courage to get over there and confront him, and I guess I thought once I did that, all the struggle would be over. Instead I feel like it's just beginning."

"You honestly thought just talking to him would somehow erase all those years of hurt?"

Jami smiled sheepishly. "Not very practical, huh?"

She eased to a stop at a red light just as a heavy gust swept through, blowing debris across the street in front of her. A stray leaf landed on the windshield and stayed behind, trapped against one of the motionless wiper blades.

Sam continued. "Things like this take time. And lots of prayer."

"I guess I want it to be instantaneous. I encouraged Grant to let go of the bitterness he's been hanging on to, and now I'm having a hard time listening to my own advice. I feel like a hypocrite."

"You're the least hypocritical person I know. You just need a little time, that's all."

The light changed, and she made a right onto the highway, some of the heaviness lifting. Sam was good at that. She was tough—growing up with three brothers, she'd had no choice. But in spite of her sassy attitude and sarcastic sense of humor, her well of compassion ran deep.

"Thanks for the encouragement. So what's up with you?"

"Well," Sam began, stretching out the word, "I was planning to send another e-mail to Hank tonight and wanted to run it by you. But if you don't feel like doing it right now, that's fine."

"I don't mind." Something to take her mind off both her father and Grant would be a good thing. "I'm having second thoughts, though."

"Don't tell me you're getting cold feet."

"It's not that. It just doesn't seem to be working. With every e-mail, she's adding another quality to her secret admirer, and the picture she's got now doesn't bear the slightest resemblance to Hank. I ran into her in town yesterday, and she had brochures from a company that does

African safari tours. One advertised the opportunity to explore remote areas on the back of a camel."

Sam giggled. "I can't picture Hank on horseback, let alone bouncing along on the back of a camel."

"My point exactly. I think it's time to just throw them together and see what sticks before our plans go any further off base."

"Sounds good to me. What do you have in mind?"

"I say tonight or tomorrow morning we send them each an e-mail to meet at the park Tuesday evening." She eased to a stop in her driveway and shot a glance at the sky. She'd beaten the rain, but not by much.

"That sounds good. When no one shows up except the two of them, they'll probably accuse each other. They'll both claim ignorance about the notes and gifts, but neither will believe the other's denials."

Jami smiled. Maybe their scheme would work out after all. "Are you going to be there to see where the pieces fall?"

"I wouldn't miss it for the world."

—⚉—

Jami sighed and doubled back toward Ingles's paper-goods aisle. She needed paper towels and had even been thinking about it when she entered the aisle the first time. Then she'd walked right past them. And she'd done the same thing with the ketchup and hand soap.

Focus. But the silent scolding didn't do any good, because her brain wasn't listening.

She'd done what she needed to do yesterday. She'd talked with her father and sent him home with at least some hope there might be reconciliation in the future. There were a lot of years of hurt, and healing took time. Maybe somewhere down the road, she would be ready to see him again.

But this evening, it wasn't her father who kept intruding into her thoughts. It was Grant. And he had no business there. She'd told him a final good-bye Saturday morning, when he'd shown up at her house. Each word out of her mouth had shredded her heart a little further, but she'd gotten them out and hadn't caved to his pleading words and incredible blue eyes. Now she needed to just pick up the pieces and move forward.

She skidded to a stop just past the paper towels and turned her buggy around. She'd almost done it again. She sighed and tossed a three-pack into her cart. Now for the oregano. When she stepped into the baking aisle, Hank was in front of her, hurrying to catch up with Bernie halfway down.

Hank chasing Bernie? That looked promising. Jami smiled. Maybe she and her coconspirators were giving up too soon. Just last night, she and Samantha and Holly had composed the e-mails. If everything went as planned, Bernie and Hank would both show up at the park and be convinced the other was the secret admirer. Samantha had promised to be there. It was easy to picture her hiding out in the bushes in full camo gear. Jami and Holly would be there, too. But without the fatigues.

Hank had caught up to Bernie, and they stood in the center of the baking aisle, heads tilted together. Maybe Operation Bernie Match-Up was bearing some fruit after all. And Jami wasn't above eavesdropping to find out. She ducked behind an ethnic-food display.

"I can't be at Doyle's. Something came up." The voice belonged to Hank.

"You have to." Bernie was speaking in an undertone, a rare occurrence. Of course, an undertone for Bernie carried two aisles over instead of five. "One of us has to be there, and I got something important going on at the park. It's something I can't miss."

"That's where I'm going to be."

"What are *you* doing at the park?" Suspicion laced her tone.

"I can't tell you."

"Why not?"

Jami peeked around the display. They both stood in profile, facing each other.

Hank crossed his arms and affected a stubborn stance. "I'm not telling. What are *you* doing at the park?"

Bernie matched his stance. "If you're not telling me, I'm not telling you."

He stood in silence, shifting his weight from one foot to the other. Finally, he uncrossed his arms and leaned toward her as if ready to spill some big secret. "I'm meeting a woman."

Bernie didn't even try to match his hushed tone. "You're meeting a woman? Who?"

"Shh! You don't have to announce it to the whole county." He took a step back and again crossed his arms. "It's not anybody you know."

She stared at him, brows raised behind her jewel-framed glasses. Then a slow smile crept up her cheeks. "I'll be. Hank's got a girlfriend. Well, *I'm* meeting a *man*."

His jaw dropped. "You are?"

She sniffed and raised her chin. "Don't look so shocked. Someone out there thinks I'm a real catch, whether you believe it or not."

"I didn't say I didn't believe it."

"Well, one of us has to be at Doyle's and make sure everything goes down like it's supposed to. And since you were the first one to mess everything up, I think it needs to be you."

"Why does it have to be Doyle's? Why not the park?"

Bernie's eyes widened. "Hank, you're brilliant. I could kiss you. We'll set this up at the park. Then you won't miss your date, and I won't miss mine, either."

Jami straightened and approached them. Bernie saw her first. She started and reached a nervous hand to her hair. "Jami!" False cheer infused her tone. "How are you?"

Jami looked from Bernie to Hank, who seemed intent on taking a mental inventory of the cake mixes. "Fine. What are you two up to?"

"Oh, nothing much. Hank and I were talking about a project we're working on together. Weren't we, Hank?"

His head bobbed. "A project. Yep, that's right. Well, I better finish my shopping." He gripped the cart handle with both hands as if waiting for the starting gunshot, then ambled off down the aisle.

"And I've got to get going, too." Bernie followed Hank's retreat, but turned the opposite direction when she reached the end of the aisle.

Jami shook her head. What was Bernie up to now? And how in the world had she dragged Hank into it?

EIGHTEEN

Jami arched her back, enjoying the satisfying crack of the bones loosening up. She'd been sitting too long, but it was worth it. Another article written and ready to upload. Although she was getting more confident with her journalism skills, she would probably still have Bernie do a quick read through.

If Bernie ever got there.

It was almost ten thirty on Tuesday morning, and no one had seen or heard from her. She'd been known to lose track of time at the Grind, but even Bernie couldn't stretch out a coffee and Danish for three hours.

The lobby door swung open, and surprisingly, it was Donna's voice that reached her first. "Wow, Bernie. You look . . . nice."

"Thank you, Donna. It's a special day."

Jami swiveled her head that direction and watched Bernie approach. Her steps were light and faltering. Jami put her hands on her hips. "All right. Who are you, and what have you done with Bernie?"

First was the makeup. The fact she was even wearing any was earth-shattering in itself. But eye shadow, eyeliner, mascara *and* lipstick? Bernie had fun coloring her hair, but referred to the daily beauty routine as nonsense. And her sentiments on dresses weren't any better. But here she stood, decked to the hilt in a deep forest-green tea-length dress, cream-colored high heels and several pieces of clunky costume jewelry that were over the top, even for Bernie. The hair added to the fashion fiasco. It was teased into a tangled mass large enough to hide a pen, her checkbook and a couple of small children.

"It's really me." She stopped to pose. "How do I look?"

"Is there a costume party going on today, and I missed the memo?"

"I wore this to work to get your opinion." She hobbled to her chair, grimacing with each step, then plopped into it with a groan.

"Bernie, how long has it been since you put on a pair of high heels?"

She thought for several moments, lips pursed. "I think it was Missy and John's wedding."

"That was four years ago."

"I don't wear 'em often." She pulled off one shoe and wiggled her toes, then freed her other foot. A huge rock glittered on each hand, complemented by equally gaudy bracelets. "I keep 'em in case I have a funeral or wedding to go to."

"Well, I haven't heard about any engagements recently, and I don't think anyone's died. So what's the occasion?"

Bernie lowered her voice and spoke out the side of her mouth. "I'm meeting *him*."

"Who?"

"You know, *him*. My secret admirer."

Jami nodded. If she hadn't composed the e-mail herself, she would have thought Bernie was headed off to some swanky dinner theater. She couldn't be planning to wear that getup to the park. "Where are you meeting him?"

"At the park."

"Don't you think you might be a tad bit overdressed?"

"But I want to look my best."

"You want to look good, but he's also expecting you to be yourself." Her gaze swept Bernie from the top of her bee's-nest hairdo to the bottom of her protesting feet, which she was alternating massaging. "That is definitely not you. And it shows. You look about as comfortable as a hobo in a tuxedo."

"So what do I wear?"

"What would you normally wear to the park?"

"I'd wear shorts and a comfortable tee. But I can't wear that to meet *him*. One look at these chicken legs, and he'd be headed for the next county."

"Then wear some pants and a casual blouse. And put on some comfortable shoes, for Pete's sake. My feet hurt just watching you."

Bernie dropped her foot to the floor. "So you think this is too much?"

"Definitely. He already likes the Bernie he sees. If you show up like that, he'll be disappointed."

"In that case, I can't wait to get out of this dress and these shoes. What about the jewelry?"

Jami shook her head. "It's gotta go."

"The hair, too?"

"Definitely."

"Then I guess I better leave a few minutes early this afternoon to undo all the damage I did this morning."

"That's a wonderful idea." If there was one thing Bernie had, it was confidence. Staying dressed like that all day instead of rushing home to change took a lot of guts.

Bernie huffed out a sigh. "Now that that's settled, I have a great idea for a story, and you'd be the perfect one to write it. I wanted to tell you yesterday here at the *Scout* but never caught up with you. A couple days ago, I learned there's a businessman who has plans to move to North Carolina and open a bed and breakfast."

"Here in Murphy?"

"Here in Murphy or somewhere nearby. He wants to cater to people who are looking for a quiet retreat, a place to escape the stress of the city and enjoy nature. He also wants to open a restaurant. The restaurant would be for everyone, not just the guests of the bed and breakfast."

Jami nodded, an unexpected pang of nostalgia hitting her. She had a lot of good memories of the years she worked at the bed and breakfast with her mom and Aunt Lily. And though it wasn't doable now, the thought that she would one day open one herself, in memory of her mother, always rested in the back of her mind. This businessman was going to be living her dream.

"Okay, I'll interview him and write an article about his plans. Any particular slant you think I should take?"

"Nope, I'll leave that up to you."

She slid a notepad into the center of her desk and picked up a pen. "Okay. Where is he from?"

Bernie's eyes fluttered away. "He's from somewhere up north, like Chicago or Philadelphia or somewhere. You know, one of those crowded big cities that stays frozen half the year."

"You got a name and number for me?"

"I might have a card." Bernie fished through her oversized bag. "I think his name's Edward. Edward something. Or maybe something Edward." She removed a wad of receipts with an ink pen wedged between them and placed it in her lap. After fishing through them one by one, she added a checkbook, wallet and pack of tissues to the stack. "I don't seem to have it right now. But don't worry, I already set everything up. You're meeting him tonight at seven."

"So he's here now?"

"Yup. He's staying somewhere in the area."

She jotted *interview at seven* on the pad. "And where are we meeting?"

"The park."

"The park?" She laid down her pen. "Isn't that an odd place to do an interview?"

"Well, it's either the park or his motel room. It's not like he has an office here or anything."

"No, but wouldn't one of the restaurants have made more sense?"

Bernie shrugged and stuffed the items back into the zippered pockets of her purse. Everything went back inside in even less order than it had come out. "He liked the idea of meeting in the park. Maybe it fits better with his whole retreat-to-nature idea."

"Okay." That made sense. "So what does this mystery businessman look like?"

"Well, he's young."

"How young is young?"

"He's younger than me."

Jami frowned. "That doesn't help."

"Well, he's not over forty. And," she added, "he's hot."

"Bernie, you think all men are hot."

"Not *all* men."

"Okay, most. So what else can you give me?"

"He has dark hair, like black or brown. Or maybe it's light brown." She pursed her lips, brows drawn together in concentration. "It's not blond. I do know that much."

Jami shook her head. "I hope you're never an eyewitness in a big criminal case, or the prosecution is doomed."

Bernie threw back her head and laughed, the throaty guffaw that was so Bernie even though the hair and clothes weren't.

Jami picked up her pen and wrote *park* beneath the note she'd scrawled earlier. "If you find that card, let me know. I know I'm looking for a hot man under forty who doesn't have blond hair, but even with all those details, it wouldn't hurt to have a name."

Bernie's hearty laughter once again filled the huge, open space, and Jami shook her head.

There was only one Bernie.

Grant eased to a stop in one of several parking areas along the Murphy River Walk. This one was on the stretch of trail running along the southern bank of the Valley River. He'd chosen it for a reason. Jami wouldn't be likely to park here. Since her interview was to take place at Koneheta Park, she would choose one of the parking lots near the ball fields.

He swung open the car door and stepped into a world shining with a postrain brilliance. The sun sat low on the horizon, peeking through the clouds that still blanketed the western sky. On the path ahead of him, a flock of Canada geese waddled toward the water's edge.

He set out walking in the direction of the small bridge that would take him across the river. He had plenty of time. The interview wouldn't be for another thirty minutes. The wait would do him good, give him a chance to prepare. One side of his mouth cocked up in a wry smile. No amount of preparation was going to help him face the evening with confidence. His whole future happiness hinged on the next two hours.

He lifted his eyes and sent up another one of those selfish prayers. He'd prayed quite a few of those over the past couple of days. *Lord, I need your help. Give me the right words, and please make Jami receptive to them.*

Bernie had called that morning, all apologetic she was going to have to change the location of the interview. But meeting at the park was a brilliant idea. It would give him the opportunity to stroll with Jami while she waited for her interview subject to arrive. If she would let him. It wouldn't have been so easy at Doyle's. The minute she showed up and was led to his table, she would have known Bernie had set her up and would have left without even giving him a chance.

Of course, he had no guarantee she wouldn't do the same thing at the park. She would still suspect Bernie had sent him there. And if he was lucky, he would have all of two minutes to break down the protective wall that encased her heart.

As he started across the bridge, he pressed his hand over the pewter piece resting against his chest. He'd put it back on earlier today, and he wasn't taking it off. It would stay close to his heart, a continual reminder not to give up hope. Somehow he would win her back.

He had a plan, or more like a shell of one, a vague idea. He would rather have had a full script, the magic words that would guarantee a path to her heart. He wasn't good at ad lib. Every concert he'd ever done, he'd relied on the sheet music. Tonight he was going to have to wing it, to face the most important performance of his life blind and unscripted.

He stepped off the bridge, and to his left, a chain-link fence sectioned off colorful playground equipment. Kids sailed down tubular slides amid squeals of pleasure while parents sat nearby on wooden benches, watching their charges work off all that excess energy. The activity would be a good distraction.

But instead of approaching, he turned to walk in the other direction, following the paved trail that led toward the park. A couple strolled some distance ahead. Trees cast their lengthening shadows across the landscape, and every so often, a bench or picnic table offered repose.

Eventually, the path forked, the right branch continuing its route along the river and the left passing through a large, grassy area dotted with picnic tables, benches and plantings. A monument stood at the fork, erected by the Cherokee County Chapter of the Compassionate Friends, according to the words engraved on its base. A little farther down, a waterwheel and wood flume were displayed behind a split-rail fence, and beyond that, a parking area. That was where Jami would be.

He strolled across the grass to a bench where he could watch for her to arrive. Within minutes, the red Sunbird pulled into the parking lot. His pulse quickened. Jami was early, too. She stepped from the car, and a gust of wind blew reddish strands of hair across her face. Emotion surged up within. Somehow he had to convince her to give him another chance.

He pushed himself to his feet and watched her head up the path toward the river, purse hung over one shoulder and water bottle in her other hand. She wore a tailored suit with moderate heels, her usual work attire. But beneath the confident, professional exterior was a warm, caring woman. How could he get her to once again let down her guard and trust him with her heart?

He squared his shoulders and drew in a steadying breath. He was a lawyer. Being persuasive was a big part of his job. But tonight, he had all the confidence of a nerdy, pimpled teen getting ready to ask the beauty queen to prom. He stuffed his hands into his pockets, and when his left hand met the small box tucked away there, his heart began to race. Maybe his purchase was a little premature. And maybe he was a little crazy. But he'd never been more sure of anything in his life.

He walked in her direction and sent up another one of those selfish prayers.

Lord, help me do this right.

NINETEEN

Jami strolled down the path, scouting out a place where she could keep an eye on the parking area. She had no idea what kind of vehicle her hot, not-blond, younger-than-forty businessman drove, but so far, she recognized every car in the lot, including Bernie's and Hank's. Even Samantha was there. At least her car was. She hadn't seen either Sam or Holly herself.

Meeting in the park hadn't been a bad idea. If her big-city businessman wanted the tranquility of the outdoors, this was the ideal time of year to get it. The weather was perfect, the temperature a balmy seventy degrees with the faintest hint of a breeze. The grass was still wet from the afternoon rain, a soft floor of green velvet.

Movement in her peripheral vision drew her attention to her left. A familiar figure moved toward her across the grass, and her heart fell. Grant. He was the last person she wanted to see. So why was her pulse racing and this crazy warmth spreading through her chest?

When he reached her, he turned and fell into step beside her. She didn't slow her pace. Someone told him she was going to be at the park, and she could easily guess who. A certain meddling newspaper reporter needed a muzzle. "Bernie told you I was going to be here tonight, didn't she?"

He flashed her a grin, one of those warm smiles that made her stomach do somersaults. "I admit it. She did. And I didn't want to pass up the opportunity to see you."

"I'm meeting someone for an interview in about five minutes, so I can't talk." She pulled her gaze to a wooden swing overlooking the river, which was a lot safer than letting that dazzling smile wreak havoc with her defenses.

"Well, if it's okay, I'd like to walk with you until it's time for your interview."

She shrugged. It was a free country, and the park was public property. When their path met the river walk, she made a left. So much for finding a comfortable place to wait. With Grant beside her, she would never be relaxed enough to sit still.

"So who are you interviewing?"

"Some businessman from Chicago. I don't have a name. Not a full one, anyway." She glanced over at him, even though she shouldn't.

The corners of his mouth quivered upward, as if he were trying hard to hide amusement. "You're doing an interview in five minutes and don't have the name of the interviewee?"

"That would be Bernie. She lost the guy's card."

He nodded, obviously still amused. "So this no-name Chicago businessman, what's special about him?"

"He has plans to open up a bed and breakfast with a restaurant and is considering Murphy."

"That sounds interesting."

Up ahead, a picnic table sat off the left side of the path. Bernie stood next to it, Hank a short distance away. Fortunately, Bernie had changed clothes before coming. The dress was likely tucked into the back of her closet again, the shoes in a box slipped far beneath her bed. Her hair had even recovered from its trauma nicely.

As they got closer, Bernie looked past Hank and waved enthusiastically. "Jami, Grant, it's good to see you. Hank and I are keeping each other company while we wait for our dates to show up." Her words overflowed with excitement. "Would you believe Hank has been getting the same kind of notes and e-mails I have? It even started around the same time."

Jami lifted her brows in feigned surprise. Maybe thinking they'd assume the notes came from each other was expecting too much. "What a coincidence."

"I know. What are the odds?" She shook her head. "So what's happening?"

Bernie's gaze went from her face to Grant's. She had questions much more pointed than *What's happening?*

"My interview subject hasn't shown up yet." She studied Bernie. "You haven't heard from him, have you?"

"No, I sure haven't." She looked at Grant, then focused on some point beyond them. "Maybe he got held up."

Jami nodded. Bernie was up to something, and it wasn't simply letting Grant know she had an interview at the park.

Maybe the assignment was a setup. Maybe there *was* no Chicago businessman, no bed and breakfast or new restaurant, no interview at all. Maybe Bernie had orchestrated the whole evening to throw her and Grant together. She wouldn't put it past her.

Jami put her hands on her hips and nailed Bernie with a glare. "I don't have an interview tonight, do I?"

Bernie's jaw went slack. "Are you accusing me of making this up? I wouldn't do something like that. You really do have an interview. I guess you'll just have to wait until he's ready to talk." She plopped onto the bench behind her. When Hank started to sit next to her, she planted one hand on the small of his back and gave him enough of a shove to reverse his momentum. "You can't sit here."

"Why not?"

Bernie sighed and rolled her eyes as if he'd asked the dumbest question ever. "If we're sitting on the same bench when he gets here, he'll think I'm with you and won't even come over and talk to me."

"Good thinking." Hank circled the table and sat on the opposite side, his back to her. "I don't want *her* to think I'm with *you*, neither." He cast the words over his shoulder.

Moments later, Sam peeked out from behind a bush some ten feet away. She winked and waved, then put a finger to her lips, commanding silence. Jami hadn't seen Holly yet, but she was probably somewhere nearby.

"If there's really an interview, I'd better head back." She could still see the parking lot, but just barely.

Grant waited to speak until they were out of earshot of Hank and Bernie. "I take it you ladies are responsible for them being here tonight."

"Yep. We decided to throw them together and see what happens." She frowned. "So far it doesn't seem to be working."

"The night is still young." He scanned the park while they walked. "What does your interview subject look like?"

"He's not blond."

"That's it?"

"He's also under forty."

"Well, that narrows it down a little bit."

She grinned. "And he's hot."

Unexpected laughter burst from Grant. "Bernie said that?"

"She sure did. Of course, coming from Bernie, it's not unusual."

Jami slowed her pace and looked around. They had reached the point of the river walk where they'd started. She stepped off the path to sit on the swing, turning sideways so she could still keep the parking lot in view. Her interviewee was probably a no-show, but it didn't hurt to watch for him.

Grant sat on the other end of the swing and set it swaying with one foot. "You want to practice?"

"Practice what?"

"Your interview. You know, ask me the questions."

"I don't need to practice. I already know what I'm going to ask."

He flashed her a teasing grin, the same one that had almost reduced her to a quivering puddle of Jell-O on the sidewalk when he'd arrived a short time earlier. "Just humor me."

"All right." She took a deep breath and matched his smile. "Mr. Successful Chicago Businessman, I understand you're considering opening a bed and breakfast and fine restaurant right here in Murphy. Is that true?"

"Yes, I'm quite serious about it."

"And do you have a location picked out yet?"

"In fact, I do. It's a huge old house several miles outside of town, and although it's pretty run-down, the place has a lot of character. I think it's the perfect location for a venture like this."

They were only playacting, but Grant was so convincing her heart skipped a beat, and whatever question she planned to ask next slid from her mind. She took a long swig from her water bottle while she recomposed her thoughts. "That sounds appealing. How soon do you plan to get started?"

"As soon as possible. I've got a few things to wrap up at home. Then I'll be coming back to stay. I'd like to open both the bed and breakfast and the restaurant before next summer."

Longing stabbed through her, so intense she almost doubled over. She wasn't so sure she liked this game, but Grant didn't seem to have any problems. That warm, teasing grin held on the entire time. She pasted on her own smile and tried to focus on the soothing back-and-forth movement of the swing. No matter how much this playful exchange shredded her already-raw heart, Grant would never know.

"That's a pretty ambitious goal. So tell me something. Why would a successful businessman leave his life in the city and come to a quaint little town like Murphy to open a bed and breakfast?"

"That's a good question." He paused. "A month ago, I never would have considered it. But once you experience the tranquility of nature, the clean mountain air and the friendliness of the local people, city life becomes less appealing."

Jami studied him. He didn't *look* like someone who was playacting. Was it possible . . . Could he really be thinking . . . *No, don't get your hopes up.*

"Why Murphy?" Her voice was barely above a whisper, cold professionalism gone. "With all the quaint towns in the North Carolina mountains, why would you choose Murphy?"

"It's a beautiful area, popular with the tourists. There's a lot to do, from hiking to horseback riding to whitewater rafting." He turned toward her and took both of her hands. His knee rested against hers, and all teasing had fled his gaze. "And there's this certain newspaper reporter who entranced me almost from the first moment I saw her. And now it seems I can't convince myself to leave."

She stared at him, jaw slack, her heart pounding out an erratic rhythm. This was no act. He was staying, because of her. How was she supposed to hold on to her defenses?

Finally, she found her voice. "Bernie wasn't lying. I really *am* meeting a businessman planning to open a bed and breakfast. You're not blond, and you're definitely under forty."

He flashed her a teasing grin, accompanied by a mischievous glint in his eyes. "What about the hot part?"

"Without a doubt."

She drew in a shaky breath. He was staying. It didn't seem real and probably wouldn't for a while. Over time, maybe it would sink in. Now it felt like a dream, one that would vanish like a vapor come morning.

She looked up at Grant. "What do you say we check on Bernie and Hank?"

"That sounds good. Do you think things are progressing back there?"

"Truthfully? I doubt it."

Grant stood and took her hand to help her to her feet. When they approached Bernie and Hank, the two of them still sat on opposite sides of the table, but they were now facing one another. Bernie's eager gaze dipped to their hands, still joined, and a knowing smile climbed up her cheeks. "Looks like you got the interview."

"I did. Grant is going to turn the McAllister mansion into a bed and breakfast. But I guess you already knew that."

"I might have known a little something."

"Admit it, Bernie. This assignment was nothing but a ploy to get Grant and me together. In fact, I think that's all the other assignment was, too. You were plotting to get us together right from the start."

Bernie shrugged, but the devious grin gave her away. "Getting you the McAllister feature was completely innocent on my part. But when you told me you'd dumped Robert, I was so afraid you were going to change your mind. I'd set everything in motion with the assignment, but I had to jump in there a few times to keep the ball rolling in the right direction."

Jami shook her head. "Bernie, you're a mess. And a little devious."

"I never said anything that wasn't true."

"Yes, you did. You said he was from Chicago."

Bernie planted one hand on her hip. "No, I didn't. I said he was from a big city up north, *like* Chicago or Philadelphia."

"Okay, you squeaked by on that one. But you also said his name was Edward."

Grant answered this time. "My name *is* Edward. Grant Edward McAllister."

Jami looked from one to the other. "Why do I feel as if I've just been snookered?"

"Because you have." Bernie grinned. "But I don't hear you complaining." She slapped her hands against the wooden slats of the bench and turned to Hank. "It looks like we both got stood up tonight. Are you okay?"

Hank shrugged. "I'm all right. How about you?"

"I'm good." Bernie sucked in a deep breath and pushed herself to her feet. "Since both of our plans got messed up, what do you say we have a late dinner at the Waffle House? I'll even treat you."

Hank stood, too. "Are you sure? I don't mind paying."

"You can pay next time." She looked up at him, uncertainty in her gaze. "I mean, if you want there to be a next time."

Hank smiled down at her. "I think I'd like that."

"You two want to join us?"

Before Jami could open her mouth, Grant answered for them. "We might join you later."

She watched Bernie and Hank leave, then smiled up at Grant, happy for the choice he'd made. Dinner with Bernie and Hank would be fun. But nothing appealed to her more than time alone with Grant. He was staying. Planting roots. Deep roots—he was starting a business. It couldn't get much more permanent than that.

"So why did you do it? What made you decide to come back and pursue your dream?"

"You planted the seed that one night at dinner. I kept thinking about it and finally decided it was time to make my dream a reality. The restaurant is definite, but the bed and breakfast is up in the air. It's dependent on whether a certain spunky newspaper reporter is willing to work with me."

Her heart jumped to double time. "You want me to be your business partner?"

"Yes, I do."

She began walking, mind swirling with questions and doubt settling in her chest. She would never be satisfied with just being his business partner, because she had fallen hopelessly in love with him. If that was all he wanted, she just couldn't do it.

But if he wanted more, could she do that? Would she be able to lower the walls around her heart and risk the ultimate rejection?

He grasped her shoulder and guided her to a stop before turning her to face him. His eyes locked with hers, warm and tender, and he placed both hands on her shoulders. "I want you to be my business partner, but that's not all I want. I want you by my side as I pursue my dream. I want to spend the rest of my life with you." He hesitated but didn't look away. When he spoke, his words were filled with emotion. "Jami, I love you, and I want you to be my wife."

Wife? Did he say *wife*? Grant McAllister, who was never going to fall into that trap again, never going to let a woman touch his heart? She studied him, afraid she hadn't heard him right while at the same time scared to death she had. "Did you just ask me to marry you?"

"No."

He let his arms fall, and her heart wobbled to a stop. Then he took both of her hands in his and dropped to one knee. "But I am now. Jami Carlisle, will you marry me?"

Conflicting emotions tumbled through her, a love so powerful it almost took her breath away, with panic pounding close on its heels. She needed time. What if she was making a mistake? What if, after he thought about it awhile, he realized he couldn't do it after all? Or even worse, what if he went through with marrying her, and then decided it was a mistake? The ring and marriage vows would mean nothing. He would still leave. Just like her father had.

God, please help me to know what to do. If this is right, help me let go of my fears and grasp hold of your will for my life.

She pulled her lower lip between her teeth and met his gaze. He was looking up at her, awaiting her answer, love shining out from eyes as dark as sapphires in the waning light. A silent plea floated on the air between them, begging her to drop her guard and let him touch her heart.

Samantha had said life was full of uncertainty, that she needed to be willing to take some risks. If she allowed Grant to penetrate the barriers protecting her, there would be risk, the potential for heartbreak. But the alternative, life without him, was unthinkable.

She gave a slight nod.

"You'll marry me?" His face filled with hope, and he straightened to his feet without releasing her hands.

This was her second proposal with no ring, no elegant setting, no candlelight or romantic music. But it didn't matter. Because it was coming from Grant, the man she loved with all her heart.

She tipped back her head and drew in a deep breath. Actually, his proposal couldn't have been more perfect. There was no fancy restaurant with white linen tablecloths, but all around them, trees stretched leaf-covered boughs skyward. Instead of flutes, oboes and violins, calls of whip-poor-wills punctuated a katydid serenade. And no candle ever compared to the dazzling display stretched across the horizon. Orange, pink and lavender colored the sky, painted in giant strokes.

And the ring . . .

Grant released her hands and reached into his pocket to pull out a hinged velvet box. "If you don't like it, I can take it back, and you can pick out something you like better. I went to Paula's Jewelry yesterday and bought something they had in stock. I had no idea when I might propose, but when the opportunity arose, I wanted to be prepared." He slipped the ring onto her finger. "So, Jami, *will* you marry me?"

She stared at the diamonds capturing the slanting rays of sunlight and reflecting them back in a glittery display. Two baguettes flanked a large center stone, all set in a yellow-gold band. She lifted her eyes to meet his. "It's perfect."

He still stared down at her, brows raised. "So is the answer to my question yes?"

"Yes." She wrapped both arms around his neck and pulled him toward her until her lips met his. "Yes, yes, yes." She punctuated each word with a kiss.

Then Grant wrapped her in an embrace that left no doubt about how thrilled he was with her response. Love swelled in her chest, strengthened by the assurance that, after a whole series of heartbreaks and disappointments, this was the man God had for her. The last of her doubts drifted away on the gentle summer breeze.

Grant had told her to hang on to her dreams. She had. And God was granting every one of them.

Her novel was shaping up nicely. With Grant's encouragement, she would see it through to completion.

Sickness had snuffed out her mother's desire to run a bed and breakfast, but Jami had claimed that dream as her own. Now she was going to be half owner of one, sooner than she ever thought possible.

But she'd almost given up on the dream she'd clung to the longest—that Prince Charming would one day sweep in and turn her world upside down. She'd begun to believe he was nothing but a fantasy, a mystical figure that resided solely in the fanciful imaginings of starry-eyed young girls.

She'd been wrong. He wasn't a fantasy.

He was real, flesh and blood.

And he was standing right in front of her, ready to carry her away to her own happily ever after.

ACKNOWLEDGMENTS

My sincerest thanks to David Brown, publisher of the *Cherokee Scout*, for the informative tour and for patiently answering all my questions.

Thank you to my wonderful sister, Kim Wolff, for driving me all over Murphy and helping me get the information I needed. You made researching this book a real joy.

Thank you to my family for your unending support.

Thank you to my critique partners, Karen Fleming and Sabrina Jarema. Your amazing insight always makes my writing better.

Thank you to my editors, Erin Calligan Mooney and Colleen Wagner, and my agent, Nalini Akolekar. I am blessed to be working with each of you.

And lastly, thank you to my husband, Chris. After thirty-five years, you still put romance in my life.

ABOUT THE AUTHOR

From medical secretary to court reporter to property manager to owner of a special-events decorating company, Carol J. Post's résumé reads as if she hasn't yet decided what she wants to be when she grows up. But one thing that has remained constant through the years is her love of writing. She started as a child, composing poetry for family and friends, then graduated to articles for religious and children's publications. Now she pens fun, fast-paced inspirational romance and romantic suspense stories. Her books have been nominated for an RT Reviewers' Choice Best Book award and selected as an RT Top Pick. When Carol isn't writing, she enjoys sailing, hiking, camping—almost anything outdoors. She also plays the piano and sings with her music-minister husband. Their two grown daughters and their grandkids live too far away for her liking, so she now pours all her nurturing into taking care of a fat and sassy black cat and a highly spoiled dachshund.